LIBRARIAN WITCH

Flutterbye Trail Press
797 Sam Bass Road #2541
Round Rock, TX 78681

First edition

Chapter Art by Etheric Tales
Cover Design by Covers by Kellie Arts
Discreet Cover Design by Gombar Cover Design
Editing by Red Loop Editing
Hardback Case Design by Olga Sauchenia
Printed Interior Design by Enchanting Covers
Published by Flutterbye Trail Press

ISBN: 978-1-954582-08-8 (E-book)
ISBN: 978-1-954582-52-1 (Discreet Paperback)
ISBN: 978-1-954582-13-2 (Paperback)
ISBN: 978-1-954582-28-6 (Hardback)

Feedback: Encounter a problem with this book? Let us know at ellahendricksauthor@gmail.com

BOOKS BY ELLA HENDRICKS

Fated or Knot

LIBRARIAN WITCH

MOONGROVE ACADEMY: WICKED SPELLS
BOOK 1

ELLA HENDRICKS

CONTENT OVERVIEW

This is a paranormal RH romance, meaning that the main female character does not need to choose between love interests. There are graphic sex scenes (some including more than one partner) between consenting adults. *Librarian Witch* is book one of a trilogy with a cliffhanger ending.

Please be aware that this book includes a death (murder) of a friend and depictions of grief because of it. Also contained within are fight sequences that include death, gore, and magical violence. This trilogy is classified as dark academia because the main antagonists have magic that affects the souls of others.

This trilogy does not include a pregnancy for the FMC or MM content.

If you find anything in the contents of this book that should be added to this page, please let me know at ellahen dricksauthor@gmail.com.

1

CRESS

Thirty-some witches sat in a dimly lit classroom with auditorium-style seating. Gum snapped, and young women giggled quietly, paying little heed to the elderly figure at the front projecting her raspy voice over the group via a tiny microphone taped to one ear. She had one gnarled hand resting on the surface of what looked like a pure-black tabletop. "This device will determine what you study at our esteemed university. It will tell you which branch of witchcraft you are best suited for."

I shot a glare over my shoulder as a girl said a little too loudly, "Can we hurry this up?"

I'd met her at orientation, learning that she was one of many legacy witches attending this university like their parents had in the past. Unlike her and a disruptive handful of her friends, I didn't come from an established witch family who'd specialized in one kind of magic for generations. Every word from the venerated Dr. Evanora Heartwood was news to me. That was why I was one of three people who'd sat themselves in the front row.

While today was a formality for most of the students

here, it was vital for me. I couldn't stop my fidgeting as I waited to learn what kind of magic was the right fit for me. Today was my stepping stone into the supernatural world, which I'd just learned about a couple short months ago.

Dr. Heartwood acted like she hadn't heard the pointed question. Considering that she was at least two decades past retirement age, maybe her aging ears made her immune to the impatience of the younger generation. "I hope you are ready to learn your affinity! Even those of you who have already bonded your magic to a chosen affinity will be required to step forward and confirm it for the university's records," she said. She perched a tiny pair of eyeglasses on the tip of her nose before consulting a clipboard. "Merrill Blackwood, you're up first."

A guy with shaggy, clay-colored corkscrew hair descended the steps. He wore a polo and a pair of khaki shorts, looking for all the world like a normal college student.

That's what was still so surreal about Moongrove Academy. To me, witches were supposed to be green-skinned crones bent over bubbling cauldrons of goop, who rode brooms across the night sky and owned irritable black cats. They weren't guys like Merrill, who had the good looks and swagger of a future popular man on campus.

"The Blackwoods are a verdant witch family," the girl next to me whispered behind her hand. She was the only witch I'd talked to in depth since I'd arrived two days ago. I hadn't connected with any other witches, who all seemed to scoff when they realized I knew next to nothing about being one of them.

Luckily, I had a roommate who didn't mind I was completely new to magic. Lanie Graygazer had greeted me with an enthusiastic wave and an effusive, "Hi, Cress! I've seen we're going to be best friends." There was just something candy sweet and earnest about her, so I listened to her explain how she'd already known my name. Which, of course, involved magic.

Lanie was from a big family of augury witches that traveled all over helping others, sometimes before they realized they needed help. She'd come into her powers at fourteen, which was incredibly impressive by witch standards. While I was angsting over boys and pimples in eighth grade, she'd been busy viewing the future.

Lanie had already spent half her life in Europe and Asia, learning from her parents about how to use her augury magic. She could speak several languages fluently, starting with her family's native Korean, due to being homeschooled all that time. She'd learned everything she needed to know by doing it. Next to her, I felt like a talentless potato.

She took her family's calling to heart—she helped answer some of my questions before I asked them. "That thing up there looks like it's a table, but there's a machine in the center that'll prick your finger with a tiny needle. Inside it, a computer will read all the bits in your blood and then will turn on a light under the symbol for your affinity," she explained since Merrill had his back to us while he completed the process. A fresh-faced assistant had popped up out of nowhere to ask him a few questions first, recording his responses by tapping on a tablet.

After a few minutes, Dr. Heartwood announced his affinity. "A verdant witch. Congratulations, Mr. Blackwood." She led the group in a smattering round of applause.

One by one, the other witches completed the process. I started to sweat as the group went in alphabetical order.

Usually, my last name, Rollins, meant I was comfortably in the last third when it came to roll calls and classroom assignments. I'd never complained about it until the minutes crawled and the walls pushed in around me.

"Are you sure you can't tell me what my affinity is?" I asked Lanie.

She shook her head rapidly, flapping the dark hair of her bob. A reassuring smile crossed her face. "It's not my place to say. You'll like it, though," she said.

My lips formed a nervous twist, and I rubbed my clammy palms over my thighs. What would happen if I went up there and the machine couldn't find any potential in my blood? Other than my cats, I had no proof I was someone special and supernatural.

Cats don't just say "hello" to you. Not like Milo had when I'd walked by his cage at the shelter.

If that hadn't been enough, the brown tabby in the cage under him had pawed at the metal bars that separated us. "Get me out of here!" she'd howled.

I had two cats now. They talked. What explanation did I have for it if I wasn't a witch?

Lanie, too, had a cat for a familiar. Just one, though, an opinionated scrap of black fur. I couldn't understand what she mewed, only that she squeaked a lot for attention and food. I wondered if we were matched as roommates due to our familiars, considering how I'd seen a few of my witch peers walking around with wolves by their sides or falcons on their wrists. How many familiars fought one another despite their tamer natures? I had more questions than answers.

I drew myself out of my reverie to watch the different personalities come take their affinity test. The way someone walked up to that machine told me a lot about them. I looked at the slope of their shoulders and the fit of their clothes, drawing on years of people watching from the other side of a cash register as an ex-fast-food worker.

A slim brunette approached the podium like a timid mouse, her hands clutched before her. She took nearly five minutes with the assistant, whispering her answers and hunching her shoulders further when it looked like there was about to be an argument between them. Dr. Heartwood stepped in and announced the girl as Willow Frost, oceanic witch. I made sure to applaud more sincerely for her.

"Those without compound last names are new witches," Lanie told me. "They're probably going to try renaming you, too."

I scowled, my mouth forming a reply, when Lanie was called up to test next. It was brief, so she was soon skipping back to sit beside me again.

"And if I don't want a witchy last name?" I asked in an undertone.

"Oh, c'mon. There's no harm in it," she said. "It means you're one of us. And we don't go by the whole thing around humans. Like, my family introduces ourselves as the Grays, not the Graygazers."

I crossed my arms, not about to budge on my opinion. We would've argued had the double doors into this room not shot open and another woman who looked about our age walked in casually.

She had a post-workout glow on her tanned complexion. A towel hung around her neck, and she'd elevated a wavy mass of red hair into a springy high tail, highlighting a face with strong features and a constellation of freckles. She was muscular in a way most women weren't, with obvious pride in her body, which was barely covered by a neon pink pair of shorts and a matching crop top with the word "Tuff" in white lettering between two cartoon flexing arms.

She glanced around and announced loudly, "Sorry I'm late! Lost track of time."

Dr. Heartwood and her assistant were deep in conversation the moment the redhead appeared. The professor beckoned. "You must be Miss Ashbough. Let's test you next, then."

"Eh, no need. I'll go last. It's only fair," the redhead replied. She crossed the room to sit on my other side, her muscular arm scooting mine off the armrest.

To my shock, Dr. Heartwood nodded and called the next witch in line rather than make this girl respect her judgment. I glanced at the newcomer in disbelief, and she jerked her chin up. "Sup?"

Lanie came to my rescue, leaning past me to say, "Roe, this is Cress. She's a new witch."

A toothy white grin split the newcomer's face. "No way? Just learned about your powers?" she asked me. I nodded. "Coulda fooled me with that hair!"

I twirled a lock of hair self-consciously. The box color was "radiant orchid," but I wasn't sure such a bold change suited me yet. My little sister and I had dyed our hair in different intense shades before I'd left for college, and my palms were still purplish with lingering pigment.

"Yeah, I just thought it was a nice color," I said. Plus, purple was Carly's favorite color, and every time I looked in the mirror, I remember the joy on her face when I pulled out "radiant orchid" from the shopping bag. Carly was getting ready for her senior year of high school with a head of electric blue locks as we spoke.

"Cool, cool. Nice to meet you, new witch. I'm Rowena

Ashbough, but you can call me Roe. My family is *ooooooold* witch blood, so there's no real surprises here." She hitched a thumb toward her chest. "Ninety-nine percent chance I'm a guardian witch."

I asked something that'd been burning a hole in my thoughts. "How can you be so sure? Like, if you haven't bonded to your affinity yet, couldn't you be something else?"

"In that case, I'd ask to be bonded to the earth anyway," Roe said. "I'd embarrass my family if I didn't come home a guardian witch, no matter what."

"Right, you could do that." I nodded to myself.

I already knew this, sort of. The university had sent me a welcome package that included an informative video on the seven affinities, which were the official and safe wells of power witches could draw from. Generation after generation had honed down what worked and what didn't.

Along with the video, the university sent a thousand-page tome with details on the supernatural world. The kind of things the other witches in this room learned in their special supernatural-only private schools. It was *a lot*. Since I'd been busy working all summer to help support my family, I hadn't had a chance to read it in depth yet.

Witches could be any affinity they wanted to be, but the purpose of having our blood tested first was to find the best fit. Our magic was naturally drawn to just one of the seven sources we can safely pull from.

"But don't follow my lead. If your magic wants you to be a blood witch and you get afraid of that and pick the verdant path instead, then it's unlikely you're going to be a successful witch," Roe continued. "The moment you tap into a well of power for the first time, you're locked to that kind of magic for life."

I felt myself sweat. The fact that this was a permanent choice still made me quite nervous. I had enough trouble choosing what to eat for dinner, and I was soon expected to pledge myself to one of the seven affinities for life. No pressure at all!

"Whatever the machine shows you, you should accept it," Lanie agreed more quietly on my other side.

Easy enough for these two witches from established families to say. But I kept my lips clamped on that thought. "Blood magic seems dangerous," I pointed out.

Roe shrugged. "It's bad in the wrong hands. But it's regulated as tightly as vampires are, and many great witches have been blood witches. I won't think any less of you if you turn out to be one too."

I held back from saying that she barely even knew me yet to form an opinion, locking it behind a practiced customer service smile. "Great, but what if—?"

"Next up, Cressida Rollins," Dr. Heartwood announced.

"Hey, that's you!" Roe exclaimed. There was a twinkle in her bright green eyes.

Lanie flashed me a knowing smile. "Good luck."

I took a deep breath and stood, feeling like the whole auditorium had its attention on me. Wiping my forehead, I told myself I was imagining things.

The attendant consulted her tablet as I came to a stop before her expectantly. "Hi, Cressida. Just a couple questions before we find out what your affinity is," she said. "We update the SPDI registry on all our witches regularly, in accordance with supernatural law. Your file is mostly blank right now."

I licked my dry lips as she launched into the first question. "Do you have any supernatural relatives that you know of? We can link your file to theirs, and it'll save you time at the SPDI office later when you change your license."

"I wouldn't know. I'm adopted," I answered.

She nodded rapidly and tapped on her screen. "How were your talents first identified?"

"One of my teachers was secretly a supernatural. He was a talent scout and recognized a change in something about me after I found my cats." He'd also convinced me that I wasn't a total loony for being able to converse with a pair of felines.

"Of course." She drew out the words out as she documented what I'd said. "You found your familiars. How many cats do you have?"

"Two."

"Okay, Cressida. That's it for now. Best of luck," she said, gesturing to the machine next to us, which still resembled a black tabletop.

Dr. Heartwood beckoned me over. For the first time, I got a good look at the machine, seeing that it was mostly gears and wires underneath a black varnish. There was a raised lump in the center, and seven symbols were spread in an arc around it.

"I know you must be very excited," the professor said in an undertone. "May I give you a generic last name based on your affinity to begin your witch line?"

"No thank you," I said stiffly.

"Very well. Put your hand on that knob. You'll feel a little pinch, and then the machine will do its work and identify where you belong." She gave me a warm, grandmotherly smile.

This was the moment of truth, and my heartbeat roared in my ears. I had an understanding of the affinities and what kind of witch came from each, but up until this moment, I'd considered myself an imposter, a "normal" human who'd accidentally gotten an invitation to the university. When was I going to wake up and realize I'd never heard a cat talk and there were no such thing as supernaturals?

I needed a sign that this was real. I needed to know my affinity. Swallowing past the lump in my throat, I studied the seven symbols as my hand descended toward my destiny.

Half of all witches were verdant witches, powered by the green things out in untamed nature. They mixed potions and healed even the direst of wounds. The verdant symbol, a wand intertwined with a patch of flowers, was the first one to the left of my hand.

Immediately to the right was the second most common type, guardian. Drawing from the solid strength of the earth, they were tough as stone, with the magic to fight for and protect what they believed in. They were represented by an image of a rocky shield and a jagged cluster of crystals.

Third was the symbol for oceanic witches, a wave and trident together. They commanded control of the weather and summoned ice to defend themselves. Of the seven, I least wanted this one. Despite living in chilly Massachusetts my whole life, I hated the cold.

My hand closed around the knob on the table. I waited a few anxiety-filled seconds before a little needle poked the center of my thumb.

Would the machine read that I was a blood witch, the most feared affinity? They could steal power from almost any supernatural if they got their hands on a single drop of blood. I watched the dagger and cup symbol on the machine, hoping that one wouldn't light up either.

I knew the least about the last three affinities, the rarest ones. The tarot symbol was for augury witches like Lanie, wielding the kind of power only a chosen few should have.

The librarian witch's symbol of an open book and unsheathed sword also remained dark opposite of the augury mark. All I could remember was that librarians tapped power beyond mere mortal understanding. The witches with this affinity weren't busy filing away books, but instead dealing with darker powers.

And finally was the strongest affinity, that of celestial witches, who channeled the raw power of the sun and moon. Its crescent moon and staff symbol only lit for the privileged few that ruled witchkind, or so I'd heard.

My expression began to fall as the seconds ticked away and nothing happened. Maybe I really was dreaming, or this was all one big, elaborate mistake. I glanced at Dr. Heartwood, whose smile was rapidly shading toward pity. Then, a patch of brightness lit up in the corner of my eye with a mechanical *ding*.

2

BEN

I KNEW it was going to be a bad day when a politician visited. The strutting and puffing and doublespeak. Exhausting. Master Garroway inevitably gained the upper hand every time, fleecing eye-watering amounts from his clients in exchange for his discreet services.

Garroway required that his whole "coven" of blood witches attend every meeting when he negotiated with clients, if we weren't out on missions. Today, oddly enough, there was an actual coven of seven lining the far wall, standing in order of seniority. From Seth, the tough old salt who'd served here the longest, to my little brother, Lucas, who'd recently joined us with his blood witch affinity. He was only sixteen, with a boyish tousle of blond hair atop his head and soft cheekbones that'd never grown more than a bit of fuzz. Too young to be called an assassin, in my opinion.

We were the muscle and the reminder of which spider owned this parlor. Today, the fly was none other than Blaize Starsurge, a middle-aged celestial witch. He was an old client who'd wised up to some of Garroway's tricks.

He'd left his steaming cup of tea untouched on the low table between them and angled his chair away from the seven of us assassins without a single nervous glance in our direction.

The man was a member of the Crown Coven, the ruling body of witchkind. He had the air of old money about him, clear in the crisp cut of his suit and his fair hair professionally styled to comb over the balding patch creeping across his head.

After only ten minutes of pleasantries, however, Crown Starsurge seemed tired of avoiding the subject of his appointment. "Do you remember the Darkmore job, Garroway?"

I watched my vampire master as he calmly sipped from his cup of tea, eyeing the man opposite of him from over the rim. He placed the priceless china back on its dish with a little hum. "That was many years ago." As always, Garroway spoke in a hypnotic cadence, soft and precise. His deep voice had lost its power over me, but many female clients relaxed utterly in his presence.

"I paid you a fortune to send your best man to kill the Darkmore family."

"It rings a few bells," Garroway said smoothly. "Did you call on me to reminisce over your successes?"

"No," Starsurge muttered. He slapped a folder on the table between them, scattering a few glossy photos. "Whomever you sent on the job half-assed it. One of them survived."

My brother shot me a worried glance. Lucas had attended maybe two of these meetings. He didn't know yet that we were easy scapegoats should anything go wrong. "Accidents happen," I murmured.

Garroway, with his inhumanly good hearing, shot me a quick warning look.

He shuffled through the contents of the folder. "And what makes you believe that this girl is a Darkmore?" the vampire asked.

Starsurge flipped an impatient hand. "Without a genetic test, it's all the evidence you're holding. Orphan witches with potential like hers don't just *appear.* You were supposed to take out the whole Darkmore family for me. Four people! Eris Darkmore, her husband, sister, and baby."

Garroway covered his lips with a hand, glancing through the folder a second time. "So, you believe this girl is the baby, miraculously returned to life. Well. You have certainly done your homework on her, Crown Starsurge. Her adoption papers, plus an augury reading that says she'll be a celestial witch." His cunning blood-red gaze flashed toward the politician's face. "But this doesn't tell me why you're here."

"Isn't it obvious?"

"I do not operate on assumptions. They are bad for business."

"Your best assassin *failed.* I want what I paid for." Now he flashed a sneer over his shoulder at us, his gaze fixed on Seth. As one, the seven of us tensed, muscles flexing, hands drifting for weapons. I drew one of the knives at my belt. He raised an unimpressed brow and turned back to Garroway. "I want the last Darkmore dead before she can inherit the full might of her family line. For free."

"Free," Garroway echoed with a low chuckle.

"I have a contact in the university who will sabotage her affinity test. She will be an easy target for you." Starsurge sniffed.

My fingers tensed on the hilt of my knife. I couldn't

stand the superior smirk in his words. It was like if the girl wasn't a celestial witch, she was a defenseless nobody. He must not have been paying attention during his own schooling.

Celestial witches didn't wield offensive magic until they learned complicated astrology and some of the most laborious runes. They were insanely powerful when fully trained, but the drawback was slow casting speed. If his proposed mark became a blood or guardian witch, she'd be able to fight back much more effectively.

All seven of us were trained by the same playbook. Even my little brother shook his head with a little snort. We knew how best to fight most anything in the supernatural world.

"And if you're wrong about her? What happens then?" Garroway asked.

Starsurge lifted his shoulder. "People die every day."

The vampire threw his head back and laughed. "Very well. Due to our long friendship, I shall send someone to remove your little enemy for free."

With a nod, Starsurge got to his feet and pointed. "I do not trust your best anymore. I want her for the job."

We weren't actually lined up in order of age, but price. Next to Seth stood the woman he pointed to, Bianca. She flashed her signature vicious smile.

Bianca had dressed in her femme fatale wannabe leather today, posing sexily on the wall. Male clients liked her, and she loved going on missions. I was past worrying for her. We were about the same age, but she'd taken to her blood witchery much faster than me. Master Garroway usually picked her for one of the other services he provided, monster hunting. She was adept at killing man and unnatural alike. Just give her a blade, and let her go.

"Very well. Will this conclude your visit, Crown Star-surge?" Garroway asked, getting to his feet as well. When the politician nodded, our vampire master led him out.

Lucas gave a soft breath of relief, but the rest of us knew not to relax yet. Garroway's smile was nonexistent when he returned alone and swept up the folder and all its contents so quickly the paper made a snapping noise. His long face was drawn in an irritated snarl, fangs pearly white underneath the dark shadow of his mustache.

My heart drummed at double time as his bloody gaze swept over us. It landed on the boy standing next to me. "Lucas," he barked. "It's time for your first mission."

"But Master, he wanted *me* to do it," Bianca whined.

He shot her a look that could boil her blood. Her pouty red lips snapped closed, and she bowed her head in acknowledgment. Mollified, Garroway dismissed us with a wave of his hand, leaving an eager Lucas. I remained at his side, feet planted, waiting to receive the same treatment as Bianca.

"May I attend my brother's first briefing?" I placed a hand on Lucas's shoulder and flashed my best smile, earning a sullen look from him.

I squeezed him more firmly, trying to express my urgency with a single glance. He hadn't been old enough to see what had happened to some of the older witches in Garroway's employ, but I could still see their faces. They'd been caught. Executed. Our blood runes wouldn't leave us alive long enough to share Garroway's name and whereabouts. The most dangerous time for him was now, with his first assignment, especially since it was supposed to be "easy."

Garroway watched this brief exchange far too keenly. Somehow, some way, he'd use my concern for Lucas against me. But for now, he gestured us back to the living room where he'd been negotiating with Crown Starsurge. "By all means," he said.

Lucas jerked out of my hold and sat on one side of an unused couch, closest to Garroway's favorite chair, and I settled next to him. Everything in this room was hand-crafted to resemble antiques, just as the vampire liked it, with upholstery in red and black patterns.

I didn't know exactly how old he was, but Garroway seemed ancient beyond any measure of understanding. He liked things only in his exacting way, and that included the position of the furniture down to the angle and the flavor of the black tea he sipped on that never had even a wink of sugar.

"Little Lucas. Finally earning his keep," Garroway said, a hint of mockery in his precise cadence. "You are to remove a new enrollee in the Moongrove Academy division of the Northern Supernatural University. Here's what she looks like. Hard to miss."

He passed Lucas a few photos of a young woman from several angles. Discreet, paparazzi-style snaps of her that my brother let me see over his shoulder. "She's hot," Lucas commented.

Garroway flipped the folder over Lucas's knuckles. "You're going to kill her, not fuck her. Focus."

"Yes, Master," he grumbled.

Secretly, I agreed with my brother. Her most striking feature was a head of dark purple hair, freshly dyed by the looks of it. Since these pictures had been taken without her noticing, she wasn't smiling in any of them. Even with a serious case of resting bitch face, she was a looker with soulful brown eyes and a heart-shaped face.

The only time she looked happier was a photo with her

walking next to a petite girl with a dark bob. I took that picture from Lucas for further inspection, happy I didn't get this mission. I'd only gone on a few missions and could justify taking out all of my marks by twisted logic. It was hard to validate killing this woman, though.

"Her name is Cressida Rollins. She's an upcoming freshman with signs of great potential already," Garroway said. "Before you make a plan, find out which affinity she picks. If it's blood, I want you to bring her back to me alive, Starsurge be damned. We will find out together if she gains the Darkmore hereditary power."

From the glimmer in his eyes, I could tell he was dreaming of having control of a witch with access to the Darkmores' power. She'd be deadlier than Bianca, maybe even Seth. I shuddered to think of what Garroway would do with her. He made most of his money in lending, but it was the threat of his deadliest agents that kept a flow of income pouring into his pockets.

"And if she doesn't pick blood, I kill her," Lucas confirmed.

"That's right. Don't get yourself caught. Any other creative details are at your discretion." The vampire bared his fangs with a bloodthirsty smile. "See, isn't that an easy job? Go earn your place here, Lucas."

"Yes, Master," he said eagerly. "I won't let you down."

My brother didn't turn to see the concern flashing over my features. The easy jobs rarely ended that way.

3

CRESS

The light flickered under one mark before switching to another. I waited, my brow drawn, to see if the machine would change its mind again about what kind of witch I should be. For the barest moment, I swore it'd said I'd be a celestial witch, but now the light held steady under a different mark.

The book and sword of a librarian shimmered before me. I could hardly believe it. Not only was I a confirmed witch, but I was one of the rarest three types. Dr. Heartwood peered at it before nodding to her assistant, who tapped on her screen to record the results.

"Everyone, welcome Cressida Rollins, a new librarian witch," the elderly professor announced, and I received a smattering of applause. Even though the group's enthusiasm was flagging at this point, I still grinned like I'd received a standing ovation as I crossed the room to take my seat again.

My gaze caught on a reflection of light, and I realized there was a phone camera pointed at me from one of the back rows. Elation turned to a scowl immediately, aimed toward a blonde girl popping gum as she looked down at her screen.

Roe clapped me on the shoulder as the testing continued. "Congrats, librarian! One of the coolest affinities, if you ask me. Right behind being a guardian."

"You might be biased," Lanie teased.

"Girl, I've watched my mama juggle boulders as a preworkout. Tell me guardians aren't cool," Roe said with a belly laugh.

"Sure, but my parents have saved hundreds of lives just by slightly altering the timeline of fate," Lanie replied.

I was barely listening. The blonde was called up to test next, and I stared daggers into her back as she approached the table with an obnoxious snap of her gum. Her name was Wren Starsurge, and my eyebrows rose in surprise when she was announced as a celestial witch. She was the second one in this whole session of affinity testing.

On her way back to her seat, I noticed Wren walked confidently in the kind of stiletto heels that would break a lesser woman's ankles. Her satiny dress was a deep blue, matching the shade of her eyes as our gazes locked. It was only a fraction of a second before her attention flicked over my two companions and her lips twisted into a smirk. She flipped a wave of thick hair over her shoulder and moved on, leaving only a lingering hint of sweet perfume behind.

Roe's elbow nudged my side, bringing my attention back to her. "You wanna grab some food after this?" she invited.

"I guess," I said noncommittally. "Shouldn't we be getting started with our affinities, though?"

"That's after orientation. Two days from now," Lanie supplied. Well, the augur would know. "Dr. Heartwood will share this too, but we get time to think things over before committing to our affinities. If we have any lingering questions over what the test said, there's time to test again and seek answers."

I chewed thoughtfully on my lower lip. Not that I'd question a good thing, but the flickering symbol of celestial magic came to mind. Was it normal for the machine to change its mind like that? Or perhaps being a celestial witch was a viable option for me as well?

"Makes sense," I said mostly to myself.

Roe tested last and was quickly announced as a guardian witch. She pumped her fists in the air like she'd won a huge prize. I applauded for her like she had for me, surprising myself. I didn't make friends easily, but I could see myself hanging out with Roe.

As soon as Dr. Heartwood finished telling us what came next, which echoed Lanie's wisdom exactly, we were released to acclimate to campus life for our last two days free of the pressures of classes and deadlines. "Take us to the best grub, Graygazer," Roe said, flanking the petite girl as we walked out into the late afternoon sunshine.

"I know just the place," Lanie said, a skip to her step as she picked a direction.

I soon gained a skip too, smiling to myself. I knew my affinity now, doubts notwithstanding. I was a real witch, soon to bond to whatever "dimensional energy" was, and had the opportunity to stay here and study magic alongside a more normal college major. Giddy bubbles floated in my belly as we crossed the campus together.

Northern Supernatural University was a massive complex, and I kept my head on a swivel as we headed toward a corner I hadn't explored yet. The air gained a salty tang, and the path we took wound its way around a massive grassy field and ended at a roadway, where we waited for a red light to cross.

Everything seemed ordinary until we passed a marina and I realized some of the buildings along the lakeside were actually deeper in the water than any human would design. Sidewalks ended with lapping, green water where they submerged and presumably continued the campus underwater, if the gleaming spires of a few buildings further into the lake were any indication.

We'd entered the mer side of campus, where the merfolk and oceanic witches had class. I tried not to gape too much. I hadn't had enough time to have it sink in that nobody here would be hiding their true natures. My introduction to NSU had been walking through a gate that was apparently a portal or a seam in reality. My guide had called it both. One moment, we'd been in Salem, Massachusetts, and the next, we were on the other side of the gate leading to this campus. It was a safe place for supernaturals to be themselves.

Lanie led us to a building with a brightly painted sign declaring it Poseidon's Kitchen. "Here it is, the kind of food you were craving," she said to Roe.

The redhead licked her lips. "I love your magic."

We were seated quickly, and Lanie was sure to ask for a lakeside table. The back of the building was a massive deck with a water-level bar. With only a railing between me and a dunking in the green lake, I leaned over to get my first look at a group of giggling mermaids cracking oysters below us.

"Wow," I murmured. They were mostly what I was expecting, except instead of wearing shells and seaweed, they had flowy shirts that covered the seam in their bodies where human torso met flexible, iridescent fish tail. They were every shade of the rainbow, with scales and fins lining their arms and cheeks.

I sat up straight before any mermaid could notice me gawking. When I'd worked in fast food, I'd learned when and where to make eye contact and how long was considered uncomfortable. Customers started getting weird if you stared at them, unblinking, while they complained about something.

Roe glanced my way. "Takes a minute to get used to it all," she said. "I get it. I just saw my first cupid the other day."

Self-conscious, I turned my gaze down to the menu. I'd just confirmed for her that I was a gaping newcomer compared to most of the people on this campus. Hopefully she wasn't judging like some of the other witches I'd already met.

It was an honor to be here, like I'd fallen into one of my favorite books, where the most incredible creatures and magic both existed and thrived just under the nose of humanity. At the same time, I was one of the only supernaturals here who'd grown up with no clue about this secret world. I had so many misconceptions to correct.

I cleared my throat, searching for any topic other than my own ignorance. "So, uh, how do you two know each other?" I asked.

Lanie and Roe exchanged a glance. They'd both sat across from me. "Our parents go back a long way," Lanie answered. "The Ashboughs guard some of the Graygazer family's relics in exchange for our augury services."

"She's told me a lot about my future. Good and bad," Roe added. "Including that we'd be close friends."

"You too?" I laughed.

She nodded, pausing to put her order in with the

waiter. He was obviously merfolk of some kind, with shiny green scales lining his hands and face, complete with a set of flapping fins under his aquamarine hair instead of ears. When his slitted pupils turned my way to take my order, I was momentarily catching flies.

Don't ask him what he is. Don't be weird, I told myself.

I ordered the first special on the menu, ignoring the snickers coming from Roe until he walked away.

"As I was going to say, it must be nice to know your friends before you meet them," she said instead of teasing me, nudging Lanie in the side.

"Can you tell me about someone, actually?" I asked suddenly. "Wren Starsurge? I think she was recording me earlier."

The smiles erased from both of their faces. "Yeah. She's from another old bloodline. Her dad's a member of the ruling coven of witches," Roe answered. "My pops runs security for some of their family artifacts, and he hates working with the Starsurges. They've got money and entitlement, and Wren's no different. I only know her by reputation, and it's the same as the rest of her family. I wouldn't mess with her."

My frown deepened. "And if *she* messes with *me*?"

There was no immediate answer, as I expected. When a girl had power and money, there was no stopping her if you were an ordinary person. And a nobody like me might as well have a target on my back for someone like her.

"Gotta play it cool for now. Let's see if she tries something, and then maybe Lanie and I can help," Roe offered.

The waiter returned, dropping off a basket of seaweed chips. We took a moment to sample them, and I pulled a face at how salty they were. I let Lanie and Roe have them.

"What majors are you picking?" I asked. The university's piles of information had suggested that it wasn't common to get a degree in magic unless one was good at it and intended to stay exclusively in a supernatural community. That was the kind of thing I couldn't plan for yet.

Roe rolled her eyes. "Business," she answered in a grumble.

"You already know this, but I'm in world cultural studies," Lanie said, glancing to Roe. "Your dad won that argument, huh?"

"Yeah," she sighed, glancing at my puzzled expression. "I'm the eldest kid, so I get to inherit the family business. Means I get to babysit other people's important things for the rest of my life."

I tried to look sympathetic, but there were worse fates than getting a successful business from one's parents. "What would you do otherwise?" I asked.

She started to brighten again. "I was thinking physiotherapy. Don't you know how hard it is to find help if you have an injury in your wings or tail? It's not like you can walk in to see a human doctor for things like that."

"Yeah. Limited clients, though," I said.

"Please. The supernatural world is *huge*. There's a need for a supernatural physiotherapist somewhere." From the way she puffed up, I imagined she'd argued this point before with less sympathetic ears. "What about you? What are you majoring in?"

A tinge of pink lit my cheeks. "Well, I picked fashion design. The professors are still reviewing my portfolio and 'extenuating circumstances,'" I said, making air quotes. "But all my designs were for humans. They're looking for, like, more creativity."

I still hoped to hear back from the committee making the decision soon. Attending a university wasn't even in my five-year plan, not when I'd been gainfully employed and helping support my mother and sister.

Yet life had thrown me a curve ball, so here I was, trying to get accepted into one of the more competitive degree tracks at NSU. From the moment I'd been identified as a supernatural and ordered to attend a school to properly develop my powers, the authorities had made it clear this could be a two-year deal if I wasn't feeling the college environment.

So, if the committee didn't accept me, I would just leave in two years. There was nothing I wanted more than to bring my sketches to life. Mermaids, winged fae, and other assorted supernaturals needed to wear clothes, too.

I know most people my age would sneer at the decision to leave NSU two years early, considering that I'd been put on a full-ride scholarship. Newcomers to the supernatural world all received the same perk. If we *had* to be here and had no means to pay, it was the least the university could do.

"Do you have any designs on you?" Roe asked curiously. "How about it, Lanie? Is she going to make it?"

Lanie's dark eyes twinkled. "I can't give away everything, can I?"

"C'mon, the suspense is killing me!"

While I was busy thumbing through my phone for a photo of a recent sketch, the two girls leaned together and whispered behind their hands. "Hey, if you're going to tell her, tell me too," I complained.

The huge grin on Roe's face seemed to be answer enough, though she tried to hide it by cramming more seaweed chips in her mouth. I showed her what was on my screen before I could regret it. I was so worried about offending other races that I hadn't started drawing clothes for their varied body shapes yet, so I'd made a design I wanted to bring to life for myself. It was a little black dress with an empire waist and elbow-length sleeves. What made it unique was the insert of spider-web-shaped lace to expose shoulders and collarbone. Simple, sleek, and witchy.

Well, my conception of witchy. So far, none of the witches I'd met seemed like the type to keep spiders and other creepy crawlies.

"Cress, this is super cool," Roe said. "You drew that yourself?"

"Yeah. I have a whole sketchbook full," I said, wishing I could show her some of the more whimsical designs I'd drawn before ever knowing of the supernatural world. I dreamed in flowing dresses and beautiful fabrics, all the premium kinds my adopted family couldn't afford.

But I didn't share with my two new friends that I'd learned to make my own clothes out of necessity. I didn't need pity, just a place for myself in this supernatural world.

4

CRESS

THE NEXT MORNING, a tiny sprite thumped against my dorm's door at eight sharp. Bleary eyed, I opened the door to see a floating person at eye level, holding the edge of an envelope three times its size. I scrubbed my eyeballs and then confirmed, yup, normal-sized envelope, mini-sized person.

"Thanks," I said, taking the letter it offered. A feline chirp behind me turned into the quiet chattering of a cat who'd spotted something it wanted to hunt. With a squeak, the tiny person zoomed off on its diminutive wings. I closed the door before Bella could run after it.

"That was a friend," I said, plopping back onto my nest of blankets, all thrown askew in my rush to get the door. I gathered up one corner and pulled them off Milo, my black and white boy cat, who licked the fur prickling against his side in disgruntlement at getting buried.

Bella, the brown tabby girl cat, paced the doorway as if the sprite would come inside at any moment. "I just wanted to play," she complained.

Where anyone else would hear meowing, I heard a

high-pitch voice as she whined her frustration at losing access to what must've seemed like a living, flying toy.

"Was it food?" Milo asked, his voice only a little lower than my other familiar's. He looked at me, eyes rounded expectantly. As he grew to adult size, his black spots had been engulfed in white fluff. I was probably feeding him too much, as he was developing a chubby belly.

"No," I giggled. I tore open the envelope and scanned its contents before releasing a sound somewhere in the octaves of a dog whistle. Milo and Bella scattered.

My dorm room was set up like a cinderblock box. There was barely enough room for two beds, two desks, and two closets for Lanie and me to share. So when I popped up and screamed, Lanie, sitting a couple feet away at her desk, earphones on so loud that I could hear the beat of her music, still startled.

"What happened?" she asked, resting a pale hand over her chest. She was already showered and ready for the day, while I'd been passed out with no alarm set.

"Don't you already know?" I laughed and passed the letter to her.

She rolled her eyes before reading it. "My magic doesn't tell me *everything*," she said, brightening and turning a smile my way. "Congratulations!"

She gave me my acceptance letter back. I was officially in the fashion design major and invited to the building where classes were held for a little meet and greet at lunchtime. "Everything okay?" Milo squeaked, peeking out from under my bed.

"Definitely," I answered, making kissy noises until he hopped up onto the bed and barreled into my lap for a snuggle. Bella settled at the foot of the bed, curling up into a loaf. She resumed her favorite pastime, staring daggers at

Lanie's cat, Jin. Her cat was barely bigger than a kitten, but she was apparently three years old. She didn't seem bothered at all by Bella's stink eye.

"Are you going to the event?" Lanie asked. I realized again that I was assuming she already knew the answer and was just asking to talk me out of my decision. I cast her a side glance and a shrug. "It'd be a great opportunity. See the campus, meet some non-witches that share your major..."

I groaned and flopped back on the bed.

"Plus, you can take your familiars out! I bet they're dying to see the campus too," Lanie added.

My heart rate stuttered. "Out? But have you *seen* the other familiars walking around? It's dangerous for a little cat out there."

Jin let out an opinionated meow. "She's right, we can take care of ourselves," Milo agreed with the other cat. Both he and Bella turned pleading faces my way, complete with him making soft pats of my arm when I tried to avert my gaze.

"You could even take Jin. She's already explored," Lanie offered.

Bella released a little growl. "Sounds good," I said just to watch her fur lift. I couldn't feel any emotions from her and Milo like other witches do with their familiars. That was supposed to come after I attained my magic, apparently.

I spent the time until then showering and sipping on an energy drink while reading over the massive book the university had sent as a welcome gift. It was the third time I'd reread the requirements to be a celestial or a librarian witch. It wasn't too late to ask for a redo of the affinity test and see if the machine really meant for me to be the former. But did I want that?

The more I read over what celestial witches had to learn, the less I wanted to be one. They had the most rituals of the seven affinities. Though it was possible a celestial witch could call down the full wrath of the sun to scorch away her opponents, her day-to-day life involved preparing for hours to be able to unleash that kind of power.

When would I have use for magic like that? Honestly, the more I thought about it, the less the decision seemed to matter in the end. I was a confirmed witch with the need to train in one of the seven affinities, but I wanted to design clothes, not read star charts or fight the dangerous super-natural creatures called unnaturals that plagued our world in secret.

On the other hand for my decision, though, librarian witches handled artifacts and beings from other dimensions. They wielded silver swords instead of decimal systems, even though, for the most part, the job still involved books. Books of occult knowledge that might drive the reader insane, but books nonetheless.

It sounded really *cool*, and that cemented the decision for me. I was going for the affinity the test had decided on and becoming a librarian witch. As I pet Milo, I daydreamed about the kind of outfits a proper librarian wore. Maybe it was tweed jackets and polish, or tank tops and grit. Depended on how much they actually used the swords associated with the affinity, I decided.

When a distant clock chimed eleven o'clock, I set the book aside and took the cat trio outside on a walk. I occasionally glanced behind me to make sure they were still around...they were. Sniffing flowers, rolling in the grass, or giving strangers' ankles a brush of soft fur, but still following me.

I smiled to myself at their antics and consulted a paper map several times. The campus was shaped like a big egg from above, with the center serving as a multicultural center where most races studied together. But on the outskirts, there were sections of space for each individual race. Witches had the largest space, actually, labeled "Moongrove Academy." Considering we were located in Salem, Moongrove was first built as a haven for witches and still had the biggest enrollment of them of all the supernatural universities.

But we shared space with vampires, shifters, and fae, with smaller sections for cupids, merfolk, and dimensionals. Each race had their own academy to learn the ins and outs of their place in the supernatural world. Considering how our individual spaces were pushed to the outskirts of the university grounds, I could tell we were meant to mingle and learn from each other just as much as we were here for magical training and our degrees.

I stopped briefly at the Voidbinder Building, a three-story structure where the witch professors had their offices and most witch-related classes were held. Dr. Heartwood was in there somewhere with the affinity-testing machine. This was my chance to change my mind and get tested again...but I was pretty sure of my decision, so I kept walking.

I kept my eyes peeled for the Margot E. Frederick Building, and along the way, my phone vibrated in my back pocket. I fumbled it out and answered, "Hello?"

"Cress!" It was my sister, Carly. I felt my expression stretch into a big smile. "You don't text, you don't call. I was wondering if they'd turned you into a frog or something!"

"Sorry," I said quickly. "It's just...it's been a wild ride already."

Truth be told, I was waiting for something concrete to tell her and Mom. But now I knew what kind of witch I was going to be and what my major was. Her call couldn't be better timing. "Well, you won't believe who asked me out," she practically squealed.

I listened and made encouraging noises, glad to hear her voice again. She babbled on about her new guy as I finally spotted the building I was looking for. It was as modern as any other human campus would have, with a front of smoky glass and chrome. The double doors were thrown open, a banner over the threshold to welcome all the newbies like myself.

I ducked to the side of the stairs and leaned against their cool surface. "How's witch school?" she was asking, a teasing lit to the question.

"I made it into the fashion design major." This time, we squealed together. It felt like I'd never left home.

"Are you going to be making, like..." She dropped her voice to an awed hush. "...*magic* clothes?"

Due to my circumstances, the first people who'd learned I was actually a supernatural were Mom and Carly. It was heavily frowned upon to have "normal" people made aware of this kind of thing, but I trusted my adopted family. They knew everything I did about NSU and the students who attended it.

"If I do, I'll let you try them on first," I promised her.

We giggled together before I let her go, heading up the steps in high spirits. Just on the inside of the building stood a statuesque woman. She was straight out of an earlier era, wearing a billowing maroon ball gown and classic, understated makeup with gently curled brunette hair. Her red lips spread and...she flashed a fanged smile my way.

I stopped short of shaking her hand for a split second before realizing...of course. A vampire. Yeah. "So pleased you could make it," she said politely as I gave myself a mental slap and closed the gap between us to shake her hand. "Dr. Margot Fredrick, at your service."

My mouth hung. "Like...*the*..."

"One in the same," she drawled. "Who might you be, darling?"

I shared my name, and she nodded. Her long, pale fingers tweezed a lock of my hair, and she turned it with a curious eye. "This will fade in a couple weeks. If you have a verdant witch friend, I know the most delightful potion recipe for vibrant, long-lasting colors."

"Oh, um, thank you, ma'am," I said.

"Please, come inside. We have refreshments." She gestured me into the lobby, where a few clusters of students were already chatting away happily. I went a few yards in and stood, a little petrified to join in somewhere. I wished I had more of Carly's bubbly personality right about now, since she was capable of wading into the middle of a crowded room and joining any conversation.

An upperclassman came to my rescue and looped her finned arm through mine, sweeping me off for a big round of introductions. She was an amethyst-toned mer woman, but ordinary legs replaced her tail for now. She wore a tunic and the tiniest shorts possible, which seemed to be a common style amongst the mostly female crowd getting to know each other.

With a lemonade in one hand and the other free for handshakes, I dare say I was having a good time until I heard a pointed voice say, "What is *she* doing here?"

I turned and made eye contact with a smirking blonde, dressed up from the college casual the rest of us sported. She'd spoken in a loud aside to the umber-skinned witch next to her, who I recognized from the affinity test as a fellow freshman and the other girl to reveal an affinity for celestial magic.

I quietly cursed my luck. Really? Wren Starsurge had to have the same major as me?

Well, this just confirmed that she had some chip on her shoulder. She and her friend moved into the crowd to start socializing too, but the draw for me was gone. I said my goodbyes, ducking away from confrontation before it could get ugly. But something told me I was making a mistake showing my vulnerable back to a girl like her.

BESIDES THE BRIEF unpleasantness of realizing I might have several classes with Wren, I enjoyed the time learning my way around the NSU campus and hanging out with Lanie and Roe. We sat together toward the front of the double-tiered auditorium waiting for Convocation to begin. We'd gotten here early since the whole place was due to fill with all manner of supernatural students.

Roe, it turned out, lived in a multi-race dorm. She'd brought her roommate, a slender fae who might be about five feet tall if her horns grew in more. She had the upper body of a woman, which met the furry hindquarters of an animal, complete with dainty cloven hooves painted with silvery sparkles.

Her skin was a warm, earthy brown, complimenting curly auburn hair woven with a myriad of fresh pink flowers. Two bell-shaped deer ears poked out of either side of her head, flickering toward any loud noise. A pair of two-inch-long horns were starting to grow upward from her forehead, and her nose took on a blunted slope and ended in a damp, textured button that connected to her lips by a thick cupid's bow.

The fae gal, Áine, didn't tell me what kind of fae she was, and I didn't ask. That seemed super rude. She did clarify that her name was pronounced "Anya" and spelled it out for me, accent mark included. When she learned my major, she'd turned around and showed off how the flag of her deer-like tail stuck out awkwardly above the line of her shorts. "Remember to make more comfortable clothes for your tailed sisters."

"Of course," I'd said, too surprised to have a fae shake her tail at me to have a better response. But my mind turned around a few ideas as we waited. I'd noticed how her fur puffed out under the cuff of her shorts, brown with white spots like a fawn's.

Convocation began with a speech by the Dean of Magical Studies, an ordinary-seeming gentleman. Lanie leaned over and shared that he was a shifter. "How can you tell?" I asked behind my hand.

"He has an aura of magic. You'll see it too when you bond to your affinity," she promised.

The Dean spoke briefly before gesturing off stage. "It is my greatest honor to welcome our esteemed University President, Dr. Melinda Aurina, to the stage. For nearly fifty years, Dr. Aurina has seen to the modernization and continued privacy of NSU and its esteemed academies of magic." He led the crowd in a round of applause as a winged woman joined him at the microphone.

There was an audible murmur of awe from the audience

as the spotlight caused her rose gold feathers to shine. Dr. Aurina didn't look like she'd even reached fifty, let alone earned a doctorate and clawed her way up the academic ladder to helm a university the size of NSU. Her pink hair flowed around her to waist length, lending her a nearly ethereal beauty.

An elbow jabbed my side hard. It was Roe, and the moment I glared at her, I wondered why I was angry. "Rule number, like, five hundred of the supernatural world...never look at a cupid for too long," she whispered.

"I wasn't," I said defensively.

She bent and placed the program we'd all gotten at the door back into my hands, flipping it over to a section I hadn't bothered to read before putting it under my chair. I scanned it, and my eyebrows rose. "She's a demigoddess?" I gasped. "That's possible?"

"It means she's got *very* strong emotional magic. Any of us can get to demigod or demigoddess status if we get enough power, so...don't look at her directly," Roe said. The audience was listening in silently as Dr. Aurina's flute-like voice and beautiful looks kept them spellbound.

"Show me your schedule again," Lanie suggested when I started fidgeting. We'd just picked up our schedules from a small army of upperclassmen outside who'd had the documents separated in alphabetical order by last name.

We exchanged schedules. Regrettably, I only had one class with my two friends, Introduction to Witchcraft. Lanie hadn't been happy to see it on her schedule, considering how she was the furthest from a newcomer, but I was just happy she'd be there too.

On Mondays, Wednesdays, and Fridays, I had Introduction to Witchcraft, Drawing for Fashion, and Library Science 101. Tuesdays and Thursdays were dominated by

Introduction to Supernatural Society and Beginning Fashion. And then there was the class I wasn't thrilled with... Latin I, my foreign language requirement. Apparently, all librarian witches were required to take Latin, and the first semester of it was hosted bright and early every day.

It was a full schedule, and Roe's was bursting too. Oh well. If we took eighteen hours in our first semesters, we would have less to do by the time we were in our later years here.

By the time I was done reviewing Lanie's schedule, Dr. Aurina was saying goodbye to us and bidding that we go do well in our first semester at NSU. She received a standing ovation on her way out. I glanced at Roe, and she shrugged. "Want to go hit the gym?"

5

CRESS

On Monday, I'd already gone and gotten my Latin I class syllabus by the time I glanced up from my campus map and beheld Moongrove Library for the first time. It was right in the middle of the general campus, accented by a strip of garden paths and a fountain of geometric shapes where a pair of students were already sitting and chatting.

I hoisted my backpack higher on my shoulders, stopping just past those students so they weren't watching me awkwardly as I took a moment to admire my destination. I was a little starstruck. It was the biggest library I'd seen in my life, with gothic towers framing an arched entryway. Even from a distance, the shiny panes high above reflected colored light in circular mosaics or tall, skinny windows.

It was the oldest-looking building on campus, and as I shook off my awe and neared it, I noted crouching figures along the high eaves. Gargoyles. Shading my eyes, I tried to view the ugly, snarling face of one, just to realize it was a little too human-looking for my taste. Whoever was in charge of this library must've added the gargoyles in later. They weren't worn down by the elements yet.

I consulted the email I had up on my phone. The instructor, a man named Lars Eriksson, wanted us to meet in the foyer to begin our tour of the library. My heart raced faster as I read the last line a few times.

We were also bonding to the magic of the library today, so I would officially be a librarian witch when I walked back down these steps. The moment I'd been waiting for. I would have magic soon!

One of the wooden double doors into the library was propped open by a block of concrete. Cool air conditioning blew my purple-hued hair back as I stepped into a modern foyer complete with a coffee shop and bank of computers. A group milled by the circulation desk, so I assumed that was where I needed to be.

The desk had a barcode scanner flashing steadily and a little gate blocking anyone from coming and going into the heart of the library. Leaning against the gate was a pale man with fine, feathered platinum hair. He had a clipboard jammed into his armpit, flashing a white grin when some of my fellow students giggled at something he'd been saying.

My attention flashed to the sword he held. This must be our instructor, considering his business casual clothing. He didn't seem much older than me, but there was no mistaking he had magic of some sort when he pulled the sword a few inches out of its sheath. Its metal glowed from within, throwing off a silvery aura.

"In two years, you'll have yours too," he said to the students closest to him. His voice held a generous accent.

The girl next to me released a dreamy sigh, masking the sound of disappointment I uttered at the same time. It would really take two years before I could have a sword of my own? That sucked. I hoped that meant we'd be practicing in the library for those two years before we were trusted to take a sword out of its confines. I'd be okay with that.

Our instructor started counting the group with one finger extended. "This looks like everyone," he said cheerfully. "Welcome to Library Science 101, my students. Or as you're called in my country...my pages."

I fought a losing battle for being a respectful listener at that point, rolling my eyes.

"I am Lars Eriksson, this year's Distinguished Guest Professor at Moongrove Library. Here to teach you all the way from Sweden. You are my first group of pages ever." He flashed his bright smile proudly over the group. "Every year, many compete for the chance to teach and work in this position, but I was the lucky victor this year due to my many accomplishments. We can talk about those later.

"NSU has the largest dimensional powercore in North America. You will draw from it several times over the course of your first month here to nurture your affinity in pure power. Under my care and guidance, you will discover your potential as librarian witches. Who's ready?" He drew out a cheer from the class, and I waited for a cliché librarian shush to come. Yet, the only librarian around was Mr. Eriksson himself.

He scanned his ID to unlock the gate barring us from going deeper into the library before laughing and smacking his forehead. "I need to take attendance." He drew the clipboard and its battered sheet of paper from his armpit and quickly checked us off.

A cramp rolled through my belly as the group started moving. I placed a hand over it, willing it to wait. I wanted to see the powercore and get my magic, and a trip to the bathroom wasn't going to stop me.

"The Moongrove Library has existed in one form or

another since the Salem Witch Trials," Mr. Eriksson said at the head of our group. He led us like ducklings down a grand hall with a vaulted ceiling. I craned my neck upward to catch glimpses of the colored glass far above us.

I needed to come back here on my own and really take in the art lining the walls as well. Expensive, authentic pieces captured the history of this place and what I presumed were the exploits of past librarian witches.

"It is built atop a seam of power invisible to human eyes, otherwise known as a ley line. Only with a partnership with the beings from beyond our world was it possible for us witches to find it," my instructor continued. For a moment, I thought he was mentioning aliens and was halfway to accepting it. Aliens, no problem. Just like vampires, cupids, and mer. "I'm talking about dimensions, of course. It is only possible to have a library and a dimensional powercore with the permission of the dimensional travelers who have come to call our planet home."

Our group reached the end of the hallway, where it joined the kind of library I was expecting. Endless stacks lined each direction I looked, momentarily distracting me from Mr. Eriksson's explanation. I inhaled the scent of aging paper and ink with a wide smile.

The instructor took a sharp left turn. I swiveled on my heels and noticed a pair of brightly polished elevators at severe odds with the aged, austere environment of this part of the library. "We go down," he said simply.

My belly gave another grumble, and I crossed my legs impatiently. I didn't want to miss a second of this and raised my hand, trying to butt in before he continued talking. "Yes?" he said, pointing toward me.

"Can you explain what a dimensional is? It sounds like you're saying they come from another planet," I asked, hoping I didn't sound too stupid. A few of my classmates stilled and glanced my way. One guy hid a smile by glancing down at his phone.

"We will talk about dimensionals in great detail over the course of this semester." Mr. Eriksson gave me a patient smile. "Most humans know them by a different name: demons. They first traveled to our lands evading creatures spawned in the darkness of their world. But in the process of meeting humans, many were hunted and feared by us for how closely their likenesses evoke our own ideas of evil."

The elevator arrived behind him with a bell tone. "Half of us will go down at a time," he continued as if he hadn't just blown my mind. There were real demons around somewhere? But they came from another world? Perhaps sensing that I was bursting with more questions, Mr. Eriksson waved me into the first group to head into the heart of the library...thirty floors down.

The bay of buttons went down to negative fifty, however. A scanner sat prominently next to the buttons, implying that not everyone could go down fifty floors into the earth, even if they wanted to. The elevator started descending smoothly, taking me and nine other students down.

"I've seen a dimensional once." A guy interrupted the rules of elevator etiquette by talking and glancing my way instead of at the wall. "There's, like, a lot of them on campus."

"But you've only seen one?" I asked.

"Yeah. They hide in shadows with their magic. It's pretty cool, actually."

I hummed, pondering this mysterious race that hid on an open, accepting campus like NSU. Could it be that even supernaturals feared their demon-like appearance?

We stepped off the elevator and waited quietly for the other one to deliver Mr. Eriksson and the other half of our class. The lights were dim overhead and the air here felt... different. Static charged each breath, tingling in my lungs and over my skin.

"Okay, my pages," Mr. Eriksson said as soon as he joined us and clapped his hands. "It is time for you to touch the powercore for the first time and take its magic into yourself."

My heart leapt with excitement. I was one of the first people to follow him through a door he unlocked. On the other side, there was a huge open space. Stone columns straight out of another era supported the ceiling. Instead of manmade lights, the air was lit by the eerie purple-black glow thrown off by a massive orb at the center of it all.

A set of stairs led up its side, so someone could place their hands on it where it was suspended a few feet above the ground by a stone loop. I inched closer, squinting to get a better look. As I watched, tiny white strikes of lightning zapped the underside of the core.

"All true libraries have a powercore, which fills its librarians with magic to keep its day-to-day functions running," Mr. Eriksson explained. "In becoming a librarian witch, you take in dimensional power. It makes you much more resistant to the charms of dangerous, unknowable magic and able to fight back against the monsters that followed our dimensional friends to our world. Now, who's first?"

He fumbled out the battered attendance roster and answered his own question...calling on the first name in alphabetical order. I barely concealed a groan of dismay. I'd need to watch about two-thirds of the class go before me and touch that thing. Curse my last name. I should've let Dr. Heartwood name me Cressida Book-something.

At least on the sidelines, I could watch how this actually worked. My peers didn't touch the surface of the power-core...they stuck their hands inside it. Purple mist swirled around the newly anointed librarians, and the powercore pushed their hands back out when they'd had enough.

Since it was reasonably fast, my turn was up sooner rather than later. I regretted not using the restroom before coming down with the group, though, because every second was becoming agonizing.

I approached the powercore with caution, hearing it crackle with electricity. If I wasn't worthy, what would it do? Electrocute me? I hadn't even cleared the steps before I felt a tug on my arms. The powercore drew me forward like we were magnetized. It felt like jelly when my hands submerged into it to the wrist. Cold and wiggly.

Static crawled over my skin, setting every hair straight up. The other students had mentioned the powercore talking to them, but I only understood when it whispered into my mind.

"Hmm. Stars and shine."

I tried to open my mouth, to somehow converse with this object of magic. However, I was frozen, only able to breathe shallowly.

"My, my, aren't you a special one?"

I got the feeling it was inspecting me. Its magical eye peered into my very being, turning over the bits of fluffy dreams and jagged emotional edges. Nothing was private between us...but it wasn't malicious, either. I felt it rummaging around with gentle fingers, picking up memories like mementos and turning them over with care.

"Such a bright soul has found its way to me. Tell me, why do you want to be a librarian witch?"

It read my thoughts like we were conversing. Of course, thinking it was cool and fitting for me was my answer. I felt both vain and vapid standing before the powercore. I had the impression I was touching something ancient beyond comprehension. Immobile but precious, in need of librarians as much as they needed it.

Tinkling, almost feminine laughter echoed in my ears. *"Perhaps you will find a more serious reason than fashion, with time. My librarians are, without a doubt, more polished appearances and tweed jackets, by the way."*

I nodded slowly. I did prefer that look myself.

"You have the potential for greatness, once you shake your more youthful endeavors. I gladly accept you into my service if you will pledge to defend this library."

No sound escaped my lips, but it must've sensed the agreement in me past the embarrassment of this conversation. At least it'd called me out in a private way.

"There is no judgment here, only power. Accept this gift and thrive."

Electricity flowed over my palms, sending numbness up my arms and through my body. It was over within a split second, and the core left me panting and looking down at my unmarked palms as its mysterious magic sizzled its way through my every pore. I stumbled away from it, soon filled with giddiness I could barely express. The powercore had accepted me...I was a real witch now!

Another student took my place at the core while I drifted to Mr. Eriksson's side. He glanced my way and raised a brow. "I need to use the restroom," I whispered.

"Oh." He gave a careless wave. "Go back up to the first floor for that. We'll go back up when everyone's done."

"Okay, sure." I nodded and forced feeling back into my numb legs by making them move back to the elevator bay. An uncomfortable pins and needles sensation followed, which I tried to shake off as one of the elevators arrived.

I went into it and faced the buttons, labeled from three to negative fifty. My inner child wanted to press every single button. I was alone, after all, with just the pressing need of my bladder to suggest that it was a bad idea. So instead, I indulged my curiosity with a single button press. Negative fifty. I expected it wouldn't depress since I didn't have a staff ID or any sort of authority in the library.

The elevator started descending instead.

"Shit," I muttered. This was a golden opportunity to figure out what was on the bottommost level, though, because I bet Mr. Eriksson would never take us that far into the library. Considering it served as a place to store dangerous magic and creatures, the worst had to be chained up at the bottom.

I was probably a moron. But I still stepped out of the elevator when it opened on the bottom floor. It began with another small, dim foyer, just like on the thirtieth floor, but this time there was already someone here. I stopped dead in my tracks as he turned and canted his head in my direction.

"At last, a librarian," he said softly. He paced my way with the silent, fluid manner of a predator. Before he'd turned around, I'd caught sight of his tail, a long and whip-thin appendage. I tried to tamp down the panic making my heart race. A half-naked demon was coming my way, and the elevator doors had already closed behind me with a tell-tale whirr of machinery suggesting it was on its way upward.

Not a demon. A dimensional, I reminded myself.

"Greetings, librarian," he said formally, stopping far too close. He had a good foot on me in height, putting my eyes level with his naked pecs. Did dimensionals not believe in clothing? His smooth skin was a cool gray, with undertones of purple veins. I couldn't help but notice he had muscle tone like any human man, with defined ridges down to the pair of dusty pants he wore.

Blushing hard, I edged back from him and craned my neck to meet his eyes. I almost regretted it. His eyes were a shocking yellow color and glimmered like well-cut topaz. Catlike slits marked his pupils, which drilled into my skull with unsettling intensity. "I apologize for my state of undress." He had the smooth, deep voice of a devil to match the hint of fangs I noticed behind his lips. "Something terrible has occurred to wake me from stasis. I have been trapped here, unable to escape. Might you be able to assist me?"

He tilted his head with the request, sending a sheet of glossy black hair free from the trap of his horn. Two of them framed his face, curved into spirals. When his gray lips spread into a smile, my heart skipped a beat. His angular face may not be human, but it wasn't hard on the eyes either.

I wetted my lips. *Focus, Cress.* "Um, you want help with what, exactly?" I asked. Hopefully I could escape this situation without Mr. Eriksson knowing about it. I'd just been curious...I hadn't expected to actually meet a dimensional, let alone one who needed something from me.

"The library has changed in my absence," he murmured. "Yours is the first living face I've seen. Can you take me to the surface?"

"Like, the first floor?" A breathy note wove into my

question when he slid even closer. I could feel the heat of his naked chest from here. He had the most attractive figure I'd seen in person, and now he was a breath away while fixing me with the heat of an otherworldly smolder. "Y-yeah, I was just going that way." I pawed blindly at the cold metal behind me until my fingertips found the call elevator button.

"I am in your debt..." His dark brows rose expectantly, like he wanted me to finish his sentence.

"Cress," I offered.

Two vampire-like fangs peeked out from his top lip as his smile widened. "Cress," he repeated in a low purr. I startled when his hand closed around mine and he shifted back just enough to lift my fingertips to his lips for a delicate kiss. "I am Phaeron Sudair, Prince of..." He inhaled sharply when the elevator made a bell tone and the doors opened. "...Well, it matters not."

I backed into the elevator, and my finger landed squarely on the first floor button. Hopefully the class wasn't done with the powercore; otherwise, it'd be seriously awkward to arrive after everyone else. Especially alongside a huge, half-naked dimensional man. As the elevator lurched upward, I stopped inspecting the wall to ask, "So, you're a prince...?"

But no one was next to me. I made the elevator trip alone, wondering what the hell had just happened. That man was *real*, but he'd disappeared, and I was still flushed from just how close we'd been.

Fortunately, I arrived at the first floor before Mr. Eriksson and the rest of my class. As my head swiveled, trying to spot the closest bathroom, air drifted into my ear.

It felt like the hot breath of a man leaning right over my

shoulder. "Thank you for my freedom, Cress," whispered Phaeron's disembodied voice. I yelped and turned, but there was no one there, again.

As the seconds ticked away with no further sign of him, I had the sinking feeling I'd made a horrible mistake.

6

CRESS

I WAITED for several days in utter paranoia. I didn't tell Mr. Eriksson, or anyone else for that matter, about my surreal meeting with a dimensional prince in the bottom floor foyer of Moongrove Library. Surely there were cameras, though, capturing my blushing perusal of the half-naked man who'd gotten me to free him.

Because that's what he'd said. I'd freed him.

I was so, *so* stupid. What if that guy had been imprisoned there? I weighed opening up to Mr. Eriksson or simply leaving a note somewhere, but I cared too much for my own ass. NSU was like a dream come true, and I didn't want to get expelled within a week of starting classes. How fucking embarrassing that would be.

I kept my mouth shut and ears open, trying to catch any inkling that a mega dangerous dimensional was free and terrorizing the supernatural world. By Friday after Library Science 101, four days after "the incident," I started to relax. Maybe Phaeron wasn't some villain I'd let escape from his eternal prison. Dimensionals were an accepted supernatural race, so maybe he'd just gotten lost in the library or something.

After class, I dropped my backpack off in a corner and splayed on my bed facedown. Bella took the opportunity to curl up on the small of my back. Lanie, seated at her computer and bobbing along to her music, lifted one headphone cuff. "Rough day?" she asked.

"Long week," I said honestly. "I have, like, three essays and five chapters to read this weekend too. High school wasn't this intense!"

I watched her expression, wondering if she'd seen Phaeron somewhere in my future. She hadn't given off any hints that she knew my secret yet and just flashed a reassuring smile at me now. "Yeah, it's a lot, isn't it? I bet we'll get used to it fast."

"As long as we don't have special meetings every weekend, I'll be happy," I grumbled into my comforter.

All the freshman witches were to attend an event this Sunday evening, and I dreaded it. We'd heard about the news through Introduction to Witchcraft alongside a lesson about covens. Witches came in groups of seven, with early covens assembled carefully so each member represented one of the seven witch affinities. The strongest rituals were performed in groups of varied individuals, apparently.

In modern times, the university staff decided who was in your first coven, and their "careful considerations" were probably just random. It was normal now to double up on affinities, especially the more common ones.

"It won't be bad at all! Your coven is supposed to be made up of your closest friends, bonded by magic," Lanie said.

I muffled a groan. "Sounds like a bunch of sugar and rainbows to me."

"Okay, Negative Nancy. Know what I think you need?" She drew out the question, and when I peeked over at her, she had her hand to her chin in a thoughtful pose. There was a twinkle in her eye, and for a moment, I could tell her augury magic was actively working.

Now that I had my magic, I was starting to pick up on auras, mostly by accident. Aura reading was a touch too advanced for a newbie like me, but it came and went mostly without my input. Lanie's reading of my fate created a halo around her head and a sparkle in her eyes. Suddenly, her last name made perfect sense. Augury magic made a steely gray aura.

Her magic faded, and an excited smile crossed her face. "Ah! Tomorrow, I'm taking you into town. My treat."

I perked up quickly. "Like, New Salem?" I asked.

During the whirlwind of moving into NSU, I'd gotten a full map of the land I'd entered by portal. Though I still didn't understand exactly how I'd arrived in this magical slice of the world, I understood that there was more than just the university here. Many supernaturals entered, went through NSU, and settled in the supernatural-only city of New Salem that thrived past its gates. I'd longed to go when I wasn't so busy, to see if it was as much a multi-race paradise as my new school.

"Yup! Just you and me. What do you say?" Lanie offered.

"I'd love to," I answered. Much like magic, our plan for tomorrow gave me the motivation to coax Bella off me so I could sit down at my own desk and start plinking away at the hill of work I'd accumulated to finish this weekend. Lanie returned to her work too, typing away rapidly at whatever caught her attention.

With a covert glance behind me, I felt I had enough privacy to place a quick call to my mom. While I'd heard from Carly a few times as she updated me on her high school experience, Mom let me call her. She was too busy working for casual calls anyway.

"Hi, baby," she answered on the first ring. She sounded exhausted.

I smiled at the wall, where I'd pinned a few pictures of my little family. "Hey, Mom." I imagined her kindly face just as it had to look after a long shift at the hospital. Dark half-moons under her blue eyes, creases along the bridge of her nose and cheeks where a tight mask held her skin for hours on end.

"Did I catch you at a bad time?" I asked in concern. She worked too much, even when she was married to Carly's sperm donor. The bills piled up too fast, and I knew things had to be tight without me working at the fast-food place up the street anymore.

"No, no. It's nice to hear from you. How are you doing? Carly's told me you've got magic now," she said.

"I do. I'm a librarian." After a short pause, it occurred to me that that didn't sound all that witchy to someone who wasn't supernatural. "That means my magic is made to help me contain dangerous spells, books, and creatures that don't quite come from our world."

"Wow," she breathed. I'd gotten my love of reading from her, so I knew she had to be imagining what kind of things I was getting into. I wish I had something even cooler to tell her, like if I'd held a book of black magic or something, but so far, Mr. Eriksson hadn't let us get a sniff of anything even remotely dangerous outside of the class-room tucked into the corner of floor negative one.

"And I also made it into the fashion design major," I added.

"Are you going to be a fashionable librarian, then?"

I stifled a giggle. "Well, no. I still want to design clothes. The supernatural world requires everyone get trained in their unique magic for two years, but I doubt I'm going to do more with it. Most witches do normal human things after university," I explained.

She hummed, and I imagined her tilting her head back and forth as she considered more deeply. "Never say no to opportunity," she replied.

"I know, Mom."

I mouthed her response, I'd heard it so much. "That's how I got you, and I've never regretted it," she said.

"You did a few times when I was in high school," I joked.

"Never," she repeated firmly.

When I'd been surrendered by my birth parents as an infant, it'd been my mom who'd immediately wanted me. She'd been as surprised as I was when I suddenly developed the ability to speak to my two cats, but like in all things, she was supportive of who I was. My gaze traced the outline of her in one of my family photos, and for the first time, I missed the normalcy of home.

I stuck out from Mom and Carly in every picture. While they were both fair and pale, I had a complexion a few shades darker and chestnut brown hair when it wasn't dyed. Mom was five-foot-nothing and naturally slim, Carly not much taller, while I'd been blessed with curves and above-average height. But with the two of them, I had acceptance and love. For me, there was no other family.

And if I wasn't a witch...I wouldn't be the odd one out again, nearly alone on a campus full of mythical beings straight from fairy tales and the imaginations of paranormal romance authors. I'd never wonder if I'd made a grave mistake meeting and releasing a dimension prince named Phaeron.

As I caught her up on what'd happened so far at NSU, I skirted mentioning anything about him. I didn't want to hear her warm voice go stiff with disapproval. So, when I let her go, I nursed a quiet tinge of shame. If I couldn't tell the woman who'd raised me what I'd done, I knew deep down that it was truly wrong.

I blew out a breath and resolved to tell Mr. Eriksson about Phaeron after class on Monday.

Lanie and I took the shuttle into New Salem the next morning. She let me take the window seat, knowing I'd be pressing my nose almost to the glass to watch the supernatural world scroll by.

"There is a distinct lack of puns," I commented after a few blocks. "Like, why isn't the blood delicacy store called 'Fangs for Everything'?"

"Most supernaturals don't take places like that seriously," Lanie said, shrugging. "This is one of the only cities where we don't have to hide what we are behind clever puns and a wink."

"Well, when you put it that way..." I just felt my lack of experience again.

"You're in for a treat. Promise," she said.

I looked over at her to see if her gray magic aura was flaring up again, to see if she was viewing my future with a statement like that. A smile creased the skin around her dark eyes, but if she was using her magic, my sense of auras was too weak to spot it.

She must've realized where my thoughts went and nudged me with an elbow, Roe-style. "I just know that. I love New Salem," she clarified.

The shuttle dropped us off in the heart of it, several buildings looming around us. Lanie set off in what seemed like a random direction, passing a couple parking garages with storefronts lining the ground level. I counted three pubs and a sandwich shop that leaked the scent of garlic and herbs when someone exited with a brown paper bag.

In other words, completely ordinary until it wasn't. The next block held a few stores we browsed, from a general store for merfolk, selling enchanted seashells and pearls alongside clothing tailored for their unique body shape, to a witch-run shop with tools for all witch affinities.

I spent a lot of time in the latter building, exploring at length with Lanie there to explain what was useful and what to do with it. Verdant witches had the biggest section, with candles of several colors and an expansive selection of dried herbs and pickled bits from various animals. "Ugh," I muttered upon picking up a bottle just to see a frog's eyeball staring back.

"Come over here," Lanie practically giggled. She directed me to the section for librarians, which was quite short, covering half a row. It had some stuff I expected to be junk, like talismans against malicious and dark magic, but I stopped to scan the spines of the books lining one shelf.

I pulled one, surprised to see the pages it bore were battered with use. It was a hardback with no jacket, dark brown leather with golden letters embossed on the front and spine. "Is this something I need?" I asked Lanie, showing her the title: *The Librarian Witch's Handbook*. Cute little symbols surrounded the title in the same embossment. It was the only copy here, and someone had committed the grave sin of putting a discount sticker on it.

Lanie brightened and nodded. "Open it and see if it speaks to you!" she said.

"It talks?" I echoed uncertainly, getting a vivid flashback to the powercore I'd touched and how it'd somehow seen into me and spoken to my mind.

Still, I cracked it open to the first page. It was completely blank, and I skimmed through the rest with a thumb. Nothing, just cream-colored paper. "Weird," I said. "It doesn't even have lines like a jour—"

I cut myself off abruptly as color leaked onto the page where I'd stopped. A thin band of cursive ink darkened to read "Henceforth and Always."

I said it out loud, glancing at Lanie in confusion. "You should buy it," she said immediately.

"Because I see words on the page?" I asked. The book flipped a page on its own.

A new line of cursive text appeared in the middle of the new page. *Just do what the augur says.*

"I've heard about books like it. A strong librarian will hold on to it through his or her travels, and it records everything they learn," Lanie explained. "When another librarian gets it, the book is there to help them. It can give advice and continue to learn as it's passed from witch to witch."

"Like a hardback Wikipedia," I said mostly to myself. "I wonder why it's here, then. Surely these kinds of things are a family heirloom." This one was discounted, no less.

The book flipped another page on its own. *Are you going to buy me, or what?*

"Ask it who its former owners were," my friend suggested.

I echoed her, and it flipped another page. *Don't you want to know?* wrote its ink.

My eyes narrowed. "Yes, that's why I asked."

Maybe do something of note with your magic and I'll tell you.

"It's kind of...sarcastic," I said, shutting it with a huff.

"That's cool, it's got a personality! It must've had a lot of owners," she said cheerfully.

In the end, I bought the snarky magical book. The cashier stuck the receipt right under the front cover and told me I could return it, no questions asked, within a month.

The moment we walked outside, the cover flipped up, and I scrambled to catch the receipt before the wind could snatch it away. *Only $19.99?* the book wrote out.

"You were on sale," I informed it. I closed the cover again to remove the sticker on its front.

It opened again of its own volition. *Hey, that tickles.*

"You're a book. How could it tickle?" I asked.

It flipped another page. Instead of answering, it asked a question of its own: *You got a name, toots?*

"It's Cress."

Watercress?

"Cressida. Do *you* have a name?"

The Librarian Witch's Handbook. Duh.

Rolling my eyes, I snapped it closed and tucked it under my elbow to end the conversation.

Lanie took me to a spa next and covered a special for us both with a swipe of the Graygazer family's credit card. One relaxing massage later, and we were next to each other in pedicure chairs, our feet submerged in hot water.

"Thank you for this," I said, humbled by her generosity.

A pair of shifter women wheeled over carts of tools to start our pedicures. This time, there was no questioning what they were since they both had fluffy white tails and softly rounded ears poking out of their fur-like hair. With the sly tilt of their eyes, they resembled arctic foxes quite heavily.

"Of course. I could tell you needed to relax and see more of the supernatural world than the university," Lanie said.

"You were spot-on, of course. I bet your magic helps a lot with that."

For a moment, Lanie's expression fell. Gray magic swirled around her head and sparkled in her eyes. It was over before I could even blink. She shook herself off with a heavy sigh, her shoulders slumping like they held a weight too heavy for her to bear. "What? What is it?" I practically demanded.

She smiled. "Hmm? Nothing happened. Just enjoy the moment," she said. "You never know exactly when life will throw you another challenge, even as an augury witch."

No matter how I phrased the question, she didn't explain that statement further and assured me she meant nothing by it.

AFTER SPENDING MOST of Saturday in town with Lanie, I devoted my Sunday to catching up on my studies. We stayed in most of the day, with Lanie practically chained to her laptop, typing away rapidly while her cat pawed at her for attention. I sat on my bed, my lap crowded with both Milo and Bella forming a warm pile as I studied my textbooks.

It was a peaceful time, only broken by quick trips to the dorm cafeteria for food and the special evening event in the Voidbinder Building. I didn't dress up for it, and to my surprise, neither did Lanie. Since the evening was unseasonably chilly, I popped on a pair of jeans and a hoodie.

"We match!" my roommate announced, sliding on a hooded jacket of the same navy blue shade.

"Nice," I said with a laugh.

The sun was setting as we left our dorm and headed to the three-story building along with a shuffle of other freshman witches. "Remember, this isn't your only coven ever," Lanie said.

"Good. I hate the idea that we're slapped with a random group of people," I muttered. I would've been much happier without a coven at all and just keeping my head down and passing my time at NSU with only a couple close friends. Being forced to socialize with the expectation of friendship just didn't sit well with me.

"It's not quite random," she said. "The augury professors get together and see who would work best together for coven spells and events."

I grumbled to myself as we came up to the Voidbinder Building, which was alive with activity. In the front office, upperclassmen were running back and forth, making sure everyone received an envelope with their name on it. Elderly Dr. Heartwood directed us to check the letter inside and head to the room it indicated.

Lanie and I both had the same room: 204. We entered together to see two different circles of eight desks, each with an upperclassman wearing a Moongrove Academy t-shirt and a few freshman witches already seated.

"Over here," one of the upperclassmen called, a dark-haired witch who was all smiles. She checked off a list of names and indicated that we sit down in her circle.

To either side of our upperclassman, who introduced herself as Yasmin, sat what I supposed were two other members of my new coven. I slipped into the desk next to the girl who I recognized from affinity testing as Willow Frost, the mousy oceanic witch who looked as uncomfortable to be here as I felt.

The other person introduced himself as Heath Storm, another oceanic witch. He was tall and obviously built, barely fitting into the desk to Yasmin's left. He had rich, tawny skin and a big grin that offset his skin tone with a sparkle of white. "Hello, ladies. Looks like I'm a lucky witch if this is my coven."

I was prepared to ask if it was because we were all women when another guy joined our ranks. "Grant Norwood, of the verdant Norwood line," he introduced himself, immediately looking bored with our company.

Two more empty seats. I craned my neck to watch the door and felt myself pale when in clicked the designer heels of Wren Starsurge, her hair perfectly coifed for this event. Her closest friend followed her like a shadow. "There has to be some mistake," I heard her tell Yasmin as the upperclassman gestured for her to join the rest of my coven. "I don't see Sanna's name on that list!"

"Here, then!" the other upperclassman called, motioning for Wren's friend to come over.

Wren's face reddened. "I won't join a coven without—"

"Hey, guys, am I too late?" burst out a loud voice from the doorway. Roe came in with a big smile and narrowed in on the two empty seats in the circle where my coven was. She turned to Yasmin. "Rowena Ashbough—is this my coven?"

Yasmin checked the list and confirmed with a nod. I breathed a huge sigh of relief that transformed to a grin as the big redhead practically squealed and came over to pull Lanie and me into an enthusiastic hug that felt more like a headlock. "We're in the same coven!" Roe exclaimed.

In the echo of her excitement, I heard Wren mutter, "Please switch me into the other coven."

"I'm sorry, Wren. The university wants you here," Yasmin replied, gesturing for the sour-faced girl to take a seat.

"Don't you know who my father is?" she practically growled.

"Can you just sit, please?" the upperclassman answered impatiently.

When Roe and Wren took their seats, my coven was completely in attendance. It was great to have both my friends in this circle, but there was Wren too, and she was glowering over at me like this was somehow my fault.

Lanie went rigid and clutched at her face. "I...I need to go," she said, turning to Yasmin. She pointed to her own forehead. "I saw something with my familiar. Forgive me, but I need to go now."

"Do I need to come too?" I asked, concerned. I assumed our familiars were together back in our dorm room.

"No!" she said, louder than her usual tone. I blinked in surprise, and she softened her voice, "I mean, no. It's okay. It's just Jin."

Lanie stood and rested a hand on my shoulder. "Bye, Cress. I wish you the best of luck," she said. Before I could reply, she pulled up the hood of her jacket and sped out of the room.

My jaw sat open, my hand lifted toward her retreating

figure. That little doe that represented my subconscious told me something was very wrong.

Yasmin started saying something to the rest of us about our happy new coven family when I drew to my feet and left the circle too. "Hey!" I heard her protest behind me.

I didn't hesitate, instead plunging out of the room and whipping my head left and right. A little thread of doubt wove into my thoughts. Maybe I was overreacting. But *"I wish you the best of luck"* had held a weird, final note in Lanie's tone. Besides, what an odd thing to say in the first place.

I left the Voidbinder Building and started jogging toward my dorm, sure I was going to overtake Lanie at any moment. She hadn't had much of a head start, maybe a minute on me.

A woman's shrill scream pierced the night, and I stopped short, my chest icing over. Was that Lanie? I turned, realizing the sound had come from the opposite direction. Heart leaping to my throat, I tore into a serious run toward where I'd heard the scream. All the while, I catalogued how prepared I was for this.

Self-defense? I'd taken a couple classes as a kid.

Magic? I didn't know how to use it.

Weapons? None.

In short, I was hurtling myself straight into danger with no plan. I should've gone straight into the Voidbinder Building to get a trained witch to help me. But Lanie was in trouble *now*, and I didn't let anything stop me, not even the strange curls of white mist that started lapping at my ankles.

The sidewalk was coated with the glowing mist, centered thickest around a figure crouched a few yards ahead of me. I skidded to a halt when I realized that person was on their knees in front of a prone body sprawled on the cement. A hood was knocked askew from Lanie's distinctive bob of dark hair...and there was a growing puddle of blood spreading from underneath her.

The kneeling man lifted his head and met my gaze with eyes that gleamed like pure topaz. "This isn't what it looks like," Phaeron said.

7
PHAERON

I awoke somewhere into eternity with Morgana's name still on my lips. Laid out on my back, the world swam in double images, turning the array of librarian witch symbols engraved in the ceiling into an unreadable tangle.

The most important part, though, was that they were ruined. The dancing ink was black and fading, not an active violet-like color. This didn't fill me with glee, but dread instead. If I was awake, that meant something awful had happened, and indeed, when I found the strength to stand and feel my way around my former prison, I found the exit unsealed.

I felt the crumbling edges where a door should be and winced when my fingertips found the last remnants of silver that'd formed an impenetrable line to one such as me, a dimensional traveler. I sucked on the smoking wound even the touch of crumbling silver left on my skin.

Morgana was gone, I realized, crumpling to my knees mere steps into freedom. With my eyes closed, I saw one image, her face. The pain in her stark white face as she clutched the mortal wound in her gut and used the last of her magic to seal me in with a fiend.

"Why, Morgana?" I murmured, asking a specter at this point. I'd felt her death like a nightmare at the beginning of my long rest. She was no longer around to answer for locking me away with...with an unnamable creature. An "it," a true demon hiding within a race humans mistook for their monsters.

If I was free, that meant *it* was as well.

And I was truly alone. My mate had forsaken me and died, leaving me the sole hunter left that knew the devastation to come if *it* was not contained or destroyed.

The disorientation I felt was a lingering failsafe of librarian magic. I wandered alone for days, knowing my new prison was the size of a small rectangle. Over-bright lights stung my sensitive eyes and reflected off a section of the wall, which was lined with silver-like metal. Time slipped by, filling my dry mouth with the taste of frustration and lingering magic.

Things had changed in my absence. Modernized. If I could just escape this room, I'd see for myself and begin my new hunt. *It* had to have the help of another living soul to have a head start on me, else it'd be stuck and wandering like I was. We could meet in clumsy combat, claws and shadows and fangs.

I was still wandering without purpose when she arrived, the first living person since I'd opened my eyes once more.

The two swirling halves of my disoriented world swung into full focus as I turned to take her in. Weak librarian magic haloed her aura in purple and soaked into her violet locks. She was a lovely woman with the shapely figure and wide-set brown eyes.

My mind said, *Mate?* No, she wasn't Morgana. She wasn't nearly strong enough yet, but I felt the potential in her where her soul pulsed to my enhanced sight. It blazed with curious youth, shining with fractals like a diamond in the sunlight. Its brilliance was stunning to this creature of shadows and dark spaces, a shadowborn with a calling to defend the innocent and pure from their shadows.

She was my key to escaping. I nearly pushed her into the metal wall, half-seducing her to free me. The moment a bell sounded and the...shiny door opened, full clarity returned to me in a heady rush as the spell fogging my mind faded. We returned to the surface of the library in the modern contraption, Cress and I.

Cress. I memorized the taste of her name even as I fled into the stark brightness of a world changed.

In fact, the light seemed to do something to me as I drifted out of Moongrove Library as a nearly invisible curl of shadow. Blinded by brightness, I closed my incorporeal eyes and drifted into a bank of darkness. Black winds caressed me, and then nothing.

I awoke *again* from that state, lying on my back in a stinking alleyway with rats nibbling on my toes.

"You okay, man?" asked a man sitting a few paces away, smelling pungently of alcohol.

Clutching my aching head, I sat up and fixed him with a stare. "How did I get here?" I demanded.

He put his hands up, one holding a bottle concealed in a brown paper bag. "Hey, man, this is my place. You just got here and passed out," he said.

Frustration bubbled in my gut as I took a look around. I doubted this drunkard had any idea of what else was wrong with me, but perhaps he could be of use.

"Very well. When is it?" I sighed.

He checked the bright screen of a little metal device he had concealed in his pocket. "About three o'clock."

"No," I practically growled. "*When* is it? What is the year?"

"Chill, my dude." The drunkard simply laughed and told me the date. This time, the world lurched because I swayed with disbelief rather than from any spell to confuse my mind. It'd been nearly two hundred years…

"You need something to take the edge off?" He offered the bottle across the alleyway.

I took it and drank a hard swig of the swill. It burned a path down my throat, and I nearly choked. That was strong stuff. After another sip, I passed it back with a gruff, "Thanks."

For the first time, I took a closer look at this other man. His aura held the ever-changing nature of a shifter, though it was subdued with how much alcohol was in his veins. His soul bore cracks at the edges, its existence much more understated than the brilliant spirit within Cress. Well, that didn't surprise me, if he was hiding in an alleyway with a bottle of swill. Shifters on their own were lonely, often broken creatures.

"Is this still Salem, Massachusetts?" I asked.

"New Salem, actually. Do you want directions to the portal?"

"No." I scraped myself back to my bare feet with a groan. "This is exactly where I want to be. Thank you."

I took to the shadows, looking for all the world like I'd disappeared in the span of a breath. There was a fiend to hunt and a city aged forward two hundred years for me to explore.

Thus started days of wandering the world a stranger. I spoke to no one, instead letting conversation drift over my incorporeal ears. How different the tongue of mortals sounded! And their technology was completely foreign. Perhaps the most jarring change was when I came across others of my kind being treated like ordinary supernaturals rather than suspicious demons.

I drifted in and out, waking in strange places with no rhyme or reason. Had I dreamt of finding a shop full of clothes and merchandise all emblazoned with the letters NSU?

One glance down at myself proved that was real. I'd stolen a set of clothes, the material fuzzy and impossibly soft. A bright white "NSU" stood out in the middle of my broad chest. I didn't care too much, not when I was comfortable, warm, and fully dressed for the first time since my prison was unsealed.

That evening, I picked up the first traces of *it*, the creature I hunted while my mind was sane and cooperative. Its dark presence stalked circles around one side of the university campus, where witches came and went. I found a patch of shadows and waited, invisible, for it to show its sorry face.

The witches were active tonight, all converging on the same building. I spotted Cress amongst them, a navy hood pulled up over her head and only allowing a few violet strands of hair to frame her heart-shaped face. Her laugh sounded tense as she focused her attention on another young woman with a similar hood pulled to hide her face in shadows.

My invisible brows arched. Significant augury magic blazed around the other witch, turning her into a beacon of pure power. Despite myself, my mouth watered. I wondered what a little taste of her blood would be like and whether I could borrow a hint of her magic for my cause.

Abruptly, darkness closed in around my vision. It came and went when it wished, and this time, I fought it desperately, worried what kind of nightmare I'd experience with the augury witch fixed so firmly in my mind.

I blinked and lost the battle of wills with myself, reemerging into coherency a step away from a corpse. Magic hung heavily in this area, tasting of *it*. It must've abandoned its kill upon sensing me, because the young woman it'd killed still had an intact soul.

The navy hood hung askew and for a moment, I thought I was seeing Cress lying on her back, unseeing eyes staring into the night sky. I knelt before her, taking in the messy gash in her neck where a weapon—or jagged teeth—had torn it open and left a smeared mess of crimson turning her clothing black. Her expression was permanently locked somewhere between horror and determination.

Not Cress, but her augury witch friend. I released a guilty sigh of relief that it wasn't the bright-souled woman lying dead before me. My kind believed in life debts, and I owed a measure of gratitude to the librarian who'd freed me, even if I was in no shape to repay her now.

"I'm sorry. I was a moment too late," I whispered over the dead girl. I closed her eyelids with gentle fingertips and set her soul free at the same time. It disappeared into the afterlife just as rapid footfalls approached. Through the obscuring mist left behind from the fiend's attack came Cress.

She stopped short a few yards away, her wild gaze flashing from the body to me kneeling beside it. "This isn't what it looks like," I said, knowing damn well how guilty I seemed.

"Lanie!" she cried, her pupils ballooning in horror. "Did you—? Is she—?"

"Dead, I'm afraid. But I reached her before it could consume her soul," I said, getting to my feet. There was nothing else I could do for the augury witch, but there was still a chance *it* lingered here, waiting for a second chance to feed.

Cress was going into shock, her breathing pattern erratic. "What do you mean, she's dead? She was just..." She gestured to the building behind her. When she turned back to me, something shifted in her expression. Growing realization and rage. "You killed my friend!"

Voices shifted toward us, undoubtedly drawn by her appearance and sudden scream.

"No, I had nothing to do with it," I said. "*It* did."

Her face creased further. I knew it sounded like an excuse, but if I said its name, it would come back and attack us both.

"I released you, and you killed her! Fuck you, Phaeron," she spat, stabbing a finger in my direction like a deadly silver sword.

She may have said more, but half a dozen witches were approaching, and at least four of them had the auras of experienced, powerful magic. She looked over her shoulder, and I took the opportunity to go incorporeal and sink into the shadows.

Cress broke into sobs as she explained what she'd seen to the group of witches. Surprisingly, she didn't mention me by name, just as "a dimensional with yellow eyes."

I stayed to watch them as long as I was able, to ward off the true monster from reappearing and making a feast of them.

8

GEO

Something shifted in the world's bedrock, and I came back to awareness faster than the slow transference of patient rock. Had I friends or kin, I would tell the story about how one moment, I slept, and the next, my sightless eyes transformed from solid crystal to working and flesh-like.

It was so fast, actually, my senses returned before my muscles and tendons regained their mobility. I was trapped in the prison of my stone flesh, but I didn't panic. All things came around in time.

Besides, this patient rock remembered the first time it woke from sculpted perfection, animated by the soul of a witch demigoddess. I owed my very existence to her sacrifice, so I could take the care not to damage my vessel.

Unblinking, I took in my surroundings. I'd entered stasis guarding the eaves of Moongrove Library, loyal to the same structure my witch's soul had once served. Someone had painstakingly scraped me off my resting place and relocated me to a perfumed study warmed by sandy wood, with rugs and upholstery in a rich ruby red.

I was positioned perfectly to loom over a trio of chairs

facing a broad desk. Someone shifted on the other side of it, and I caught the hint of pink shining off the figure's hair. I'd spent years of rest not on standby for the defense of my library, but instead protecting this room. If I were a fleshy, irrational being, I might be angered by the audacity.

Instead, I was tolerant. I waited for sensation to return to my fingertips, toes, and wingtips. Soon, I would be able to move and explore the sensation of danger pulsing where my heart should beat. I was needed. I woke abruptly with the knowledge that somewhere beyond this pretty wooden room, my presence was desperately required. Nothing less could wake a gargoyle fatigued by a century of unceasing service.

I was still immobile but aware when there was a knock at the door. "Come in," the pink woman said, her voice hitting a sweet, musical tone.

In walked a middle-aged man, his clothes barely containing a paunchy belly. "You wanted to see me, ma'am."

"Yes." Her slender hand gestured to one of the chairs. "Callum, I need you to explain this to me." She gestured to a packet of paper that rested on her desk.

He sat and took the packet, skimming it quickly. A flush covered his face, and a fat bead of sweat formed on his temple. "What about—?"

"All of it," she snapped. Her flute-like voice turned to an angry shriek, and the man, Callum, recoiled into the back-rest of his chair. "How did a dimensional creature escape the most secure library in the world?"

"A-Aurina, y-you're quite..." he struggled and wheezed. "Y-you're..."

With a feathery snap of what sounded like wings, the

woman leaned out of the edge of my line of sight. "My apologies," she said stiffly.

Callum covered his chest with a hand, gasping for air. "An unusual chain of events has occurred…"

Aurina's graceful hands balled into fists, and he flinched.

"The security cameras facing floor negative fifty were caught in a loop. It was very clever, actually, since we rarely need to inspect the seals." He tugged at his collar and released a tense laugh. "We think the seal broke about two weeks ago, with assistance from someone with access to a stolen card key. All dangerous dimensional creatures are spelled with our heaviest disorientation effects, so it follows that someone else helped it escape once the seal broke."

"And your cameras caught no hint of who that person was?" Disbelief coated Aurina's voice.

"Well, no. They came and went like a shadow. Even our best cameras have a hard time capturing dimensional magic at work. They did make one teensy mistake…" He held up two fingers pinched close together. "They didn't lock the elevator after them. It's been going down to restricted levels no matter what access badge is scanned."

"I don't see how that helps us at all," she said.

"It means the access code belonged to one of my master librarians. We fixed the elevator and identified the code used… It was from a woman I trusted," he said.

There was a shuffling of paper. "The librarian witch that was found dead in a corner of level negative twenty-two yesterday?" She made a sound of disgust as she read over a report.

"Yes, ma'am." He bowed his head. "The SPDI are

conducting an autopsy, but we suspect it was the same monster."

Aurina blew out a sigh coated in frustration. "How could this happen? I need you to mobilize your master librarians and bring in this dimensional *before* it tries to eat another one of my students. I can hardly believe the incompetence that's led us to this point."

"My apologies, ma'am. I'll just be going to—"

"No. We have to make an official statement to the students and the greater New Salem population, and I'll be dead before I admit to anyone that Phaeron Sudair, the goddamned Hungering Darkness himself, was set free from Moongrove Library." She stood and paced with a rustling of soft feathers. "We contained him for two hundred years, and we will re-contain him for two hundred more. Bring your most trusted librarians directly to me, and we will spell them to secrecy as to who they are truly hunting."

Callum wrung his hands. "And what do we tell everyone else?" he asked.

Aurina stopped her pacing, standing over him. She was a gorgeous cupid with rose gold wings and wore a shimmering, curve-hugging gown that displayed generous cleavage, but my stone heart was unmoved. I was needed elsewhere, not here, listening to these two scheme.

"As for your librarian witch's death, we will tell the family that it was a containment breech and an unfortunate accident. For the student, we will announce a blood witch committed the murder. The Hungering Darkness fed on the victim's blood, so anyone on the scene saw the evidence of it," she said.

"We have a witness who described a dimensional man looming over the victim." Callum flipped to a certain page in his files and stabbed his finger at the tiny text printed there.

"Well..." Aurina's lips twisted slyly. "Tell her that she was mistaken. And if she asks any more questions, send her to me."

"Yes, ma'am," he murmured.

"Dr. Callum *Voidbinder*. I sure hope you put your all into finishing this business quickly," she continued. "The legacy of your family name rests squarely on your shoulders. You know what this very dimensional monster did to your ancestor."

"I do know," he confirmed. Both of them glanced toward me.

Aurina walked out of my line of sight. "Her soul lives on. Isn't he magnificent? A demigoddess of Morgana Voidbinder's power deserved a vessel as special as she was."

"That old thing has never moved," he said.

"Do you really think I'd display a fake gargoyle?" Aurina scoffed. Her hand felt like a brand against my cold stone as she rested it on my chest. "This vessel holds Morgana's soul. Your predecessors gave her the honor of animating the Quartz Gargoyle."

Identity and thoughts filled the empty space in my mind. Quartz. My pupils were a cloudy white, but the mineral also formed the spikes lining my back and accented my finger and toenails. Were I capable of moving my lips, my teeth would flash white, also formed of it. My hair was made of sparkling smoky geodes that grew into thick tubes. The rest of me was magically formed of pure obsidian and cured to be as resilient as any ordinary granite gargoyle.

I was special, beautifully made in memorial to an exceptional woman. I remembered now.

Crack! Stone bent and moved like flesh until I was chin

to forehead with Aurina. She jumped back with a startled yelp.

I rolled my shoulders with the obnoxious grind of old rock moving for the first time in ages. My wings spread with the motion, and I drew myself up from a century-long slouch to take my full height once more.

"H-hello?" For once, the cupid woman sounded meek. I took a step, knee and ankle scraping internally with the requirements of motion. My heavy foot thumped onto a rug far down. I'd been resting on a pedestal here for her entertainment for who knew how long.

My lips parted in a jerky motion, stale dust escaping on a grinding inhale and exhale. Aurina and Callum stared at me like I was a horror come to life right before their eyes. "Greetings," I said, my low voice reminiscent of grinding rock. Both of them winced. I'd need to work on loosening my lungs and vocal cords again. Each word was a struggle to utter. "I. Am. Needed. Elsewhere."

I took blocky, thudding steps toward the door. Each one slackened my body a bit more. By the time I arrived to where I was required, hopefully I would resume the smooth semi-living motions this vessel was capable of. If not...my magic would return now that I was active, and I could shift into my flesh form for everyone's benefit and comfort.

"Now, hold on. The Moongrove Library needs your help," Callum said as I reached the door. My stiff fingers struggled to turn the knob. He didn't assist me with his more flexible digits.

Rock was patient, but not for whatever this man needed from me. I heaved the considerable weight of my stony body into the door, reducing it to splinters in moments.

"We are kin. I'm a distant relative of your brother," he said in my shadow as my neck ground left to right. We were on the top floor of a building, and one end of the hallway shone with a sheet of glass. I moved in that direction.

"I. Am. Not. Your. Kin." Each word was punctuated with a step. It was true; though I held the soul of one of his family members within me, it powered the existence of a new, duty-bound being that animated when it was needed. And I could tell that, despite the plan he and the woman had created right in front of me, I was not awake because of them.

Someone else called to my waking mind. As I smashed the window and took to the sky for the first time in a century, I swore I'd go find...her. I propelled myself through the air like a fledgling bird, determined to meet the female presence that needed me.

At least, I attempted to fly to her like a storybook hero, ready to swoop in and save her with a gargoyle's flare.

Instead, I crashed, unable to carry my weight through the air further than the length of a few buildings. My body formed a crater in a small rectangle of grass, spraying dirt in every direction. "Hey, watch it!" snapped a passing fae, glaring with a draw of his leafy eyebrows.

I righted myself and clomped onward by foot, sparing the grinding of my rocky lungs as an apology. This would be considerably slower than flying, but my purpose beckoned like a beacon in the distance. I would find her one grinding step at a time.

What had happened in my absence? Roaring carriage-like monstrosities passed me on the tar-black surface beside the sidewalk. Meanwhile, supernaturals of all sorts maneuvered around me if they weren't too busy staring. A late-summer sun cast a glare overhead, heating my obsidian body considerably.

I tried to ignore it all. I was not a spectacle, and if I needed to know how Moongrove Academy gained such a medley of individuals, I would be informed along the path to serving my purpose.

At least along the way, the struggle to breathe and move smoothed out. My chest rose and fell, my stone heart beating more steadily. In this form, my heart was the soul of my honored witch, and her energy infused my limbs with magic, movement, and life.

Perhaps my long walk was a blessing in disguise, because by the time I found a four-story building with an attached garden, I was no longer moving in the short jerks that made my animation so disconcerting. My stone feet touched the ground without breaking it under my body's considerable weight.

Still, with the tug of my purpose taking me into the garden, I walked with a *thump* of each step on grass. I glanced around, not seeing any immediate danger. Instead, in the heart of the garden, I found a decorative pond filled with lazing koi and a woman seated on a bench beside it, her knees tucked up and forming a cradle for her to hide her face. The first feature I saw was an unkempt mass of dark purple hair, so I assumed she was fae of some sort.

My approach was the opposite of stealthy, so when I took a closer look, her shoulders hitched up and she lifted her head. Red-rimmed but human eyes turned toward me, and she swiped under her nose with a wet sniffle. Faint tear tracks traced down her pale cheeks. Fatigue lined her young face and marked the skin under her eyes with bruise-like shadows.

The stone heart in my chest released a pulse of recognition. *She* was my purpose and duty, the reason I'd woken ready for combat. My heart resonated on a low level. It was my reward for fulfilling the first of what may be several steps in resolving what this young woman needed from me.

She stared at me. I knelt before her, bowing my head in deference to the woman I sensed to be either a weak or inexperienced librarian witch. Taking a deep breath, I tested the dusty depths of my newly exercised lungs. "Greetings, librarian. I am here to serve you."

"You...you're..." She cleared her throat and lowered her legs to the ground.

"I am the Quartz Gargoyle, animated to your service," I stated. She must be *very* new, for she did not immediately order me to the task she required.

All she said was a faint, "Huh?"

"Your need awoke me. What do you require?" I asked.

Her lips moved soundlessly, repeating what I'd just said to herself. Her shoulders tensed. "You know what I did."

I didn't budge an inch, gazing at her unblinkingly. "I know nothing of you yet. Direct me to your service."

"So...no one sent you?" She directed her gaze over her shoulder. "Can you keep a secret?"

"As long as it does not endanger Moongrove Library, I swear myself to secrecy," I said without curiosity. It wasn't like anyone attempted to pry idle gossip from a gargoyle. Even at the height of my service, I had the autonomy to refuse answering probing questions that infringed on others' privacy.

"I..." Her eyes welled up with tears, and she hiccupped a sob. She struggled to speak past her grief. "I made...a terrible mistake."

A mortal might be able to comfort her as she cried, but I

simply stared and waited for her to deliver a clear order. Where was a fellow witch to rub her shoulders and embrace her? A faint trickle of emotion echoed from my heart, but I didn't know what it was. Emotions weren't in the suite of skills given to me upon my creation. I felt them more clearly in my flesh form, but they had to be strong indeed to pierce the unfeeling shell of my stone body.

I carefully placed a hand on her knee but took it back when she winced from its heat. "What is the matter?" I asked.

"You really won't tell anyone?" she asked in a tearful whisper.

"I have the utmost integrity," I replied.

An uneasy chuckle escaped her lips. "Okay. I think I know why you were, um, activated? Is that the right word?"

"It is sufficient to describe my awakening."

"It's because a dimensional k-killed my friend last night." She rubbed away her tears impatiently. "And...it's my fault."

"It is your fault a dimensional killed another person?" I asked to clarify and brought on another wave of her grief.

"Yeah," she mumbled. "I guess that's all you really need to know. I did him a, uh, favor. And in return, he killed her last night. I-I...found him over her body."

No wonder she grieved. I waited with a stone's endurance for her to recover. I couldn't comfort her, but perhaps I could listen and provide some ease to her guilt that way.

"The supernatural police took my statement last night. They didn't seem to believe me," she said, gaze downcast. "I mean, they didn't *say* anything about it, but I got that feeling.

"But I know who killed my friend, and I'm going to get

him even if the police don't. He was imprisoned in the library until...he escaped," she continued. She formed fists on her thighs. "That's where I think you come in. Will you help me kill him?"

"You seek retribution for your friend." I considered her and the conversation I'd overheard earlier. There was a chance this young witch had broken the seals and released a dangerous dimensional, and in helping her kill him, I would also assist her in erasing her crime.

At the same time, I reassessed her aura of power and how weak it was. Any dimensional that'd reached the kind of power level to be locked in Moongrove Library would annihilate her in moments if it came to a direct confrontation. It would both fulfill my eternal duty to my home library *and* my purpose for awakening in slaying the monster for her.

"I shall assist you," I promised. "Give me a physical description of my new target."

She described the dimensional's features and, in the process, started to call him "Phae—"

I hoped my new purpose wouldn't end with me turning her in as a criminal for the release of Phaeron Sudair, the Hungering Darkness. Already, I had a developing bond to her. A mortal might call it an attraction, but I thought of it more as loyalty. Her secret was now mine, and I would serve her the head of her enemy for his trespass against her.

"It shall be done," I stated. "I will protect you as well. He may come for you next."

Her face paled further. "Maybe. Thank you..." With a shake of her head, she quirked her lips. "We've made a plan together, and I don't even know your name."

"It is Geo," I replied promptly.

"Is that short for anything?"

"No."

"Oh, well, I'm Cress," she said. "And there's something I need to do before we talk anymore."

"Is it a task I can assist with?"

"No...I need to do this alone," she sighed. "Wait right here."

And like a statue in the garden, I waited motionlessly for her return.

9
CRESS

I FELT a single pebble drop off the considerable weight of guilt balanced on my shoulders as I left the garden and went back into my dorm room. The gargoyle man had seemed more like a robot than a living, breathing creature, so I'd felt more comfortable inviting him into the messed-up situation that'd become my life.

I didn't know if Geo could kill Phaeron, but at least I had an ally now who wouldn't immediately accuse me of murder. I'd sweated my way through my statement last night, knowing if I suggested I'd known the dimensional in any way, my involvement in his freedom could come to light.

What had started as a simple curiosity for what was locked up on floor negative fifty had snowballed way out of my control. I was guilty for everything that happened afterward. Lanie's murder was my fault.

It was hard to breathe. The walls leaned in toward me in the stairwell, and I clutched my chest. *Stupid. Such an idiot,* I berated through the sudden rush of tears. I hadn't slept for a moment, instead randomly assailed by the stabbing pain of my own emotions. If I could turn the clock back twenty-four hours, I would've made Lanie stay with our new coven and walked into the night instead.

Let Phaeron have my life. It wasn't like I'd accomplished a fraction of what Lanie had. She'd traveled the world, learned several languages, and saved countless lives with her augury magic. I didn't deserve her sacrifice.

Worst of all, she'd known *exactly* what was about to happen. What was *"I wish you the best of luck"* anything but an acknowledgment of a permanent goodbye?

Her computer had been unlocked when I arrived at our dorm late last night, a document up on it that included pages and pages of her frantic typing. The top of the page was "Dear Cress," and that was about all I read before I made sure the document was saved and closed it off. I'd emailed it to myself and cried like a baby when my phone pinged with one last message from Lanie.

I was going to make Phaeron pay for what he'd done. Because I had a feeling she wasn't his original target—just a clever decoy with a similar hooded jacket. She'd thrown herself on the sword for me and left answers in a way I hadn't mustered the nerve to read.

I reached my dorm room and simply stood there, listening to the sounds of shuffling within. Lanie's parents had arrived this morning, but I'd hidden in the garden rather than witness their grief and know I'd caused it.

A school official had visited and explained that the Graygazers were here to pack up Lanie's things. At first, I'd assumed they'd seen a devastating ripple in future events and set off then and there, just to arrive too late. But no... they'd arrived by portal, traversing thousands of miles with the assistance of a talented celestial witch.

If I'd known celestial witches learned how to make real-life portals, maybe I'd have chosen to become one and side-stepped this whole mess.

Instead, here I was, hesitating with my hand over the knob. *Just go in there and apologize,* I thought viciously, cursing my hesitation.

I came in to find a diminutive, dark-haired woman perched on my bed, scratching Milo's cheeks. My two cats made a harmony of purrs. On Lanie's side of the dorm, an older man looked up from packing away her laptop, sunlight glinting off his blocky glasses frames. Both of Lanie's parents turned to me at the same time.

The only tears in the room were mine. Lanie's mother placed Milo aside gently and swept me into a hug. "Poor dear. You must be Cress... Lanie spoke well of you."

"That's me," I mumbled.

"Come, have a seat." She ushered me to sit where she'd vacated, and my familiars pressed against me for comfort. "I'm glad you chose to come see us."

Spoken just like someone with the magic to see the future, who'd known there was only a slim chance I'd gather the courage to look her in the eye. I swallowed nervously, expecting her and her husband to round on me together, but instead, she settled on Lanie's bed, and he acknowledged me with a nod before continuing to pack.

"I'm so sorry about Lanie," I burst out. "Her death was so sudden. I could tell there was something wrong, but I never expected—"

"Shh. I know." A sad smile twisted her mouth.

"We knew this day was coming," Lanie's father said through a thick accent.

My jaw dropped open. "You...did?"

"We did. Maybe not the exact date, but..." Her mother

spread her hands. "It's the burden of all accomplished augurs."

"We all know how we will die," her father said.

I bit into my bottom lip, chewing on this revelation. "That must be awful for you," I said quietly.

"Is it?" She tilted her head in consideration. "We had the chance to say our goodbyes with Lanie. Most don't get the opportunity for that kind of closure."

I stood and found my tissue box atop the modest dresser on my side of the room, just in time to blot out another wave of tears and sniffles. I had to say it, to apologize to Lanie's parents. That's what I came here for.

"It's not your fault," she said before I could muster up the fragments of my nerve.

"It is. I-I couldn't stop her in time..." As I said this, Bella wiggled into my lap, and I held on to her for comfort.

Lanie's mother shook her head. "Do you know what happens when a Graygazer denies their fate? Someone else dies instead. Often horrifically." She gave me a pointed look, and I felt the color draining off my face.

"Are you saying...I almost died in a way worse than Lanie did?" That wasn't reassuring at all. In my current headspace, I thought that would've been better.

But I saw the expression on her face and the look her husband flashed my way. It wasn't supposed to be comforting. Fate or not, they'd lost their daughter because of me.

"She told us of a being of shadows and teeth, with claws made of white fire. A dimensional creature beyond her mind's ability to understand," she murmured. "Her fate was to gain its attention, because someone would've died last night, no matter what. This thing...this-this *monster*, was going to target you. It would've consumed you, body and soul. Anyone else that got in its way would've suffered the same ending. But my daughter…"

"Her soul was eaten?" I asked in a horrified whisper.

She jerked her head. "No. She said the creature would be interrupted before it did more than attack her. That she would save your life, but you would save her soul."

My lips pressed together, head bowed solemnly. *Damn.* What was I supposed to say to that?

"The monster targeted me for a reason. It's my fa—"

"No," she interrupted. "Don't you see, Cress? There's a reason I'm telling you this. It was Lanie's decision, her gift to you and all the young witches there last night."

"But…" I said weakly. I didn't ask for this gift. It wasn't like I deserved it for causing the situation in the first place.

"My daughter met her fated end, but I will take the chance to gaze at what comes next." Magic bloomed around her head in the Graygazer's gray aura, but as I watched, it intensified and brightened until she had a halo of silver casting a glare over her inky hair.

I sat up straighter, a thick knot of emotion caught in my throat.

"You aren't ready for the full truth quite yet. But I see you standing over the creature who attacked my daughter, vanquishing it alongside three men who adore you. You will be the one to avenge her," she intoned, her voice echoing with power.

"Tell me what I have to do," I practically begged.

"Find a man by the name of Callum Voidbinder. Make him train you in librarian magic beyond what a beginner is allowed," she instructed. "And don't act foolishly. You won't get another chance to make this right."

"Yes, ma'am," I said, expecting the glow around her to

fade as she nodded and turned her attention away from me.

She asked her husband something in another language, and he fished his wallet out of his pocket, handing her a card. She passed it to me. "Call us when you lose your way." As she spoke, the sense of otherworldliness faded from her.

"I will," I promised, looking down at the card. "Graygazer Augury Services" stood out from the creamy paper, plus a phone number and email address. I caught her name as well. Hana.

"I hope you find peace," Lanie's father said. "Our calm comes from knowing that Lanie put everyone here on the right path."

Hana raised a finger. "One more thing." She made kissy noises and leaned down, coaxing out Jin. The small black cat had puffed-out fur and the most dejected expression a cat could have, her weight completely limp as Hana picked her up. "Will you care for Jin?"

"You don't want to take her with you?" I asked, fighting a sob. My dam was about to break again, seeing how heart-broken Jin was.

She scratched behind the little cat's ears, earning a reluctant lean. "It's not that at all. I have my familiars, but there's a chance you can win her over and give her a second chance to be a witch's cat." Hana's lips twisted, betraying a flicker of deep grief before she smoothed it behind an impassive mask. "It's very hard to bind three familiars to yourself, but I think you have the potential."

"In that case…I'd love to adopt her," I said. Lanie's cat would remind me of her, but that wasn't a bad thing. I let go of Bella to accept Jin, placing her on my lap. She trembled and watched me closely all the while. In all this mess, I'd overlooked how lost and terrified Jin must be with the sudden loss of her witch. Yet she stayed and let me hold her as we watched the Graygazers finish packing what remained of Lanie's things.

I wouldn't admit to understanding either of them. They'd just lost their daughter, but it felt like they'd just talked me down from the sharpest peak of my grief. I *was* going to avenge my friend. They'd seen it in the future.

I just had to make it happen, and I couldn't wait to start sharpening a silver blade.

BUT WHEN THE Graygazers left and I was alone with the cats, my motivation guttered out immediately. It was easier to promise big things and nod along as a powerful witch told me my fate. Now that it was time to, well, get out of bed and *do it*, in rushed another overwhelming wave of emotion.

This was still all my fault. Lanie had made the best out of a bad situation, but that didn't bring her back. Her cat had retreated from my hold to stretch out on the bare mattress left over on the other side of the room. Her eyes, yellow and sad, stared in my direction when she wasn't sleeping.

I shifted onto my back and watched the play of light over the ceiling. It was a Monday, and the cheerful chatter of young women going to and from their classes filled the hall. I'd gotten a week off and a promise of grade forgiveness for what I'd seen.

It didn't seem like enough. I wasn't sure I could get out of this bed in a week and go back to normal. Nothing about my life was "normal" anymore anyway.

I was apparently destined to slay a dimensional monster and avenge my friend. I waited and waited for a more heroic spirit to possess me, to push out the coward who had hidden the fact I'd been the one to release said monster.

It wasn't until the evening light was fading to darkness when a knock sounded on my door. I released a groan, shifting to sit up slowly so I didn't disturb Milo and Bella napping against my legs. The knock sounded again, timid and light.

On the other side of the threshold stood a semi-familiar brunette. She raised a hand in a brief wave. "Hi, Cress," whispered Willow, the oceanic witch who was apparently one of my coven-mates. "Can we come in?"

We? I glanced behind her to see Roe and her petite fae roommate, Áine, standing around the corner and peeking in on this discussion. Roe in particular looked like she was holding in her brash manner, the strain making her cheeks pinker.

"Yeah, I guess," I sighed, taking a few steps back.

"Uh, your phone is off." Roe sounded like she was murmuring, but her voice was at a regular conversational level. "So I thought maybe we could talk in person."

I glanced away awkwardly. Was anything more of a "do not disturb" sign than a phone turned off?

I perched on my bed, and the two witches sat on the empty mattress while Áine said with extra cheer, "Hey, are you hungry? I brought snacks."

Her little shorts looked like they didn't have pockets, and she wasn't wearing a backpack. I shrugged, but my belly betrayed me, grumbling its discontent.

"Sounds like a yes. Good thing I have…" She stuck her hand into a patch of wavering air, and I turned to stare as she withdrew a plate stacked high with brownies, plus bowls, spoons, napkins, and finally a tub of ice cream frosted from first exposure to warm air. She passed these things to Roe and Willow, who dutifully divided them equally between the four of us.

I realized I was gawking. "How…?"

"Pocket portal." The fae winked. "I have an emergency stash, and I think this qualifies."

Willow passed me a bowl stacked high with sugar. "I don't think she knows what fae magic does," she suggested in her quiet wisp of a voice.

"So, you know how New Salem is, like, separate from the rest of the mortal world?" Áine asked.

"Sort of." I stuffed a spoonful of ice cream in my mouth. It was still delightfully cold, despite its spontaneous appearance.

"That's fae magic, with a touch of other magics for stability. We can warp nature, basically. When I reach into here…" Her hand disappeared into a patch of air that rippled like a heat mirage. "…I'm reaching into a space that only exists for me. It's a natural extension of my being. Since I'm just a faun, the stuff I store away winks out of existence until I reach inside, and sometimes it's really gone for good. Were I a stronger fae, I could allow you to access it too. I could make it bigger than a pocket so you could come and go from it and we could decorate it with streets and buildings and nature. Does that make sense?"

"So you're telling me…a strong enough fae can create an entirely new *city*?" I said, imagining it. Screw castles in the sky, create a whole space just for yourself. I hadn't even an inkling it was possible until now. "And that's what New Salem is?"

"A group of fae, sure. New Salem used to be the Fall

Court, but they gave up the space after...well, you don't need all the details right now." She waved a hand dismissively. "All the fae courts are hosted in alternate dimensions like New Salem. But most of them are fae-only and thus not as big. Magic from dimensionals allows for expansion, merfolk give us stable water sources and varied weather patterns, plus verdant, oceanic, and celestial witches can help too."

"That is so cool," I said with some of my usual enthusiasm for learning about the supernatural world.

"Right?" she said brightly.

It seemed like Roe couldn't take it anymore. "I've been so worried about you!" she burst out. "Are you going to move to our dorm? Anywhere but here?"

The school official who'd visited earlier had already tried to convince me to move in with a different roommate. I thought it was standard practice, as if this room is tainted with memories. I told them the same thing I'd said to that person. "I don't want to leave. My familiars are happy in this room...and Jin might appreciate it too."

Lanie's cat was hiding under the bed right now. She hadn't even talked to my cats since we'd lost Lanie, so I wasn't sure if it was her wish or not.

"So, I convinced the school to let me have the room to myself for the rest of the year," I said. "It's going to be nice... probably."

"You're officially the host of all our dorm parties," Roe proclaimed.

"Uhhh..."

"Anyway," Willow said. "We're a coven now. If you need to talk, we're always here for you."

I glanced at Áine, who shrugged. "Roe said I'm an honorary member."

"But we have a new guy." Roe's voice turned into a grumble. "*Already!*"

"Wren attached herself to his side instantly." Willow rolled her eyes with a delicate sigh. "We're like two mini covens right now. Roe, me, and you."

"Plus me," Áine interjected.

"And the three guy witches and Wren. That girl is vicious." Willow frowned.

"You too, huh?" I said.

"Yeah," she muttered.

Roe said, "We wanted to let you know that there's another coven meeting Wednesday evening over dinner, since our first one was, uh..."

"Canceled," Willow supplied.

"And we need you to come." Roe clasped her hands, giving me her best puppy dog eyes. "I'm not about to let Wren lead my first coven."

"Me neither." I paused for a moment. "Wait. Like, are we voting on a leader? Is that more than an unofficial title?"

"Exactly. And without you there, Wren's basically guaranteed to get it," Willow said. "Can't you come and vote for Roe instead?"

I nodded slowly. "If the three guys still vote for her..."

"Well, you have to meet the new guy," Roe said quickly. She flashed me a nervous smile, the kind that came before a big request. "He came in today and, uh, seems curious about you. Maybe you could come to Introduction to Witchcraft on Wednesday and, like, convince him..."

"Curious about me how?" I asked, my eyes narrowing.

"Like, he knows you're in our coven and you're our only librarian. It's kind of a miracle he asked since Wren was shoving her boobs in his face," Roe said with a snort.

I started to laugh too. "So that's how she's getting the guys to be friends with her?"

"Yeah, well, you should meet this guy anyway." A tinge of pink touched Willow's cheeks.

"He's hot," Roe blurted.

"All right, all right. You've twisted my arm," I said wryly.

"Great!" Roe lit up. "I think you'll like him. His name's Ben."

10

BEN

Master Garroway kept me off any missions once my brother went off to assassinate the purple-haired Darkmore girl.

Days passed. I wasn't too worried. Finding the time and place to carry out a discreet mission often took time.

Then a week went by, and I would jump at any sound my phone made, hoping to see Lucas's name on the screen. It was never him.

"I suppose little Lucas is having trouble," my vampire master drawled when I brought it up at dinner that evening. He watched me without concern every night he deigned to join his coven of blood witches. Seeing him once a week was a surprise, but his uncaring remark came after his second day at the head of the table, swirling deep red blood wine in an elegant glass.

Chilled, I didn't mention Lucas to him again. All I knew was that Garroway had given Lucas a second, smaller task to complete while he was in Moongrove Library since his mark turned out to be a librarian witch. Apparently, it was a trade-off for losing money on a free deal with Crown Starsurge.

I was going crazy, though. With no missions, all I could do was sit around the manor and serve as a medic if anyone arrived injured. It was a Sunday before I got a glimmer of hope as I tended to Bianca's ears clumsily with cotton swabs and an ancient tool in the infirmary that was like a tiny water gun.

"Ow, watch it," she hissed, slapping my arm after a particularly enthusiastic squirt into her ear. Bloody water ran into the waiting basin.

"It's not my fault you didn't wear earplugs," I grunted.

"I did! And you're supposed to irrigate my ear, not blast the eardrum," she complained. "Who fucking died and made you the new medic anyway?"

"It was the master's decision," I said, applying less pressure to the trigger as I splashed water over the outside shell of her ear before digging into the crust with a swab. I'd seen a lot worse in the last week. Even though blood witches could heal most injuries on themselves with a mending rune painted on their skin in their own blood, it left a mess behind.

And I was doing a great job, thank you very much. She'd arrived deaf after hunting down a dimensional screamer, and the first thing she did after I covered her ears with mending runes to bring her hearing back was complain about me.

She made a little *tsk* noise and started scrolling her phone. "Whatever."

I made an exaggerated smack with my lips and mimicked her in a higher voice, "Whatever! Guess I'll be deaf."

Her brow furrowed hard, her death glare aimed at her

device since she was forced to lean over the padded table to drain her ear into the little curved basin that fit against her shoulder.

"It got a lucky drop on me," she admitted quietly. "I usually have two bolts in one of their throats before they can make a peep."

"Sounds sloppy to me," I said.

"Shut up, Ben. Not like you've ever been tapped to hunt a screamer," she snapped. "Stuck here while—"

An ugly gasp interrupted her, and she brought the screen closer to her face. "What? What is it?" I demanded.

"Fuck. It's Lucas, I think."

I practically snatched the phone from her as she scrolled back to the top of a page. It was a news article quoting an official statement from NSU. My gaze darted over the screen so fast I had to stop and collect myself to really let the words sink in.

It gave sparse details of a gruesome, bloody murder on campus by a "rogue blood witch." As an actual rogue, my eyebrows rose at how amateurish and sloppy the details were...almost like a first kill.

Bianca's first thought was of Lucas, and I agreed, only pausing when I saw the victim was an unnamed augury witch.

"He killed the wrong person," I muttered. "An augur."

"They're literally the worst." I could practically hear her eyes rolling. "I've been blackmailed by one before. Threatened to turn me in to the SPDI if I killed my mark."

"Do you think this one provoked my brother?" I asked.

"The fuck if I know. Probably? Why else would he have fumbled a kill so badly?" she asked.

I stared at the words on the tiny, bright screen until they ran together in a blur. No matter what, Lucas was in trouble. The SPDI didn't fuck around if they got a whiff of rogue activity. They would hunt him down like a dog.

We were specially trained in what to do if we were ever caught, but it came to one simple fact: a quick death by suicide was a much cleaner ending than having our blood boiled in our veins for even considering telling the authorities about Master Garroway or his illegal dealings. The trigger spell for a messy end was woven in through the complex blood rune all of Garroway's witches bore.

"I have to go help him," I said, handing the phone back to Bianca. "I have to find him before bounty hunters or the SPDI do."

For a moment, she turned the device over in her hands. "Do you think Garroway will give you leave to go?"

"He can always call me back," I said, shrugging. If I asked, the answer would be no. If I just slipped out, then I could make up some kind of excuse if Garroway activated my blood rune and forced me to return.

"I guess." She hesitated for a moment. "If you clean out my other ear—*gently*—I'll forge a few documents for you to get you into NSU."

"I'm not going to attend classes," I scoffed.

"You're going to look awfully suspicious, then," she pointed out. "C'mon, at least one class. Pick an old professor; they're easy to fool. Isn't Lucas's mark a student anyway?"

"Yeah."

"She might be your only lead. You should see if she knows the dead augur," she said.

Well, she did have a point. "All right. One class alongside Lucas's mark, then. I'll start with her and search the campus for any signs of him in the meantime."

"Great. It shouldn't be too hard," she said.

I suppressed a groan. It was one constant in my life: anything that seemed easy was anything but.

BIANCA DIDN'T JUST FORGE some documents for me; she slipped her way into NSU's database and brought up a list of the Darkmore girl's classes. She was taking Latin, introductory classes to witchery and the supernatural world, plus courses in fashion design.

The thought of having to sit through anything related to fashion gave me chills, so we looked up the professors in her other classes, narrowing the options down to Introduction to Witchcraft with a septuagenarian professor, Dr. Evanora Heartwood. It was a class that met Monday, Wednesday, Friday, so I made sure I was ready to attend the next day.

I ended up scraping off the scraggly beard forming over my jaw and browsing the manor's walk-in closet for a few outfits that would make me look like a casual college dude. Rack upon rack of different clothes in various sizes waited to be used, some beaten up and others brand new designer labels with the tags still on them.

Always look like you belong was one of the first rules I'd learned here. Garroway made sure we had all the tools for the job, including prosthetics and makeup if the situation required it. His greatest gift, though, was the set of jewelry I inspected after picking out my clothes. Each piece was designed to hold a tiny vial discreetly. I flipped open the nearly invisible catch on my favorite, a heavy, dark ring with a grayish sheen in the light. I slipped my vial of blood inside it and fit the ring on my right hand, adjusting it until it warmed.

Every blood witch here received one emergency vial filled with a bit of Garroway's blood. In dire circumstances, I could break it and paint myself with runes to gain a burst of vampiric strength, agility, and regeneration. Hopefully it wouldn't come to that.

I picked up a second item, a heavy necklace with an amethyst cluster as the pendant, then selected a vial of guardian witch blood to add to it, to help me pass as one for as long as I needed to complete this personal mission.

I left the manor and Garroway's pocket dimension under the cover of a newly risen sun that Monday, traversing several miles of ordinary human Salem. The shift in weather made my sinuses ache, for Garroway preferred dry and chilly autumn weather in his bubble of privacy disguised as a dilapidated house in the suburbs, while Salem had an overcast, windy day.

I rubbed my nose as I found the seam in reality at a cemetery gate and slipped into the NSU campus by touching that magic with a bit of my own. The glare of a sunny summer day hit my eyes immediately. I soaked in its warmth as I slouched my way onto the campus, hands in my hoodie and music thumping in my wireless earbuds.

To anyone else's eyes, I was another college kid with a bag casually slung over one shoulder, unhurriedly going to class along a route I'd memorized. Once I reached the right classroom, I drew out an official-looking letter and offered it to the elderly woman who smiled in the kind of way that said she recognized me as a lost young man.

"Hello, is this Introduction to Witchcraft?" I asked.

As she scanned the letter, I felt the faintest flutter of

nerves. If anything was off with Bianca's forging, this woman would notice it immediately.

"It sure is, and you're in the right place, Benjamin," she said, an odd look passing over her expression. "Do you have a coven already?"

"No, ma'am," I replied.

"Your arrival is most fortunate, then. Please sit with this row." She gestured to the far side of the room, where a couple of students sat and chatted quietly, their gazes flashing up at us more than once. "Welcome to NSU. I hope you enjoy it here."

I thanked her and went to sit at the desk at the end of the row, my back pressed to the wall. The male witch one seat up from me grinned a perfect white smile and introduced himself as Heath. He had the kind of lean muscle that suggested he was active in some sport or was the kind of fighter I'd better keep an eye on just in case.

The witch he'd been chatting with perched herself on my desk, her sparkly shirt cut to reveal a line of cleavage. She leaned just right to put me at eye level with it. "Hey there," she purred. "I'm Wren Starsurge. Celestial witch."

I met her blue gaze and smirked. Now this was awkward. I saw a hint of family resemblance between her and the blustering Blaize Starsurge, the man that was basically the reason I'd arrived here. But I doubted she knew her daddy was involved in the business of hiring my master's services.

"Ben Cross. Guardian witch," I lied, nodding to her. A bit of her interest dimmed when I didn't pull out an impressive surname. In truth, I didn't have one, just the name Cross, which all of Garroway's witches borrowed off and on.

"Where are you from, Ben?" she asked.

"Here and there." I shrugged. "Just transferred here, but I'm a little worried it was a mistake."

Her lips narrowed to a little rosebud. "So, you've already heard the news about Lanie."

"If that was her name," I said.

"Nasty business." She gave a delicate shudder. "I guess you're in my coven now. You're like, her replacement."

"Hopefully I'm not next," I said dryly.

She opened her mouth to reply when a louder woman's voice interrupted. "Hey, are you new?" A muscular redheaded woman approached, and Wren's expression turned icy in an instant.

"He's our newest coven member. We're back to seven already. Isn't that great?" the celestial witch simpered, twirling a lock of blonde hair around her finger.

The redhead recoiled as if she'd been struck. She shot a disbelieving look at the elderly professor currently deep in conversation with another student as they both looked at something on his computer screen. "It hasn't even been a day," she mumbled.

"Ben here's a guardian too, just like you. I guess you have a partner to go to the gym with now," Wren said, her judgmental gaze sweeping over the workout gear the other witch had come in wearing. I frowned to myself. Guardians were difficult opponents for a blood witch to fight due to their natural affinity for stone, and this woman looked like she was devoted to her craft, if her muscles were any indication.

The redhead made an unimpressed noise. As more of the class filed in, I was swept into a round of introductions. I memorized each name and face. The redhead, Rowena Ashbough, was the only guardian at least. Willow and Heath, both of the oceanic affinity. Grant, a verdant witch, who had a bored glaze to his eyes as he slumped into his seat. And, of course, Wren.

"Where is the last member of our group?" I asked, seeing as class was about to begin. An empty desk was bracketed in our row by Willow and Roe. Considering I hadn't seen a head of purple hair file in yet, I had my suspicions as to who was meant to sit there.

Roe turned and leaned around Heath and Wren to answer me. "Her name's Cress, and she's a librarian. I don't think we'll see her for a while," she said. A heavy sense of sadness hung over her words.

Wren rolled her eyes. "Please, save the dramatics. She knew Lanie all of a couple weeks."

"She found the *body*," Roe argued, her tone turning biting. "And they were roommates. Have some empathy."

I disguised my keen interest with a glance at my phone. Could I be so lucky? Not only did the Darkmore girl know my brother's victim, we were now in the same coven.

"I look forward to meeting her," I said.

11

CRESS

"I'm sorry I left you out here," I said when Wednesday came around. I didn't think the gargoyle had moved an inch from the kneeling position he'd settled in the last time we'd spoken.

Only a couple things betrayed that he was more than a statue placed randomly in the middle of the garden path. His chest rose and fell with slow, steady breaths. When he noticed me approaching him, his chin had tipped up with a grinding like two stones brushing off each other.

"Is. It. Time. I. Fulfilled. My. Purpose?" His voice was deep, near guttural. Each word seemed like a struggle for him to utter.

"Are you okay?" I asked uncertainly.

He drew himself off the ground and to his full height. I started assuming the grinding noises were like if I popped my knuckles or back. Once he had a good scrape, the unsettling sounds softened to the swish of sandpaper with each motion. "I am..." He blew a cloud of dust out of his mouth, aiming it away from me. "...sufficiently rested."

I supposed that was close enough and shrugged. "I

need to go to class. Do you have something else you could be doing?"

"Protecting you...is my purpose," he said. "I will... accompany you."

"Suit yourself." My mind raced to explain away a seven-foot gargoyle following me, especially into the classes with limited space. I led him into the campus, taking my time. Geo kept pace with me despite his slower steps since he had a huge stride.

I snuck an appreciating look up at him while he stared ahead, his cloudy white eyes roving constantly for danger.

A woman must've sculpted Geo, because every detail was a gal's wet dream. He had the frame to match his incredibly tall stature, detailed down to a few hairline veins of silver marbling across his bulging arm muscles. In the sunlight, his pitch-black stone skin gleamed without casting a glare.

My gaze skimmed over his perfectly formed chest. The sculptor had skipped giving him a shirt, instead outlining each abdominal with painstaking care. Fortunately for my blushing perusal, he did have a pair of stone shorts on, which moved with each flex of his generously muscled thighs.

A pair of gigantic bat wings marked him for what he was, along with the six stalactite-like spears of sharpened quartz tucked into the line of his back.

Out of nowhere, I nearly ran into his arm. My gaze flashed up to his face as a car raced past. "Careful," he said, flashing white quartz teeth.

I scratched the back of my head sheepishly, wondering if he'd realized I'd nearly walked into oncoming traffic while internally complimenting the person who'd made him. His expression was as flat as ever, though. His symmetrical face had a strong jaw and thick brow, and I hadn't seen him emote with either yet. The only expression he seemed capable of making was the serious line of his obsidian lips.

"Sorry," I said a little breathlessly.

He lowered his arm, indicating I continue leading the way.

"I'm new to the supernatural world," I told him after successfully crossing the street. "So, I'm probably going to ask you a ton of dumb questions."

"Ask," he said.

I bit my lip, unsure how to even phrase this question. If I guessed correctly, though, I wouldn't be able to offend him. He hadn't shown any emotion yet, at least. "Are you a robot?" I asked.

"No."

"Are you...alive?" I asked, holding my breath as his head turned my way with the whisper of sandpaper.

"I am capable of life."

My brow furrowed. "That's usually a yes or no question."

"For me, it is yes and no." His lips dipped, threatening a frown. "I am capable of shifting. A form of flesh and blood and feeling. But I choose not to...unless it is required."

"Why not?" I asked. The Voidbinder Building was just a block away, and I felt my palms moisten with nerves. It'd only been a few days since...

"Most gargoyles forget their duty once they've experienced living again." Geo continued speaking, oblivious to the nerves churning in my belly. "We are created to serve the library, and I have always been dutiful to my purpose."

"Oh yeah?" I mumbled, distracted.

"You need not worry. I will not abandon you to pursuits

of the flesh," he answered with all the earnestness of someone who didn't know I'd do a lot to see what he looked like when he wasn't a talking, moving rock.

I stopped before the steps up to the Voidbinder Building and turned to him. "Well, my class is in here," I said. I'd decided I was just going to attend Introduction to Witchcraft today. Dip my toes back into the water and slowly get into my normal schedule.

Geo watched me for a moment. "I shall wait here for you," he said. "Will you be gone for several days again?"

I flushed, still mortified I'd left him to wait for me for that long. And he *had,* without complaint. "No! Just a couple hours at most. After class, there's someone I need to find."

"I shall find you if it takes too long, then," he promised.

I checked my phone and hustled up the steps, mere minutes from being late. Heads turned when I walked in, several conversations quieting to whispers. *Great, they're gossiping about me.* I realized there was a change in seating. Roe waved to me from the farthest row, where she and Willow were sitting with Wren and a couple guys I semi-recognized, along with one I didn't.

Roe stood, leaving the desk in front of him empty, and mouthed the words "thank you" as she took her seat further up. Meaning I had to sit sandwiched between the new guy and Wren. I cursed under my breath as I slipped into that spot. The new male witch sat with his back to the wall, leg crossed in a casual figure-four.

"Hey," he said. "Nice hair."

"Oh, thanks," I mumbled, inspecting the ends of a lock. By this point, some of its vibrant purple color had faded. I was nearly shy when face to face with the guy Roe had so shamelessly called "hot."

Fuck, he was. He could give Geo a run for his money, and the gargoyle had been created by an expert's hand. He had a generous mane of honeyed brown hair and a crooked smile that could make a gal's heart stop. It lit up his whole face, taking away a predatory edge to his expression, because something about him reminded me of a lion, golden-skinned and hungry.

"I'm Ben. You must be Cress?" I realized he had a hand held out to shake, and he gripped mine with effortless strength despite having a lean build under a casual t-shirt and shorts.

"That's right. I understand you're in my coven now?" I asked. I shifted to put my back against the wall as well.

He shrugged. "Apparently. I just got here, so it seems a little sudden."

"Cress, how are you? No one was expecting you so early. Aren't you still in that room you shared with Lanie?" Wren interjected. Quiet venom lurked under the words, and I immediately turned a glare her direction. Her expression was sweet as can be. I wondered if she practiced it in the mirror. "Isn't it hard to sleep in that room after what happened?"

I held my breath, unpleasantly reminded that I'd barely left that room and had set aside my guilt for the moment to meet Ben.

He leaned around me, scowling at Wren. "That was rude. Don't you see she and I were having a conversation?"

She twirled a length of her hair between her fingers. "I was just curious," she said, laughing it off.

Ben turned his leaf-green gaze back to me, about to say something else when Dr. Heartwood started class. She reminded us that we had coven meetings tonight to get to know each other better and vote for a leader. I released a weary sigh, feeling the now-familiar malaise of exhaustion settling over my shoulders again. Lanie should be sitting behind me, not this guy, no matter what he looked like.

"Today's lesson is on aura reading. You may have noticed auras on and off after bonding to your affinity, but today I will show you how to focus your sight on them with a few different exercises," Dr. Heartwood said, then called for us to find partners.

I turned to Ben, who was fiddling with what looked like a chunk of purple geode strung onto a heavy silver chain around his neck. He flashed a hint of his killer smile. "Partners?"

"Yup," I answered.

"Well, I have to admit to cheating. I already know you're a librarian witch from your friends," he said, gesturing to Roe and Willow, who'd partnered up a few seats up from us.

"What is your magic?" I asked curiously.

"Guess you'll have to find out," he answered with a wink. My heart sped up a step.

"Every supernatural exerts an aura of magic, and witches are particularly adept at sensing them. With practice, you will be able to identify auras at a glance," Dr. Heartwood said.

She walked us through relaxing our gazes to see what color rose off our partner's skin. The slideshow she projected today had a guide for the seven witch affinities, since that's what we'd see today as we read each other's auras.

Ben rested his chin on his palm, gazing at me steadily. "Your aura is purple smoke, about an inch thick. That was easy," he remarked.

I had a harder time and ended up staring at him far

longer than was polite. His expression turned to an amused smirk. "It's not funny. I usually can't do this on command," I muttered.

"It's okay to admire," he replied with an exaggerated flip of his hair. "Maybe it'll help to know that not every aura is purely one color, too. It depends on the individual, how strong their magic is, and how long they've been practicing."

"Been a...guardian a while?" I asked, finally seeing an aura raising off his skin. Patterns of spiky crystals mixed in with the brownish smoke in his aura, and only the geode tips were the neon green I was supposed to look for. It rose a good two inches around him, which implied powerful or active magic according to the chart Dr. Heartwood was displaying.

He shrugged. "Long enough to know how to do this already."

I twisted my lips. "Sounds a lot like two of my friends. Already from established witch families. One even had her magic for years, but she had to take this class anyway."

My shoulders sagged. I missed Lanie so much in that moment.

Ben eyed me for a moment, wetting his lips to speak. That was when Dr. Heartwood announced that we should change partners with someone else.

I ended up reading the auras of several other witches and saw more of what I was expecting. Roe's aura was prickly and bright green, the color complimenting her complexion. Willow had an interesting one, hers an icy blue that writhed like waves in the ocean. Compared to Heath, the other oceanic affinity in our coven, hers was chaotic, while his was a deep blue and placid.

"Maybe you're really strong," I told her.

She ducked her shoulders. "I don't know. I haven't cast any magic successfully yet," she murmured.

My last partner of the day ended up being Wren, and I suppressed a sound of dismay. Her aura was blinding, three inches of pure rays of sunlight. She smirked as she looked me over. "Pretty weak, Cress."

I clamped my jaw on suggesting that she had the strongest magic out of any of the witches I'd seen today. She didn't need a bigger head.

We soon returned to our original seats, and I realized I hadn't done a thing to convince Ben who to vote for tonight for coven leader. With Wren just a seat away, waiting with barely concealed fangs, I waited for class to dismiss and caught his eye.

He jerked his chin in acknowledgment, staying in his seat as the majority of the class filed out. "I just wanted to say welcome to the coven, such as it is," I said. "Are you coming to the meeting tonight?"

"Wouldn't miss it," he said, flashing a brief smile.

"Great, because we're supposed to vote on a leader tonight..."

I drifted off when he held up a hand. "I wouldn't miss it *because* I want to spend more time with you," he said.

"Oh." A little tinge of color lit my cheeks.

"When's your next class? Maybe we could grab a coffee," he offered.

"Not for, uh..." I considered if I wanted to admit I wasn't going to any of my other classes. It'd lead to more questions than I wanted to answer, and I was going to find the experienced librarian witch Hana Graygazer told me to seek out. "...a couple hours."

"Well then." He hopped to his feet and offered me a hand up. "Show me the way."

I led the way out of the classroom. "How new are you to NSU?"

"Got here Monday. Just in time to miss the scare, apparently."

I nearly stumbled over my two feet. "Yeah," I muttered. An innocent witch had been murdered. Of course that would scare everyone on campus.

"They say it was a rogue blood witch." He fitted his hands in his pockets casually. "To think someone like that happened in a place as safe as NSU."

Well, the university was lying, but I wasn't about to tell him that. The fewer people who snooped into the details of that night, the better, as far as I was concerned. I'd seen a couple witches patrolling the campus on my way here, silver swords drawn. Someone in charge knew who they were really looking for.

I stepped outside and nearly stopped short upon seeing sunlight reflected off Geo's obsidian skin. I turned to Ben, who eyed the gargoyle with a raised brow. "I forgot to tell you. I have a bodyguard now," I said.

Geo lifted himself out of a hunched posture. "You are early," he rumbled.

"Just going on a coffee break. You don't have to come with. It'll be fine," I said.

The gargoyle looked down at me without blinking. "You are my duty. Where you go, I follow."

I glanced at Ben with a shrug. He echoed the motion. "It's not every day I meet someone important enough to have a gargoyle bodyguard." He smirked over my head at Geo.

I told myself I'd need to get used to this as Geo trailed a few steps behind Ben and me. Until Phaeron was dead, I needed protection anyway. "His name's Geo," I supplied.

"Is that short for anything?" Ben asked.

"No," came the grinding response behind me.

"Really?" the male witch glanced over his shoulder.

"Yes."

"It's not Geology or something?"

"My response to this line of inquiry shall remain the same."

Ben whistled under his breath. "Well, anyway." He directed his attention back to me. "The library obviously wants to protect you. I'm sorry for your loss, by the way. Wren told me what happened."

"Of course she did," I muttered, my hands forming fists.

"You know how legacy witches are." He rolled his eyes. "Her daddy's got money, so she thinks she can trod on no-names like us."

I cast a curious glance aside at him. "From what I can tell, most witches have some kind of legacy."

"Not me. You?"

"Same."

He offered a fist bump to that. I pressed my fingers to his before gesturing him into the campus coffee shop. Geo took up a post just outside the doors. Ben took my order and stood in line, if I would just find us a good spot. I picked a table by a window, just within sight of Geo. Though I doubted the gargoyle could experience anxiety, I didn't want to make his "duty" any more difficult.

A giddy laugh bubbled in my throat. I couldn't believe I was actually on a coffee date with a handsome guy. Carly would eat the news of this up—

My heart sank, and I fished my phone out, powering it up. I hadn't spoken to Carly or Mom since the weekend, and my device had a seizure in my hold as it buzzed continuously with messages and voicemails, most of which were from Carly or Roe.

"I'm fine. Talk later?" I texted Carly after skimming a line of messages from her. She thought I was angry with her. If only she knew what rollercoaster of emotion I was still on.

I put the phone away as Ben came over with two steaming cups. "Extra sugar for you," he said, passing me my white chocolate mocha.

"Black for you?" I asked with a chuckle.

"Nah. Extra extra sugar for me." He took the top off to show the light brown color of his coffee. It looked good, actually.

"So, about the meeting tonight. It's down to Wren or Roe," I said.

Ben glanced down at his drink with a slant of his lips. "I'll vote however you like. I have little stake in how it turns out," he said with a careless wave.

"Then you should vote for Roe," I said.

"Fine, you got it."

I breathed a sigh of relief while he took a cautious first sip of coffee. "So, why did you transfer to NSU?" I asked before the pause between us could get too awkward.

"I came from SSU. It's down in Texas. I got tired of burning up in hundred-degree weather."

I laughed briefly. "You're a sophomore, then?"

He shrugged. "I'm not the best student, so it's more like I'm a bonus freshman."

That would explain why he was still taking an introductory class.

He started asking questions about how I'd gotten here, and I ended up telling him my story. How I'd only known I was a witch when I met my familiars, Milo and Bella.

"Being here is a dream come true. Mostly." I couldn't help a bit of bitterness with how I'd nearly ruined it within a few weeks of arriving.

"Mostly?" he echoed.

"Well, you know, my roommate..." I bit my lip, feeling my eyes well immediately. It was way too soon to talk about Lanie so casually. "And I'm afraid whatever got her is still after me."

Understanding sparkled in his green eyes. "Yeah. But the library sent you that gargoyle out there." He hitched his thumb in Geo's direction.

I glanced over my shoulder, where Geo was still slouched and waiting. "I don't really know what's up with him. It sounded more like he sent himself," I admitted.

"Hmm." He tilted his head in consideration. "It sounds like you haven't experienced the best part of being a supernatural."

"Yeah?" A slight smile lit my face.

"The shows! Real magic and sometimes, real monsters. You have to know how to access them."

"Good thing I know a guy, huh?" I offered tentatively, a sprinkling of butterflies in my belly when he snapped his fingers and pointed.

"Exactly. You're going to be so happy we met."

12

CRESS

A FEW HOURS LATER, I was beaming as I headed back up the road toward the Voidbinder Building with Geo.

Of course, he had to dump cold water on my happiness immediately. "I do not trust that boy."

"He was a nice guy," I argued, flashing an annoyed look his way.

"You are my duty. I would not lie. He does not have good intentions," he stated.

"How would you know?" I muttered. It wasn't like the gargoyle had done anything but watched Ben and I chat for hours.

"Some things, I sense. Ignore if you wish. You will know I am right someday."

I glanced away, resisting the urge to roll my eyes. "I have to catch a professor," I told him, breezing into the Voidbinder Building to look for a man with its namesake. Geo didn't follow, instead dutifully keeping watch at the door.

I stomped my way to the second floor and started scanning the signs outside each professor's door. I'd identified the man I was looking for as a professor for advanced librarian students who wanted to actually make their magic a profession. To my surprise, his door was ajar when I found his office.

"Good afternoon," he said, not glancing up from his computer screen when I knocked on the door. "Office hours will have to wait, I'm afraid. Very important business in the library."

"Dr. Voidbinder?" I said.

He glanced over his shoulder, seeming annoyed that I hadn't left yet. "Yes?"

"I was hoping you could help me. My friend, uh…" I gritted my teeth, forcing the words out before I could get emotional. "She was killed by a dimensional a few days ago."

In a blink, he was on his feet and dragging me into his office. He slammed the door after him. "You can't go saying that in public," he hissed.

I stared at him owlishly, not expecting such a spry reaction from a man who looked like he'd abandoned the gym years ago. He had a middle age paunch, and sweat sheened his shiny head where scalp peeked out between thinning strands of hair.

"I'm sorry?" I asked.

He took a deep breath and looked me over more closely. "Please, have a seat, Miss…?"

"Cress," I supplied. I sat where he indicated, in the armpit of his tiny office. At least it was a comfortable nook.

"Nice to meet you, Cress. I didn't know your name, but I know *of* you. Don't get too nervous, but…" His weight hit his swivel chair, and it creaked in complaint. "You must understand that the murder you witnessed is a sensitive matter."

My eyes narrowed. "Mmm."

He sighed deeply. "The university is not sharing specific details in the case for a reason. Can you imagine the panic if we shared that a dimensional creature is loose somewhere on campus?"

"Maybe you *should*, because it's the truth," I snipped.

His watery brown eyes fixed on me with a serious expression. "Dr. Aurina wanted to meet you personally if I caught any hint that you were talking about what you really saw."

Ice snuck its way up my spine. "What? Why?" I asked quietly.

"We have the situation under control, Miss Cress. You must have faith in the librarians that run Moongrove Library."

"But—" I nearly blurted out more than I meant to and bit off the words with effort. With a furious heave of my lungs, I regrouped and said, "That dimensional was coming after *me*. My roommate sacrificed herself because she was an augur. She saw that any other victim would've been consumed, body and soul. Thanks to the circumstances, she only lost her life. Can you sleep at night, knowing a soul-eating monster is out there, free to strike again?"

"I'm sorry for your loss," he said carefully. "I will need to call for the University President if you speak out more."

"To expel me?" I asked.

"No. To make you compliant."

An uncomfortable prickle of goosebumps raised on my arms. "With her magic. Right."

A pitying look started to form on his expression. I blurted out before he could dismiss me. "I want to help. I have a gargoyle but no way to fight alongside him."

His lips parted with shock, jaw hanging for a few seconds. "The Quartz Gargoyle?" he asked.

"Yeah. Geo. He said I was his duty."

"No way," he said under his breath. "Young lady, do you know how remarkable that is? The Quartz Gargoyle was asleep for nearly a hundred years. Most of our original gargoyles have either lived out a mortal life or gone permanently dormant."

I debated replying and ended up with an indecisive nibble of my bottom lip. He nodded and continued, "Of course not. You're practically a baby in librarian terms. A page, even, as Lars says. Come, there's something you should see." He heaved himself to his feet, and I came with him.

We entered an empty classroom, and he drew me to the far wall. "The last gargoyles were created at the end of the era of demigods. The practice came under increased scrutiny and was eventually deemed to be barbaric. Do you know what animates the Quartz Gargoyle? Has he told you?"

"No," I admitted.

"Sometime in the nineteenth century, we lost one of our last witch demigoddesses, the librarian Morgana Voidbinder. And yes, she and I are related. The building we're in was named after her and her sacrifice," he said, stopping short and gesturing to a painting hanging on the wall. It was a diminutive square covered in a layer of protective glass to save it from the touch of grubby hands.

Dozens of similar paintings decorated the wall of this classroom, but Morgana Voidbinder's was first. I scanned the labels under each and realized this was a gallery of demigod and demigoddess witches.

Morgana's portrait depicted a pale, raven-haired beauty

with a mysterious curve to her rich red lips. She was posed with a leather-bound book in one hand and a silver sword in the other, her gown floor-length scarlet velvet with a slit showing her leg up to the knee. The glow thrown off her weapon illuminated the silhouettes of several horned figures kneeling before her.

I leaned in to read the little biography engraved on a plaque under her portrait.

Morgana was one of the longest-lived witch demigoddesses in recorded history. She was the first witch to discover the librarian affinity and established the guidelines for witches to create and tap dimensional powercores. It was because of her diplomacy that dimensional travelers became an accepted supernatural race and ally to witchkind. We honor her to this day for her many sacrifices, including the one that led to her untimely death in 1812 to permanently seal away an unkillable dimensional monster. Her soul elected to continue its service to mankind as the Quartz Gargoyle.

I straightened and inspected the portrait of her again with new respect. With a gasp, I pointed at one of the kneeling dimensionals. "That's him," I said, recognizing Phaeron's curled horns.

Dr. Voidbinder bent to squint at the figure. "I saw this dimensional a few nights ago," I continued in a whisper.

"Well, that would explain why the Quartz Gargoyle has returned. If he is truly targeting you...then Morgana's soul sensed it. The dimensional that attacked your friend is the same one Morgana gave her life to seal in Moongrove Library." His Adam's apple bobbed in a nervous swallow. "An evil creature that followed the dimensional travelers to Earth."

"So, Geo is actually this demigoddess?" I asked.

He sighed, shaking his head. "If only he were. We need the power of an experienced demigoddess librarian more than ever now that the Hungering Darkness is free. Geo is his own person, given life by Morgana's choice. He is more a memorial to her than anything, but you may be lucky enough to catch peeks of her through him."

"That's...wild," I admitted. Maybe she could help me fix my huge mistake.

"One reason of many our kind eventually outlawed the creation of new gargoyles," he said.

I straightened and turned to him, taking a deep breath to gather my nerve. If this demigoddess died to lock Phaeron away, then I knew I had no chance when he came to kill me. "Dr. Voidbinder, please. I need to know how to fight back if he returns. With Geo protecting me, you know Morgana's soul expects it."

His plump lips pinched as he considered. "You will still have to attend all your classes."

"Of course," I hurried to say.

"And pass them."

I nodded rapidly.

"I could tutor you in the evenings. But you do not tell anyone what you really saw the other night." He gave me a stern look when I continued nodding in agreement.

"I promise. I'll be the best pupil you've ever had," I said. "Just teach me how to put a silver sword through the bastard's face."

"Heart. They play by vampire rules. Only a strike to the heart is immediately fatal," he corrected.

"The heart, then."

We negotiated the time and place, floor negative two at eight in the evening every weekday. Except today, of course. I still needed to get Roe elected as leader of my coven.

MY COVEN MET in a building Roe had to lead me to, uncreatively called the Witch Clubhouse. I texted directions to Ben, who sent me a couple questions when he got lost too. I felt bad for him, getting roped into extra meetings when he'd just gotten here.

And yes, I was smiling down at my phone like a loon when his name popped up on my screen. We'd exchanged numbers earlier, and I'd already tentatively put a heart next to his name. After spending most of the afternoon chatting with him, it just felt right.

The clubhouse was for coven meetings, I learned, which were apparently expected on a regular basis. It was a four-story building with several small but cozy rooms, and as freshmen, we were assigned a place in the top floor with well-loved couches and scuffed floors, but I took a look around and decided it was comfortable enough. It had a minifridge and microwave, plus a couple desks to work at. I could see myself studying here when I wanted to be social.

Implying I ever wanted to be social.

I arrived to see Wren and Heath had already claimed the couch and Willow had found a comfortable corner to settle, where her presence was hidden by the shadow of the couch. Her hand shot out of nowhere to wave, and Heath nodded before turning his attention back to Wren.

Ben and Grant came in at about the same time. The latter sat alone, as far from the rest of as possible, while Ben turned around a chair and straddled it next to me. "Hey. Miss me?" he asked, flashing a toothy grin.

I rolled my eyes playfully. "Definitely."

"Did you have a good day? For real."

We were mid-chat when Roe came in, announcing herself with a loud, "Hello, friends!"

"Late, as always," Wren answered with a low *tsk*, inspecting her pristinely manicured nails.

"Who's ready to vote for me as our leader?" Roe continued, unperturbed.

"Let's give Yasmin a minute to get here," Heath said with a low chuckle.

I wracked my brain for who Yasmin was. It'd been a long few days, but when the dark-haired upperclassman walked in, I remembered that she was our guide to setting up our coven and making it run smoothly.

"Hello, everyone. How're we doing?" Yasmin asked as she planted herself in the middle of the space like a teacher warming up a class of students.

I certainly felt the mix of interest and disillusionment like we were back in high school. Where Roe vibrated with eagerness, Grant slouched in his seat and stared off into space. Maybe he was high or something.

Instead of paying attention, Ben was looking at me. I ended up being the one to answer the upperclassman's question. "Good. It's been…a good day." I felt my gaze shift to Ben as I said it, a little flutter of butterflies starting in my belly.

He flashed one of his sideways smiles like he knew exactly the kind of effect he had on me. Maybe when a guy had the kind of leonine beauty Ben gave off with ease, drawing a blush and fumble from a gal like me was completely normal.

I didn't have a boyfriend back home, and before I dyed my hair purple and learned I was a supernatural, there was nothing about my bookish and sullen self that had turned heads.

But I was a librarian witch now and destined to slay the beast that'd taken Lanie away, with the help of not one, but three men who had feelings for me. Maybe one of them would be Ben. Perhaps I should embrace the excited but nervous feeling that buzzed in my belly every time our eyes met.

Ben blinked, and I realized Yasmin was talking. "...vote this evening. Now, who's ready?" I'd completely blanked out whatever else she'd just said.

"Must we have speeches?" Ben asked on a sigh as Wren stood.

"It's like you took the words out of my mouth," I murmured.

He checked his phone while Wren spoke, neither of us particularly paying attention. "I have maybe an hour," he said.

"Yeah?"

Some quick expression flickered over his face. "Yeah... just getting settled and all."

I toyed with a lock of my hair. "Well, I'm glad you could come," I said.

For a moment, his expression relaxed. Something sad swirled in the depths of his evergreen eyes. He wetted his lips, glancing away. "Me too," he answered quietly.

A smattering of applause told me Wren was done. Roe replaced her, and I turned my attention toward my friend. Her speech told me I knew very little of what a coven actually did, as she spoke of old rituals and named a few traditional holidays like Mabon and Samhain that she wanted to celebrate.

She promised the kind of things that stirred the aching heart in my chest: friendship and togetherness, forging the kind of bonds that were like a family.

When the time came to vote, Roe won four to three. She shook her fists over her head and whooped like she'd taken home a huge trophy, not a lukewarm vote that I didn't think many of the guys cared about.

"Now we need a name," Roe said, and inwardly I groaned. "Every good coven has a name."

"Give me some time for that one," I suggested. There was hearty agreement at last for something, so we put off the idea of a name and relaxed. Willow discovered sodas and juice in the mini fridge, so we treated it like a little party.

I did what I did best at parties, staying in one place. Ben sipped his soda and didn't move either. He checked his phone every couple of minutes.

"That's my brother," he told me after catching me glancing at his phone with him the fourth time.

It took me a moment to realize he was talking about the picture on his screen. It was a sideways shot of Ben and another guy smiling at the camera. Ben let me get a good look, his gaze on me rather than the device's screen.

"He looks just like you." I laughed. "Twins?"

"Please. He's four years younger than me. Still piles all his hair on his head like that too."

It wasn't a bad look, I thought, but I much preferred how Ben wore his down to his shoulders. After my first glance, I realized his brother had a rounder, softer face, despite sharing the same striking green eyes. He had an almost goofy, carefree air in the photo, and Ben...

Well, he looked happier on that screen than in any of the sideways smiles I'd seen from him today. It was subtle, though. I hadn't realized Ben was carrying an invisible sadness, maybe because I was still dragging my own grief behind me everywhere I went.

"He's, uh, missing," Ben blurted.

"Missing?" I echoed.

He sighed, holding his forehead. "Like, he left our house a couple weeks ago and didn't come back. I'm still looking for him."

"Is that why you transferred here?" I asked.

"Yeah. My, uh, family lives close by. I wanted to get away for, like, college." He took a shaky breath and collected himself. "But Lucas means so much to me. It'd be like ripping my heart out if anything happened to him."

Sorrow gripped me as I nodded along. No wonder he needed to leave so soon. If it were me, I wouldn't have come to this meeting. "I'd feel the same way if it were my sister," I said. "I hope you find him soon. Is there magic you can use to track him?"

He sighed. "If only." With one last check of his phone, he stood and placed his drink aside. "I'd better go."

I followed him out, and he turned to me on the sidewalk outside the busy clubhouse. "Do you want a hug?" I offered, suddenly self-conscious. I'd just met Ben; maybe he didn't want me following him like this.

I felt like I understood the weight of his uncertainty, though. In a world still bright and merry, it'd felt like everyone moved on from Lanie like her murder was a bad dream. But I still felt her loss, and it was obvious Ben was worried about the unresolved situation with his brother.

He didn't hesitate or overthink like I was doing. Within a couple steps, he swept me into his arms and rested his chin atop my head. For a few moments, my mind eased its constant stream of thought and I drifted, safe in his hold.

"I'll see you later, all right?" he murmured.

"Yeah. Good luck. I know you'll find him," I said quietly.

He released me, but not before placing a swift kiss to my cheek. "Stay safe," he said before disappearing into the night.

I watched him go, releasing a breathy laugh as I touched my fingertips to my face.

13

BEN

I'd broken more than one of Master Garroway's core rules within the last twelve hours.

The first, never get to know your victims. Now when I thought of Cress, I didn't see my brother's latest mark, but a person with an unhappy smile and half-formed dreams of a future as a fashion designer for supernaturals. Someone who often looked over her shoulder in a crowded room. A woman with wide brown eyes that held an ocean of unspoken thoughts.

She was no longer "the Darkmore girl" to me. I'd opened myself up to the kind of pain unique to a witch trapped in my profession. Because if my brother lived, he would kill her, and all I'd have afterward would be the haunting strain of her shy laughter in my ears.

Shit, I was a mess. I paused somewhere in between pocket dimensions, holding my head in the darkness between streetlamps.

This isn't what's going to get you killed tonight, I told myself. *Cress is probably fine right now. She has a bodyguard and everything.*

I had no such benefit going back into the spider's parlor. Garroway strictly prohibited his blood witches from heading out without permission. Some of my fellows, like Bianca and Seth, lived for the freedom of missions. They charged out of the manor like rabid dogs let off the chain.

As I looked for Lucas, it'd occurred to me that it was possible he was out enjoying one of his first tastes of the outside world. If so, why wasn't he answering my calls and texts?

The only answer I came home with was that Cress, my only lead, had no idea who Lucas was. No matter how I'd phrased the questions and framed the conversation, she had no information of note about him. And after three days of independent searching and scouting, I had found nothing at all.

I was a failure of a brother. Unless Bianca succeeded in her promise to distract our vampire master, I would also have my head smashed into a wall for my defiance of a core rule.

I slumped my way home until my fingers were millimeters from activating the trigger to allow me to enter the manor's pocket dimension. *Better go into this with some pride.* I squared my sagging shoulders and straightened my spine, fixing a serious expression on my face to mask the nerves making my palms sweat.

Slipping into the stretch of space hiding in plain sight, I crossed the immaculate lawn and tried the back door. It was unlocked. I breathed a thanks to Bianca before soundlessly gliding it open and creeping beyond the threshold. Closing the door after me, I cast my gaze around and took the first steps that would take me to a relieved face-plant on my bed.

"Benjamin."

I froze mid-stride, my head whipping to the left. The breakfast nook was concealed in shadow with the curtains drawn over the bay windows, and hidden within the darkness was my vampire master. Now that I knew he was there, I could spot his blood-red eyes peering back at me.

"Where were you, boy?" He didn't sound angry, but that could change in moments. I'd walked straight into his trap, after all, ensnared by a simple question.

"I…" had no cover story. I hadn't bought anything to bring home with me, and he'd caught me in the middle of trying to sneak in anyway.

If I mentioned Cress and her coven, he'd know I was trying to interfere with Lucas's mission.

If I talked about Lucas directly, I'd confirm what he already knew. Not knowing if my brother was okay was torture. And I had no doubt he was already aware of it.

Over the years, I'd convinced myself that Master Garroway got his sustenance through feeding on the pain of others. He made a show out of holding glasses of blood often enough, but I'd never seen him take a drink. Even now, he had to be sucking in the despair that wafted from me at being caught with no prepared excuse.

I decided not to draw this out when he looked at me like I was a full-course buffet. "I was looking for Lucas, Master," I answered.

"Ah, little Lucas comes up again." Garroway tapped his palms together, turning on several lights. I winced, not prepared for the sudden glare coming off the polished marble table that separated us. Or for the sight of the pitch-black knife resting in front of the vampire.

Two inches long at most, the blade was darker than the deepest night and inspired a shock of fear more potent than if the lights turned on to reveal Garroway pointing a loaded gun in my direction.

I swallowed audibly. "Master, I can explain—"

He closed his hand around the hilt of the tiny weapon, giving the aged leather a squeeze. He activated its magic with a murmured word, something like "*duratus*," though once the blood rune on my chest activated, all I really heard was the hiss of air as my skin sizzled.

The magic forced me to take a ready stance, my arms pointed downward to form a capital A, my legs locked and back rigid. Crimson light leaked from under my shirt in the circular shape of the rune burning against the skin over my right ribcage like a fresh brand.

Garroway stood leisurely and circled my frozen form with a soft noise of contempt. "I told you not to interfere with little Lucas's first mission," he said. The slow, precise way he spoke was extra torture as the activated blood rune seemed to burrow deeper into my flesh with each throb of my heart.

"But you've never been good at taking directions. An unfortunate trait your brother learned from you." We stood nose to nose, and even in my frozen state, I saw the pleasure creasing his mouth and eyes. My hopes for mercy blew away on a red-stained wind.

"Never forget, Benjamin. I *own* you. I bought you from your sniveling excuse of a mother, raised you by hand into the elite ranks of my witches."

I swallowed again, the only reaction I could form. He'd carved the blood rune into me by hand, too, and shared that he'd paid the incredible sum of five million to my parents for no discernable purpose. I could only assume they wanted the chance to *not* have to raise Lucas and me. I'd been four, and my little brother, a newborn.

"Now you think you can sneak away?" Garroway wagged a finger. "There's no escape for you out there, little Benjamin. Nor for you brother. He will return eventually, even if he fails his mission."

I blinked slowly. Could it be possible...?

"That's right. I didn't give Lucas a deadline."

Damn. I was a fool. Without a deadline, Lucas probably turned off his phone and slummed it far from here. It was what I would've done on my first mission, had I not had a little brother back here to protect. None of us knew if the blood rune had a maximum distance. If Lucas got far enough away, maybe he could resist the call of the magic carved in his chest.

He could never return, his old phone disposed of, his life ripe to be lived without the restrictions of Master Garroway. But...he'd left without *me*. He'd cut and run without a backward glance.

As it sank in, the vampire's grin widened. "Imagine. Years from now, I will bring him clawing and begging back here. What do you think I should do to him if he runs for that long?"

With a gesture, he unlocked my jaw. "You'd put a deadline on the original mission," I suggested, hesitant. I knew this game too well. If I offered an over-the-top, bloodthirsty punishment, sometimes I'd override whatever he was actually planning. That was how I'd gotten Bianca lashed with a whip until she passed out from blood loss once. I don't think she's ever fully forgiven me for it.

"That's hardly a punishment," he purred. "Maybe I should sever his fingers and toes, one for every month he tried to hide from my service. Do you think that would fit his crime?"

"Y-yes, Master." If I didn't agree, he'd suggest something worse.

That must've been too easy for him, though. He ran a hand down his jawline, humming. "Or perhaps you should take his punishments for him. That is your preference, isn't it?" His tone took a mocking edge. "The noble big brother, shielding his innocent kid sibling from the big, bad vampire. Let's see how much you love him after this."

I kept my mouth closed as he waited for a reaction, for begging. It wouldn't do any good. If he wanted to punish me, he would, and if he wanted to bring Lucas back to discipline him, he could at any time. I wouldn't let him taint the last bit of family I had.

Garroway's face slanted, boredom etched in each ancient line of his face. My heart stuttered to a near-stop as I recognized that look. I was no longer an interesting plaything to help him chase off the ennui of his existence. "You will stay in the manor for the next two weeks. Your toes will not even graze a blade of grass on the lawn," he instructed, holding up the black knife to weave his will into the blood rune.

My heart sank. Two weeks was an eternity, especially when it was only a matter of time before my deception at NSU was discovered when I didn't hit its official database as a student.

"After that time, perhaps I will consider you to be the errand boy for the manor. You will not go on missions until further notice, however. And now for your punishment."

He considered me for a few moments before weaving a rune midair with the point of the knife. I watched him trace the witch rune for agony and braced myself as the crimson magic of the blood rune ran through my veins, lighting me up from the inside-out with magical fire.

My body lit with pain from crown to toes, burning brighter and deeper as the magic rooted into muscle and bone. Seconds dragged into eternity as I started screaming. If he held this spell for too long, it'd turn into his favorite form of execution, a boiling of my blood and innards.

I swear I burnt to a cinder as my vision hazed with crimson light, tears and blood mingling to trace a river of pain down my face. Through it all, I sensed the master's presence, a too-close shadow drinking in every moment of my suffering.

He did release me eventually but didn't catch my limp body as it crashed to the ground in a boneless tumble. My crisped innards gave one last spasm, one that dragged me into black unconsciousness.

A FEATHERLIGHT FINGERTIP drew marks along the skin on my face. A moan stuck in my dry throat, and my eyelids were too swollen to open. On and on someone painted the same three-lined mark on my cheeks, upper and lower lip, nose, and forehead. Tiny runes of healing.

Relief radiated slowly from each rune as my blood witchery went to work repairing the damaged veins and charred muscles left behind from Garroway's agony spell.

A firm hand closed around my shoulder, drawing a hoarse shout from me as pain spiked deep under my skin. "Hold still," Seth said gruffly.

I relaxed as best as I could, giving silent thanks that it was the experienced male witch tending to me, not Bianca. Cool wind chafed over my skin. I was probably stripped to my boxers, with huge healing runes over my chest, arms, and thighs, while Seth worked on the smaller and more delicate sections of my body with care.

"Surprised you're still breathing." Straight to the point, as always. It was more of a shock that *Seth* of all the blood witches in Garroway's coven was tending to me now. He didn't need bedside manners when he was the prized assassin and the longest surviving of all of us.

"That bad?" I croaked.

A cool lip of plastic pressed to my lips. I swallowed some of the watery energy drink, knowing it had to be terrible if Seth was giving me electrolytes directly upon waking.

"The master wouldn't let anyone approach you for three days."

I almost spluttered a whole mouthful of liquid over him. Swallowing wrong and immediately choking, I tried to sit up. He forced me back down onto the bed I rested on, maintaining that hold as I struggled to breathe amidst the deep throb of pain in my chest. "Is...Lucas?" I asked between coughs.

"Still missing," he said curtly.

I nodded, letting him go back to painting runes on me. I cracked open my eyes, letting the world come slowly into focus as my damaged eyes healed themselves. Blood witchery made us nearly invincible, but this wasn't the first time I'd woken near death in the infirmary with someone else painting runes on me with my own blood.

My blood affinity meant Garroway had more of my delicious despair to feed on, too. It sank in as I lay there, healing. I couldn't leave to search for Lucas for two weeks, enough time for him to truly disappear off the face of the earth.

The only plus was that Garroway had tipped his hand

about why Cress was unscathed. If I could convince her to skip town, maybe she would escape the plotting of Garroway and Starsurge after all, free to live her life without someone waiting in the shadows to end her life.

Deadlines were carved into our flesh just like the blood runes. If I had the strength to sit up, I would see the perfect circle of the rune on my right ribcage, plus a few black lines rising from it, pointed straight at my heart. Garroway made it a rite of passage to inflict new blood witches with a week-long deadline so we'd know what it felt like.

That line stopped just millimeters from my heart, a stark reminder against my skin every time I took my shirt off. Deadlines were slow agony spells, and to have one so close to my heart had felt a lot like the white-hot pain of the spell that'd dropped me unconscious for several days. If we failed at a mission or didn't complete it in time, we'd die, simple as that.

The only other way to survive a missed deadline was Master Garroway's mercy. And he had little of it.

"Seth," I rasped. I rolled my head to look at him. His salt-and-pepper hair was still fuzzy around the edges to my damaged sight, and the serious lines of his face seemed taut with fury as he took care of me.

He asked quietly, "Yes?"

I noted the sunlight streaming into the room. Only with Garroway resting would I dare to mention this subject. "You were the one sent on the Darkmore job, right?"

"Yeah."

"Is she...Cress...could she really be...?"

Seth sighed deeply. "The master ordered me to take care of the Darkmore family. That was the wording. So, I did."

A meaningful pause passed between us. Seth had been the one to teach me what being a blood witch really meant and how to interpret orders such as this. "Taking care of" something had several meanings.

"I killed the adults. I did my job," he said, a small catch to his usual baritone. "But the baby...she was so tiny and innocent."

I was still as he finished painting healing runes on my feet. He stood abruptly and went to the sink to wash his hands, putting his back between us like a barrier.

Well, shit. Cress may seriously be who Blaize Starsurge thought she was. If she lived long enough to access the well of hereditary magic every established witch family curated, there was a chance she could tap her deceased parents' memories. It wasn't just paranoia encouraging him to have her killed. If she knew what to do with the information, she could ruin his political career with a long overdue murder trial.

And I couldn't tell her a thing, because the blood rune on my chest would kill me painfully for sharing one of Garroway's secrets. *Fuck.*

"What did you do with her instead?" I murmured.

"I surrendered her to a local hospital." One of his shoulders lifted, but he didn't turn back to face me. "That's all I know. I never expected her to come back up or for Starsurge to identify her if she did."

"Of course."

Finally, he came back to my bedside. I tried not to stare at the broken expression on his face. This wasn't the solid assassin that Garroway sent without hesitation on the nastiest and most dangerous missions. "There are some things you don't do," he said. "And I draw the line at killing children."

"Principles. I remember."

In place of a father talking about the birds and the bees,

I'd had Seth to take me aside and talk about principles. The lines we didn't cross unless we had to, as the puppets to a vampire master who delighted in our pain. I had no doubt that saving Cress was a glimpse of salvation for my mentor.

"I wanted a moment with you for a different reason," he said, regaining the stony expression he always wore like armor. "I suspect Lucas is in a different sort of trouble than you expect."

"Do you have a lead?" I asked. My heart immediately went into a hopeful double-time.

He gave a stiff nod. "I believe I saw him a few days ago—"

"Where?" I burst out, then regretted it as pain stirred deep in my chest.

Seth's frown deepened. "In New Salem. I only caught a glimpse of him, but he ran when I called his name. I followed and lost him around a corner. But I wanted to let you know, since the master is sure Lucas ran away."

I shook my head slowly. "Why would he run from you?" I asked. Seth was practically my brother's idol, on the surface everything a dutiful blood witch assassin should be. If he was having trouble with his mark, he should've been falling over himself to ask Seth for advice.

"I've seen something like it before," he said slowly. "One of our brothers was caught right after completing a mission. His blood rune was altered with a second knife like the master's. He completed several high-profile assassinations before being captured and put on trial for his crimes. I remember him running from me, just like Lucas did. His rune compelled him to avoid everything from his life here, so he could not return to the master."

I turned over his words silently. I hadn't known that it was possible for someone else to change our blood runes and thus our allegiance. Garroway, at least, valued us when we were a resource to keep him rich and influential. "His life was thrown away," I said thoughtfully.

"It happens." He sighed, patting my shoulder gently. "I'm sorry, Ben. We won't know if it happened for sure unless he's compelled to kill someone else. If it's the Darkmore girl, we can be assured Lucas will return to us. But if it's anyone else, especially someone of political importance..."

I shut my eyes tightly, imagining what would happen if Lucas committed even one more sloppy kill. The SPDI would have him in the electric chair before I had permission to leave this manor again.

Something cold nudged my fingers. "This has been vibrating constantly. Any messages from Lucas?" Seth asked.

I took my phone from him, unlocking it with a glance and scanning the list of missed calls and messages. Most of them were from an unfamiliar number, and after listening to one message, I learned the unknown caller was Roe checking on me out of obligation as a concerned coven leader.

The rest of the notifications were from Cress. I shook my head up at Seth, who left me to heal and mull over my brother's uncertain fate. What could I do to save him from here?

I scrolled Cress's messages first, going back three days. She hadn't gotten angry or passive-aggressive with my long silence, only expressing concern for me and my brother in her last message...dated yesterday, the Friday we were supposed to have another class together.

I smiled to myself, feeling a little less alone in that moment. Which was stupid, really, for a list of reasons too long to count. I was the last person she should be sending sweet messages to, and I had a responsibility to somehow tell her to watch her back without getting myself killed by my blood rune.

However, she'd think I was crazy if I came out of nowhere saying, "Hi, change your name and leave Salem. Never come back." We'd work up to that.

So instead, I texted her a simple hey and rested my eyes.

My phone buzzed immediately. "Hi. You're back!" she'd texted.

My lips tugged. For better or worse, I was indeed back.

14

GEO

Time passed, and I did my duty. Cress was safe with me as we went class to class, day by day. She grew stronger in the evenings, her aura bolstered with librarian witch power after every private training session with Callum Voidbinder.

The library was the only place I was welcome to tromp into, so I watched Cress practice and practice and practice. She was given a wooden sword to use for now, much to her chagrin, until she was proficient with the basics of how to swing and block with it. I tended to let my mind turn off during these trainings, becoming a statue again in the place I felt most welcome.

There was no sign of the boy with the chameleon aura, though I suspected he was still talking to her via the little glowing box she liked to smile into. Her "cell phone," which she used to introduce me to the confusing pocket dimension called the Internet with all its jokes. Apparently, it could be used to talk to anyone, anywhere.

No matter. If he wasn't physically here, he was no danger to her.

My rock was patient. Undoubtedly, danger brewed, looming unseen. I was at my most alert at night, standing guard in the shadows of the garden outside the building where she slept.

In those moments of quiet, I asked myself whether I should let her rest and go off to find the creature she wished to slay. Was it my duty to simply watch her, or to fulfill her goal for her? The puzzle of that simple question lingered night after night, yet I didn't move to leave her.

Some part of me knew her monster would find me. And he did.

There was no warning. Just a voice echoing from the darkness. "Morgana?"

My neck ground to the left, where the voice originated. There was nothing there, just a stretch of wilting flowers wavering in a soft wind. "Identify yourself," I commanded.

"Of course you're not her." He was close, standing in the blind spot right over my shoulder. "I need to speak to my former mate, gargoyle."

I felt some foreboding from those words. "This unit may be powered by her soul, but she is not available for a discussion," I stated, trying to get him in my line of sight.

"A pity." Now he was on my other side, moving with silent speed.

I flexed my hand, manipulating the spines of pure quartz on my back. One traveled the length of my arm, its sharpened point sticking out a couple inches from my palm as I turned again, unsurprised to see that the bearer of the chilly, demanding voice was again gone. I let my opponents think I was slow and stupid purposefully, when it only took a split second to send a quartz spike through their fleshy forms.

"I will take the soul from you by force if I have to." This

time, he was behind me. Claws scraped over my wing, and I held it out like a solid screen as I whirled around, spotting a crouching dimensional.

Dark hair, gray skin, curled horns, yes. The only thing about him that didn't match Cress's description were his eyes, twin pools of eerie white fire. A rumbling growl escaped his fanged maw.

"Phaeron Sudair. You are a wanted fugitive of Moongrove Library," I intoned. "I am authorized to use lethal force if you do not surrender immediately."

"Give me her soul, you misbegotten construct," he snapped. Shadows rose from his form, overlaying his arms and shaping themselves into massive, pointed talons. He leapt, crossing the space between us in a blink to impale them straight through my stone shoulder. An unfamiliar feeling echoed dully from the impossible wounds. Pain.

Were I a being of flesh and bone, the damage would be debilitating. Instead, I cocked back my arm and fired my primed quartz spike. It grazed his neck, showering me with a spray of fuchsia blood.

He put a hand over the wound, and fury twisted his face into an animal's snarl. The shadows lining his arms became denser as I called on the five quartz spikes I had left, absorbing them back into my body.

As the magic in my body changed the extra quartz into the shape of a club, my preferred weapon, the dimensional's shadows crept up his shoulders and engulfed his head, becoming a formless knob except for a jagged maw of black teeth. The handle of my club emerged from my palm as he clamped down over my head and arm, creating dozens of pain-points where the shadows parted my craggy skin like cutting butter.

I swung at him as he tried to savage my body like a dog.

Bones crunched as he endured one, two, three slams over his right side. His tail caught my wrist before I could hit him a fourth time, squeezing hard like he could make me drop the club.

He released his bite, shadows dissipating fully. One arm hung limply as he sprang off my chest with clawed feet, landing a few yards away. Gasping in pain, a rivulet of his blood stained his clothing from the neck down, darkening the bright white NSU standing out on his chest in the darkness.

"Do you surrender?" I asked. I saw the hesitation. We'd savaged each other in less than a minute, and even now, I could feel magic leaking from the wounds peppering my shoulder and chest. It looked like quicksilver, the oily magic that kept my stone animated. A dimensional of his caliber would know I grew stiffer with every moment that passed.

He held his head, shaking it rapidly, and wavered on his feet, looking moments from passing out. I waited patiently for him to drop from his injuries, but instead, he lifted his gaze and regarded me with eyes of bright yellow. His gaze flashed to the dorm behind me and then down at himself.

"Noble gargoyle," he said, dipping his chin in a bow with a clear wince. "I have never quarreled with the human practice of making your kind until today. This isn't over. Morgana betrayed me long ago by sealing me in Moongrove Library. I see her within you now. She *will* answer for what she did to me, even if I must dismantle you to get my answers."

With that, he vanished into the darkness. Defeated. I waited several long minutes before absorbing my club back into my body, letting it become the quartz spines that line my back. As I bent to retrieve the spike still coated in his unusually hued blood, a twinge of deeper pain struck my lower chest. I looked down at myself in surprise.

I must've missed him scraping his claws over my belly. The fight had begun and ended so quickly, after all. Quicksilver magic poured from the equivalent of a gut wound, and I realized the slowing in my joints was reaching a critical point. I would soon be immobilized, easy prey for the dimensional by dawn.

I absorbed my last quartz spike and lifted a few extra pebbles from the ground, turning to view the bank of windows facing the garden. There was only one person I trusted to tend to me in my weakened state. I had Cress's window memorized, but getting her attention without committing vandalism would be difficult.

With a single pebble resting in my palm, I aimed and fired it with a burst of compressed air. I was created with state-of-the-art weapons in my time, including the twin cannons in my hollow arms. They were designed to injure and maim, not toss a pebble at a woman's window. But it plinked off the glass with a sharp sound. Only a small crack resulted.

Moments later, the bottom pane lifted, and Cress stuck a disheveled head of purple hair outside, looking left to right in a daze. I waved a stiff arm up at her, fearing the shoulder joint would stick like that.

She spotted me and yelped, her head withdrawing and the window slamming after her. The minutes ticked by, and I struggled to lower my arm in the meantime.

I lumbered toward the door she always exited from, not bending my knee joints to preserve mobility. She nearly ran headlong into me. "Geo, what's wrong?" She backed away, surveying the bright silver staining my obsidian form with wide eyes.

"Assist me inside. I must take my flesh form."

She held the door for me, staring all the while. "What happened? You look really hurt."

She peppered me with questions as I bowed my head, calling on the human soul within me to facilitate the shift from rock to flesh. I'd done this so infrequently that my wings rustled and shivered with obvious discomfort before being sucked into my back, alongside the quartz spikes I'd used against Phaeron.

I staggered sideways into the stairwell's railing, hunching over as my height slimmed down and skin thinned. My hollow arms became human and solid, the trickiest part of the shift, before my stone heart started beating in earnest. It absorbed the quicksilver magic in my veins rather than dispersing it, leaving me paralyzed during this part of the transformation.

Only when I was completely a being of flesh and blood did the magic circulate again, avoiding the scrapes and punctures where I was injured. I lifted my head, trying not to flinch when soft feathers of white dreadlocks slipped down my cheeks.

Cress paused in the midst of the panic attack that'd stricken her sometime when I started shifting. Her jaw dropped. "Uh...Geo?"

"I apologize for the distress." It was easier to speak, and my voice was no longer two guttural stones clashing. "Do you have an infirmary where I may rest off my injuries?"

"I have an extra bed," she said. "That's about it."

"It will suffice."

She started scaling the stairs, going slowly as I struggled behind her. My wounds echoed pain in full definition, nearly debilitating with each step.

"What happened?" she asked more calmly, fitting herself under my armpit to help heft my weight.

Air scraped my lungs, unpleasantly wet compared to the dry breeze from my stone throat. "I shall explain," I said with effort. "Soon."

I don't know why my fellow gargoyles abandoned their duties to...this misery. It took us ten minutes to climb up to her dorm room. My mouth tasted of copper. The first actual blood my construct body produced, and I was so damaged it attempted to leak from my lips.

Furry shapes scattered when she opened her dorm room and helped me inside. She spread out a few towels for me to lie on over an otherwise bare mattress. I sat on its edge, and she helped me lie down, tucking my long legs before they could dangle over the end.

"Do not be alarmed if I leak," I told her. Her face creased, and she snorted.

"You mean bleed? Of course you're going to bleed."

"There should be very little blood," I corrected. Already, a swirl of unfamiliar feeling rose to the surface of my awareness as I lay still. I didn't like that she'd laughed. It felt mocking. In my stone form, I wouldn't care in any way. "I heal most rapidly in my flesh form. Stone does not repair like flesh, even when enchanted."

Her brow knitted. "Yeah, okay. That makes sense."

My eyelids felt like they were still solid rock, slipping down without my permission. "As you humans say." I drew in a deep breath. "You should see the other guy." Her eyes widened in surprise as I repeated the line I'd learned from one of her favorite Internet videos. I slipped into the abyss of unconsciousness on a soft sigh, knowing I was safe with her.

15
CRESS

"Girl, I don't know," Roe said from my cell as I stood over Geo's unconscious form the next morning. She was the first person I called when it was a reasonable hour. I figured if anyone knew how to tend to a gargoyle, it'd be a guardian witch.

"He's, like, alive?" she asked.

"He's breathing," I reported.

That wasn't the part that concerned me. He had several gashes over his bare chest, and each sparkled with a coating of silver liquid. It was pretty but eerie, like nothing a normal guy would have. At least he wasn't a bloody mess. Other than the pink spittle I'd cleaned from the corner of his mouth, there was no blood at all unless that's what the silver stuff was.

"Do you have any idea how I could help him?" I asked with an edge of desperation. I didn't want my gargoyle guardian to die, especially not while he lay out on Lanie's old bed.

There was a pause on her end. "I could ask one of my professors. If you wanted."

"Uh, n-no. That won't be necessary." I didn't want any authority figures at the school poking around and asking questions. Though Geo hadn't said who he'd fought, I didn't know anything capable of gouging furrows in solid rock other than my boogeyman, Phaeron. He'd had claws.

They weren't as wide as the furrows in Geo right now, but he'd still had claws.

Roe wished me good luck, and I ended the call by telling her I wouldn't be in class. Over the last two weeks, I'd worked extra hard to catch up, so it was with a bit of reluctance that I decided to stay here and make sure I was on hand to help Geo when he woke.

Still, it gave me an excuse to lie back down and rest my aching muscles. Dr. Voidbinder had me doing basic drills with a wooden version of a librarian sword Monday through Friday, saying I couldn't learn any more serious skills until I knew my weapon like it was an extension of my hand. It was clear I was out of shape, too, so I'd started going to the gym more with Roe.

I was making "great strides," though. Soon Dr. Voidbinder was going to teach me how to conduct magic down a real sword and trace witch runes with the tip. The moment I learned how to do that, I'd be officially two years ahead, with the shakiest foundational knowledge a gal could have. We hadn't even gotten to the most basic runes yet in Introduction to Witchcraft.

Ben hadn't returned to class in all this time and was likely to fail his classes soon for poor attendance. He still texted, though. I'd burned down the battery on my phone late into the night rereading his messages and reliving how they made me feel until I went to sleep with my cheeks hurting from smiling so much. I yearned to see him more and more with each day that passed.

I got by in the meantime with the support of the solid women in my life. Roe, Willow, and Áine were always around to hang out, and Mom and Carly were a phone call away. I still carried my guilt silently, unable to confide in any of them about Phaeron.

Oddly enough, the only people who knew about him were Geo, who didn't care for the details, and Dr. Void-binder, who knew too much and could guess at my secret guilt over freeing Phaeron with one misplaced comment.

The last thing that troubled me stared at me from under Lanie's old bed. Jin's yellow eyes were accusing. I'd laid Geo down on her favorite sleeping spot, though under the bed seemed to be just fine for her too. That's where she usually retreated when I tried to go over and pet her.

She didn't want my assurances, and she *definitely* didn't want to be my familiar. I was starting to regret having her stay here when she could be free to do as she pleased with the rest of the Graygazer family.

"Let's go get some breakfast," I suggested to Milo and Bella. The boy cat was in the process of curling up next to me, while Bella watched me from the shadows under my desk, leery of the unfamiliar man in our space.

I cast one last glance over at Geo, making sure he was still breathing. He'd taken my breath away with his near angelic good looks as a human, but I couldn't find anything sexy about his injured form right now. While he was unconscious, he was off limits, so I left to go to the ground floor of my dorm and bring a big to-go box of food back up to him.

The cafeteria manager lit up when she saw my cats trailing me. I'd learned they got fed better than I did if they sought her out for some attention, so I loaded up on waffles and fruit while they became the bright spot of her day.

What did gargoyles even eat? I balanced a couple styrofoam cups of coffee and orange juice atop my box as I pondered that question. Geo hadn't eaten anything in the time he'd guarded me, but that was before he shifted into human form.

We'd find out soon, because he was awake when I got back to my dorm, his quicksilver eyes following my progression to his bedside. "Good morning. Want something to eat?" I lifted a strawberry out of the to-go box by its stem.

A little rumble rose from his belly. He blinked a few times. "It appears this form requires sustenance," he said.

I drew a chair to sit beside him since he made no move to sit up and jostle his chest wounds. I offered the berry, and he ate it without complaint. "Shouldn't you be in class?" he asked after swallowing and coughing a few times. He held his gut wound as his chest spasmed.

"I took the day off," I answered, loading up a fork with a piece of waffle freshly dipped in syrup. My gaze flicked to his fingers, which didn't come away with any silvery blood. It was like the damage was sealed with the liquid.

"That isn't a good idea," he said.

"Well, you need me more."

For a moment, he smiled. *Angelic indeed.* The features I'd admired so much in his stone form were preserved while he was human, but softened. No longer chiseled to perfection, but shaped by a loving hand. And when he smiled...his silver eyes and perfect white teeth twinkled in the morning light. Sunshine gilded the curve of his cheek, bringing out the warm highlights under his rich skin that was a shade of darkest bronze.

He hid that beautiful glimpse of himself under his usual

serious expression. "I shall be fine tomorrow. We will return to your regular schedule then."

I hesitated. He'd taken wounds to the shoulder, chest, and gut that would probably kill a normal person. That wasn't something that should heal within a day. "Want to tell me what happened now?" I suggested before feeding him that bite of waffle.

I felt the blood rush from my face as he recounted his brief but awful fight with Phaeron. He described the dimensional as a creature of fangs, shadows, and claws.

But one part snagged my attention. "Mate?" I echoed. "But Morgana was the one to seal him in the library in the first place."

"I care not for the ramblings of a creature such as him," he muttered. "Next time, I will kill him for coming so close to the place where you rest."

I caught the trace of anger in his deep voice. *Emotion. Real, human emotion.* I was liking this version of him more and more.

"Let me help next time," I suggested.

His eyes flashed. "Absolutely not. I am your protector and champion. When he shows his face again, I will take care of him alone."

A thrill settled in my belly at the vehemence in his voice. Maybe if I'd trained for a while longer and had the experience of fighting lesser dimensional creatures, I would be offended by this newfound macho man streak. Instead, I acquiesced with a nod and fed him several forkfuls of waffle before he had his fill of breakfast. I ate the rest and snuck a dollop of whipped cream to Milo while Bella was having her daily stare-off with Jin.

Milo jumped onto Geo's bed with a curious chirp, sniffing the gargoyle thoroughly with his jaw propped open. "He smells like the outside," he reported. My brows rose when my familiar curled up against his uninjured side and purred quietly when Geo rubbed his flank.

"Aww, you got a little nurse." I smiled and settled my laptop at the desk closer to Geo's bedside before plopping *The Librarian Witch's Handbook* atop it.

Cracking my knuckles, I put on a confident face and opened the book's front cover. For what was supposed to be a repository of knowledge, it had stubbornly refused to share a single helpful fact with me.

It had a message already printed on its first page today: *You know, it's not too late to get your $19.99 back.*

"I don't want to return you, but I do need your help."

Moi?

"What do you know about gargoyles?"

Geo stirred, rolling his head to look at me. "Are you conversing with that book?" he asked.

Quite a bit compared to you, the book wrote.

"Kind of," I told Geo before realizing I probably didn't need him to know I was fishing for answers about the mystery that he was. I told him I'd be right back and took the book out into the hall, sitting in the stairwell with it in my lap.

I'm feeling helpful today, it'd written on a new page, above a several-page description of gargoyles. The kind of thing I'd already read in a textbook, describing them as stone constructs created from the willing soul of a deceased witch.

"But book, they're described as impervious to almost all magic. Geo got cut to bits by a dimensional last night." I worried my bottom lip between my teeth as the page flipped again.

Oh, I'm just "book" to you now?

"Sorry, *The Librarian Witch's Handbook*," I recited dutifully.

That's better. What's the dimensional's name?

"Phaeron."

The next page was blank for a long minute. Then: *Oh shit. Holy shiiii—take mushrooms. Sugar honey iced tea.*

I stifled a nervous giggle as it filled the page with every euphemism for "shit" I knew and then some. "Yeah?"

You're not panicking right now? Gods above. You really are new, huh?

I frowned down on it. From how it mocked my lack of accomplishments as a librarian witch, I figured it already knew that. "I mean, yeah?"

Why do I always get the new ones? Fuck!

It flicked to a new page before I could get too offended. *Listen, toots. We're in this together. I'm not going to let you die like my last five owners.*

Nervous sweat slicked my palms. "What happened to them?"

Well, there was Chris, and he was just stupid. Got screamed to death day one in Aventuri Library by a loose screamer. Man didn't know how to read. I told him to wear earplugs.

Then there was Tammy, who just had to touch a nightmare lily. She's probably still asleep somewhere.

Eric got tricked down an elevator shaft by an illusion imp. Sad. I liked him.

And Wendy died defending Moongrove Library from a level-five containment breach like a true badass.

Sheldon was...well, Sheldon. Nuff said.

Now I belong to you.

I blinked owlishly down at the book as it recited these things rapidly and flipped the pages before I could ask what a screamer was or what a nightmare lily looked like so I never touched one.

I wanted to ask it why the change of heart, but it was still writing, going into information I didn't know. *Read this,* it instructed, writing up a page of information on power levels. I recognized its voice throughout, like it was telling this to me as part of a casual conversation.

Every supernatural has a power level, which dictates the potential they have in their respective magics. This is a measure of offensive capability, resistance to others' magic, and how much magic they can channel through their body and/or hold on to at one time. Noobs like you don't get told all this because you'll be curious what your number is and go out and try to test it and get hurt.

"I mean, I guess," I murmured. "What does this have to do with Phaeron and Geo?"

Getting there. A construct like your gargoyle friend was created with defense in mind. They have very high power levels, but only because their defense and resistance to magic is high. The average gargoyle is created to be PL5, for reference. Your friend might have a higher one since I think he's one of those fancy ones animated by a demigoddess.

Power levels are exponential. Someone at PL2 is double the strength of someone at PL1. But someone at PL3 is four times as powerful because they're the equivalent of two people at PL2, etc. etc.

You following this, toots? Your gargoyle has incredible defensive capabilities.

"Yeah, this all makes sense," I said, though I thought it was totally correct. I wanted to know what my power level was now.

Spells, too, have power levels, but that relates to ease of access. There are runes you might never be able to cast because you don't have the capability of holding enough magic to fuel them.

Now, take this matchup: a PL5 gargoyle comes up against a shadow dimensional.

It made two ink drawings of a winged gargoyle facing a shadowy creature. I saw Phaeron's true form for the first time as a wolf with lush locks of shadowy fur and a curling pair of ram horns protecting his skull. His tail was a spike strip of sharp spines.

To deal any damage to the gargoyle with magic, the dimensional has to be PL6 or higher.

The dimensional wolf leapt at the gargoyle, extending huge talons and opening its maw to reveal a stretch of jagged teeth. I shuddered, shocked Geo had survived this encounter at all. *That* was what I was hunting. That *thing* was what'd killed Lanie.

So with that out of the way, can we talk about how I keep hearing you whisper that you're going to kill Phaeron Sudair?

"I am. It's my fate," I said firmly.

Okay, toots. Sure.

My gaze narrowed at it. "What else do you know about him?" It'd picked out his last name and likeness in an instant.

Enough that, as your dutiful copy of The Librarian Witch's Handbook, *I must insist you stay away from him at all costs.*

"That's not helpful."

Neither is dying.

I scowled at it. With a slow, reluctant roll of its latest page, it wrote: *Learn how to cast the Lux rune, and I will tell you his last recorded power level.*

"Deal."

Deal. Now, why don't you go enjoy teasing your gargoyle or something? Don't you know that most gargoyles never return to their stone form after discovering human pleasure?

"Really?" I stood with its spine cradled in my palm.

It replied with a page-wide winky face.

16

CRESS

Geo slept most of the day, leaving me at loose ends. I sketched a new outfit for my Drawing for Fashion class, purposefully copying the soft-looking waves of shadowy fur in my book's sketch of Phaeron's true form. Strips of material could mimic the effect, but only a fan could make them wave like they had a mind of their own.

My mind drifted as I beheld my creation. Was it anything like the real thing? Hopefully I'd only know when I was strong enough to put a silver sword through the heart of the murderous dimensional.

My phone pinged, and a text box from Ben appeared on the screen. Even though I hadn't seen him in two weeks, my heart always pattered a little faster when I saw his name. I held the phone to my face so I could preview his text. It was shorthand, like he always seemed to send, asking what I was doing.

I put the phone back down and took a deep breath. It was about the time he and I would be in class together. Had I really missed his return?

"Skipping class. You?" I texted back.

"Wanna hang out?"

I glanced over my shoulder at the resting gargoyle, his quicksilver wounds starting to shimmer as sunlight drifted into the room. There was no way I could leave him here alone. What bad timing!

"I can't leave my dorm right now."

"Fine lol. Works great for me. Myth-Flix?" He sent each sentence as an individual text.

I asked him what Myth-Flix was, and he helped me find a website with a convoluted URL no one would think to type in. There was a spot to click cleverly hidden on the error page the URL sent me to, and up popped a big splash screen for Myth-Flix in gaudy orange, yellow, and white.

Stifling a giggle, I made an account and put in earbuds. Ben found my new account and friended me. Soon we were streaming the same episode of a supernatural sitcom and connected in a voice chat.

"Hey, Cress," he said. I immediately smiled at hearing his light voice again, with the same teasing edge as I remembered. "I told you the shows were the best part of being a supernatural."

"Hi. You did," I said, glancing over my shoulder again. A quiet inside voice didn't seem to bother Geo. "How've you been?"

More like, *where have you been?*

There was a moment of hesitation on the other end. "I've been a little sick. And, you know, my brother." He gusted a sigh. "I've missed you, though. Doing okay?"

I got a fluttery feeling in my belly. If he missed me, I didn't feel so silly about missing him despite our brief acquaintance. "Yeah. Sore from the gym. I've got Roe working me pretty hard."

"Oh, you're sore?" There was a suggestive edge to the question.

I smacked my lips. "Not like that!"

He chuckled at my expense. "Why are you hitting the gym so hard? And don't say to lose weight."

"I have to swing a sword someday," I pointed out.

He hummed. "Sure. But didn't you want to design clothes?" he asked.

"It's smart to keep your options open," I replied. Really, it was amazing how fast my priorities had turned on their head. Rather than pouring my all into my fashion design major, my best grades were now in my witch-related classes.

"Uh huh. You going to the Mabon celebration?"

"Are *you*?" I countered.

Roe had already talked my ear off about Mabon and the gratitude ritual she wanted to do as a coven. She'd fretted we wouldn't be able to do it without our wayward seventh member.

"I'll be there," he confirmed.

The whole university had this coming Friday off for the Mabon feast and the bonfire party afterward. I'd learned it was sort of like supernatural Thanksgiving, a day to give gratitude for the abundance of the earth and feast.

"Thank goodness. Have you told Roe?" I asked, looking forward to the end of the week even more now that I knew I'd get to see him in person.

"I wanted to tell you first," he said. "Though I'm going to text her now, since she's asked me about it a couple times."

"Only a couple?"

He chuckled. "I didn't realize we were electing her mother hen of our group."

That's about right. But other than absent Ben, she'd been most worried about Grant, our verdant witch. I wasn't the only one to notice how out of it and uncaring he always seemed to be. Roe was looking into possible supernatural reasons for this in concern.

"If it were you, you'd appreciate your coven trying to help too," Roe had said.

I echoed that wisdom back to Ben, and we soon fell into a companionable silence. We watched the first episodes of a few of his favorite shows, each with real magic and no post-production effects added. Before I knew it, we were well into the afternoon. I only noticed when Ben drifted off mid-sentence and covered his microphone, talking to someone else.

"Hey, Cress, I gotta go," he sighed. "Let's do this again sometime."

I was halfway through saying goodbye when I realized he'd left the call abruptly. Rude. My lips twisted. I glanced over my shoulder to check on Geo, just to see he'd propped himself up to sit with his back against the wall. His wounds were noticeably smaller, especially the one on his lower belly, which receded to show taut muscle and flawless ochre skin.

He was also making a nearly smiling expression at my cell. Quiet sound drifted from the device, courtesy of a video he was watching. I blinked in surprise, remembering that I'd left it unlocked by his bedside and forgot about it after the conversation with my handbook. I hadn't realized he was growing Internet savvy so quickly.

He caught my gaze and lowered the device. "It sounded like you were having fun."

"You're awake," I said.

"I am."

"Did you sleep well?"

"Yes."

I should've known not to ask him a yes or no question. "You're healing really fast."

"Flesh mends," he replied.

I wished he wouldn't say "flesh" so often. I was stuck between an uncomfortable shuffle of awareness and an "ew" face every time.

"This form pleases you," he added, unbidden.

A touch of heat rushed to my cheeks. "Uh, I mean..."

"Why?" His brow knitted together.

Goddamn. The nearly emotionless gargoyle really wanted me to explain how hot he was. He waited patiently for an answer.

I cleared my throat. "I, uh, guess it's nice to see you react to things more. You're not acting like a robot."

His brow furrowed harder.

"Maybe you could stay like this for a while?" I suggested hopefully.

He lifted his hands, turning them over under his gaze and flexing them. "I will not be able to protect you as effectively in this form," he said. My shoulders began to sag in disappointment. "However, perhaps you will be able to take me into your classes and along for your other activities."

"Yes!" I jumped on the idea so quickly that his brows lifted. Surprise. Another first-time emotion, I noted. "First, you need some clothes."

He glanced down at the pair of cloth shorts that'd transitioned with him out of his stone form. "I suppose these aren't sufficient anymore," he agreed.

THE FIRST TIME I took Geo to the gym with Roe, he lifted an entire weight machine and gave it a curious shake. "This was supposed to be a challenge?" he asked. His brow furrow of confusion was becoming a new normal for him as most of the other gym-goers stared and Roe and I gestured urgently for him to put it down.

He carefully set it in the same place where it'd been resting and wandered off in search of a "challenge." I exchanged a glance with my friend. "There go my hopes of out-benching him," Roe said with a laugh. She set off after him. "Geo! Come spot me!"

Physical activity, it turned out, was totally his element. He was at his most comfortable in the loose shirt and basketball shorts that constituted his workout attire. I'd bought him three sets of clothes for now. One for working out, two for casual wear. If he wanted to stay human for longer, we'd be thrifting, because my bank account held about two pennies and a cobweb at this point.

He didn't sweat much. Apparently sweat and blood are things his construct body didn't make until he'd been in his "flesh form" for quite some time. Gargoyles were weird, man.

By Thursday, I caught a pair of witches glancing at Geo, ever-present at my side, and whispering about my boyfriend. Well...he *was* carrying my backpack and holding my phone all the way to his face as he ventured down whatever Internet rabbit hole he'd found. I accepted the gossip as my due since I couldn't explain my faithful shadow any other way.

I'd taken to picking an emotion of the day for him, and

as we sat at the back of the class for another session of Introduction to Supernatural Society, I turned to him. He caught my eye and smiled automatically. I wanted to tell him he didn't have to smile every time I looked at him, but ever since I'd told him he had a nice smile, I saw it so much more. He *was* learning.

"How are you feeling right now?" I asked.

"Hmm. Content."

That was today's emotion of the day. After starting this experiment with "happy" and "sad" as the last two days, I'd printed out a chart of emotions and gave him a word to describe the patient blankness that he often displayed, even in human form.

"How about you?" he asked.

I had a much harder time answering this question, but I unpacked it for him. Eagerness to learn more about supernaturals other than witches in this class, tired from nearly a full week of classes, excited for Mabon tomorrow, and also nervous too.

A little line appeared between his brows. "You are nervous to see Ben again."

I felt myself blush. "Yeah." I hadn't talked to him much since the beginning of the week. It was a little crazy a guy I barely knew had this much of my headspace.

Geo frowned. "I do not find this pleasing."

"Yeah, I know. You don't really like him," I sighed.

"I am one call away if you need help." He reached over and covered my hand with his own, earnestness glistening in his silver eyes. "What emotion is that?"

My cheeks heated for an entirely different reason, not that I think Geo realized it was for him. Ben might give me butterflies, but Geo's steady, solid presence gave me an even greater gift: the feeling that I was safe after losing my friend so senselessly. I realized I hadn't needed to look over my shoulder since he'd joined me in his human form, sure he would be there if I needed him.

"You're feeling protective, I think," I said.

I turned my hand over and gave his a squeeze. He dipped his head before squeezing back. He held my hand without complaint through the whole lecture.

17

BEN

THE MASTER WOULD LIKE to know why you're laughing so much.

I was going to have a heart attack before I turned twenty-one, I decided. That line from Bianca had stuck with me for days, and I pretended to be the model blood witch after cutting off my chat with Cress. It'd been such a welcome change to hear her sweet voice again, but I'd still jammed that "end call" button on the computer without hesitation.

Anything to ensure he didn't change his mind about sending me out on a mission.

Friday dawned with a rainy chill, but I was not summoned before the master for a punishment. I dressed in casual college guy clothes with a couple daggers in strategic pockets, checking my phone several times as I waited for Bianca to get ready. At this point, looking at my lock screen was a nervous tick.

It'd been over a month since I saw Lucas. He hadn't miraculously returned in the two weeks I'd been confined to the manor. I'd been so horrifically bored and anxious I practically vibrated to finally leave. Not just to see Cress, or celebrate Mabon, or even search for Lucas anymore. Just… leave and breathe fresh air.

Bianca came charging down the stairs. "Let's go," she said, breezing past me. We walked out into a sunny day in regular Salem, our haste cutting in half the moment sunlight warmed our skin.

I put my hands in my hoodie's pocket, slouching strategically. "You ready for this?" I asked with a hint of sympathy. Garroway had given me a difficult mission, but it was nothing compared to what he'd tasked Bianca to do.

"I guess. Fuck," she blew out. "You know a client didn't ask for either of our tasks?"

"I got the impression. Not many people want to be on Dr. Aurina's bad side," I commented. If we didn't play our cards right, we most certainly would be. "Run the wording by me again."

Bianca's hands balled into fists. She rolled some of the tension out of her shoulders, scattering dozens of tiny braids. They were a recent addition, part of an elaborate getup in autumnal colors that made her look like she was a druid of old, arriving to the Mabon celebration fresh from the forest. She'd even stuck a few turning oak leaves in her hair.

"The master requires that I make Dr. Aurina's daughter bleed. I am to cut her while she celebrates Mabon with her family," she said from between gritted teeth.

"He didn't specify how big a cut," I reasoned.

"Yeah…but he wants to send a message to someone. He doesn't want a little poke," she said with a sigh. "I coated a knife with a numbing solution. I'm thinking of making it look like she cut her sleeve on a branch."

"I think that's your best bet," I agreed, relieved to hear the kid wouldn't feel it at least.

"And the wording for your mission?" she prompted.

"I am to bring him three rose gold cupid feathers with their magic intact," I said. I had a pair of gloves secreted away in my hoodie for the task.

"Well, that could be easy. I bet they'll sell them."

"The master probably intended for me to follow Dr. Aurina around. But you know she's going to have an entourage around to jump on any feather she sheds," I said.

We'd researched the Aurina family together, and I'd set my sights on a different cupid who had similar wings to the demigoddess. Her five mates were all cupids too, though only two were strong enough in their magic to sprout the distinctively hued wings of their kind. "I'm going to pluck a couple off her mate's wings instead. They'll still have a lot of magic and no chance of being a regular feather painted rose gold."

"Just don't be a dunce and give one away to your girl-friend," she said.

I rolled my eyes. "I wasn't going to." Actually, I'd been thinking an extra one would make a nice gift for Cress. But now that Bianca had called me out, maybe I'd just go above and beyond for Garroway instead and give him as many quills as I could steal.

"I mean it. It could be really bad news if it told her you're soul mates or something," she said, flashing a serious look at me. I put my hands up. Cupid feathers could lead someone to the real deal, a destined love match. And admittedly, I wanted a quill to point Cress my way. I could barely keep that woman out of my head, even with two weeks separating us.

I checked my phone as we entered New Salem and followed the trickle of new arrivals and motion on campus toward where Mabon had to be. Even though it was early, I tried texting Cress, hoping to see her and hang out as long as possible. Garroway had given us ten hours to accomplish our task, and the deadline twinged against my chest already, a little red line arrowing steadily toward my heart with every passing moment.

"Wow, they went all out this year," Bianca commented as we found a field transformed by a legion of picnic tables decorated with white cloth and clusters of small pumpkins and gourds. I recognized that we were in the fae section of campus, standing close to a carefully maintained forest many fae and their creatures enjoyed. The leaves were starting to golden and crisp, a few carpeting the grass.

There were baskets full of balls and Frisbees for the morning and afternoon, and a team of minotaur were assembling the kindling for a bonfire come nightfall. Also, more than a few witches and fae were already here, to my relief. We weren't too early.

My phone vibrated, and I checked Cress's message. Bianca glanced toward me and snickered at whatever she saw. Ignoring her, I turned and craned my neck until I saw a cluster of new arrivals coming in together. I spotted Cress's purple hair immediately and waved, a genuine smile splitting my face at seeing her again.

She walked over alongside Roe and Willow, whom I recognized, plus a deer-like fae girl and a Black man with shiny white dreadlocks who stuck close to her side. "Hey! About time you showed up!" Roe exclaimed.

"Sorry!" I called back.

"I let everyone know we're doing the ritual at ten," Roe said. She propped a wicker basket on the closest table and drew its cloth covering up to show row after row of pristine apples.

"Cool," I said with a nod, turning immediately to Cress.

I held my arms out first, and we came together for a hug like I'd just seen her yesterday. We lingered a moment longer than necessary. "Hi. You change this?" I fluffed a lock of her hair. Now, I wasn't one for fashion, but it was hard to miss how much brighter it was and shot with different hues of purple to make it look more natural.

"Oh, yeah. One of the professors in my major gave me a potion for it," she said, fixing what I'd mussed with a rake of her fingers. "Plus the recipe, if Grant will make it for me."

She'd done her makeup in shades of orange and red today, with glossy crimson lips I just wanted to kiss. Add in her light blush, and she reminded me of a blooming flower. "You look lovely," I said. I vowed to myself to make the most of today and spend as much of it as possible with her. "Where's Geography?"

"Ge—oh." She turned toward the man who'd watched our reunion. His arms were crossed over his chest, the clean-shaven planes of his face creased with disapproval. "Geo's human right now."

I jerked my chin in wordless greeting. He just frowned at me more intensely. Tough crowd.

"Who, uh, was that girl with you?" Cress asked.

I glanced over my shoulder to find Bianca had already disappeared, blending in somewhere as she waited for her mark to arrive. "No one." I shrugged, enjoying the flash of relief on her face. Aww, was she a little jealous? I'd take her over Bianca any day. She didn't play with knives for fun.

"C'mon, time to be grateful," I said, offering my hand for her to take. We walked into the forest where Roe had gone with her basket of apples, hands lightly clasped. I snuck a look behind us to see Geo following at a polite distance. That damn gargoyle was going to be her purity police at this rate.

Cress loosed a nervous giggle. "Have you ever done this before?" she asked.

"Nope. If Roe explained it to you, then you're ahead of me," I said.

"She did, actually. She's going to say a few words of thanks to the elements for a good harvest, and then we're going to go around in a circle placing apples out and saying thanks for what we're grateful for."

I made a little skeptical noise. There wasn't much in my life to be grateful for right now. Even Cress herself and her presence in my life were tainted with the fact that I needed to somehow warn her to leave town. I was still drawing a blank on how, exactly, to do that when every cell in my body wanted her by my side just like this.

"Think of it like you're at the Thanksgiving table. Just say what you'd tell your family," Cress suggested.

"Yeah, okay." I'd think of something.

Roe's coven ritual was far more chill than I expected. Grant, Wren, and Heath joined us right on time, and we gathered in a circle out in the forest. Even the haughty blonde listened respectfully as Roe gave thanks and planted a few apples in the dirt to return to the elements. She passed the basket around the circle. We sounded a bit like a broken record—giving thanks for good friends and each other.

Cress placed two apples on the ground. "I want to give thanks for the friends who've supported me through the unthinkable," she said. Roe pressed her lips tightly together, looking a little emotional. "And for Geo, who's helped me find a feeling of safety again."

She passed the basket to me last. Man, I know I didn't deserve to be on her gratitude list, but her giving thanks for the gargoyle didn't feel good. He was probably watching from the tree line, listening in as he received that honor.

I placed a single apple in the dirt, bowing my head for a moment. I said to the circle that it was for my friends, but in reality, I gave silent thanks that I was still alive. Every day above ground was another chance to escape the bloody hold Garroway had on Lucas and me.

"Happy Mabon, everyone," Roe said with a big grin. "Who's in for some ultimate frisbee?"

While Cress and the others were distracted with a game, I snuck off in search of a family of cupids. In the shadows of the tree line, I spotted a flash of scarlet as a winged man landed with a giggling girl in his arms. She couldn't be more than seven, with candy pink hair tied into pigtails. She was dressed in a romper to play, and off her father shooed her, toward a mixed group of kids here to enjoy the day with their parents.

Regret twisted in my gut. Bianca wouldn't fail a mission as easy as targeting that girl, but it was wrong. *Principles.* Garroway wanted Dr. Aurina's attention, and he'd get it if someone dared to hurt her daughter. But to what purpose? A random cut on the girl's arm didn't necessarily say it was him.

Like many of my vampire master's plots, I had to wait and be unpleasantly surprised later. But I hid further in the shadows as two more shapes swooped from the sky—two cupids with nearly identical wings of rose gold. Bingo. They scattered a handful of loose feathers upon landing, which I slunk out to pick up as Dr. Aurina joined the festivities between her two mates.

"Three...four...five..." I piled up my bounty in my gloved palms, shocked at my luck. One of the feathers stuck out against the others, gleaming love-me crimson against the soft pink of the other four.

I would give Cress that one, I decided. Bianca could make fun of me later for hoping it helped me get closer to the purple-haired woman. A big part of me hoped that, should we have some sort of real connection, I could convince Garroway that she had more worth to him alive. It was probably a doomed prospect, but I had to know for sure before I encouraged Cress to go and not look back.

18

CRESS

I REJOINED Ben after a couple rounds of ultimate frisbee, energized from a pair of victories courtesy of Roe's highly competitive side. She kept playing and brought in Áine to take my place. The faun was a better player than me, springing around the field with the agility of the deer her lower half resembled.

Ben was plopped on the sidelines, watching us play. It was surreal in the best way to see him again, hanging out like he'd never been away. In the early autumn sunlight, his blond highlights and gem-green eyes seemed all the more lustrous. He still carried that tired, worried edge, but it seemed to dull whenever he met my gaze.

He was casually looking at something in his hand when I returned to his side. At first, I thought it was his phone, but instead, it was something red. He snatched it out of my line of sight before I could make out what it was. "Bet Roe would love to go against you next game," I suggested, hitching a thumb over my shoulder.

He smirked. "She couldn't handle me." He patted the

grass next to him with a gloved hand. "I have something for you."

I plopped next to him. "Oh yeah?"

"Yeah, but before you touch it, know it'll bond to you the moment you do." He lifted his other hand, showing a foot-long red feather. "It's a cupid's feather. I found it..." He jerked his head toward a small gathering of people surrounding the ever-gorgeous Dr. Aurina. She held court surrounded by several men who looked at her adoringly, plus other laughing women with hair in shades of pink, red, and platinum.

They were all cupids. Most were indistinguishable from a witch who'd dyed their hair, save for a few with magnificent feathered wings.

"One of the good doctor's mates dropped it," Ben continued. "If you touch it, it'll help you find someone you connect to emotionally."

My brows rose in surprise, and I raised a finger. "Rewind for a second. Did you just say mates, as in plural?"

He shrugged. "Yeah. Fancy-ass demigods are at their most powerful with as many mates as possible. The higher their power level, the more mates they can bind to themselves. Having several is like a status symbol."

I glanced at Dr. Aurina again and started counting the adoring gazes on her.

"She has five," Ben supplied.

I whistled low. "That's...so many men. Holy shit."

His shoulder nudged mine. "Welcome to supernatural society. The more polyamorous you are, the more power you probably have," he said with a chuckle.

My gaze fell back to the feather in his hand. "So, how does this work?"

"As I understand it, the quill gets hot when you're close

to someone you might have a connection with. If you offer it to them to touch, it'll use up all the magic in the feather to tell you whether you're compatible for a serious relationship. In ye olden days, royalty used cupid feathers to find their soul mates, rather than doing it the old-fashioned way." He got a mischievous look on his face as I wondered what "the old-fashioned way" was. He whispered behind his hand, "Sex."

My cheeks burned immediately. "Oh, right."

"I know you're probably not thinking about romance or anything right now. But it's worth a lot, and I thought... well, I'd offer it to you first," he said, scratching behind his head self-consciously. "It probably won't find you a soul mate or something. You know, just for fun."

I started to smile as I waited for him to finish, holding out my hand for it. "For fun," I agreed. He dropped the large feather into my palm, and a scarlet shimmer lifted from it, absorbing into my skin with a tickling sensation.

Ben watched me hopefully as I turned the feather over into my other hand, admiring its near-metallic filaments and how soft they felt against my fingertips. It was clear he wanted me to offer the feather back to him and see what the cupid magic said about us, which snatched my breath away.

I did want to know if my feelings for him were more than a crush, but I didn't know what I'd do if it turned out we were soul mates. I was definitely not ready for something super serious. But to know there was *potential* for it?

I smiled back at him. "I'm going to take this for a walk, see what it does," I said, trying not to notice the hint of disappointment that turned down the corners of his eyes.

"Okay, I'll be here," he said, lifting a hand in farewell.

I twirled the feather by its quill, not wanting to mess up

its filaments. As I moved away from Ben, it became notice-ably cooler, like I'd just picked it up from a chilly room.

Well, that was certainly something. The magic in it was working...and it must've been trying to tell me something about Ben. I wandered to one of the tables being loaded with covered platters of food, drawing in sweet and savory aromas as I snagged a bottle of water and took a refreshing drink.

Maybe I was just teasing Ben at this point. I didn't think there was anyone else I wanted to offer the feather to. But I wandered with the feather in hand, saying hello to a few acquaintances from my major and other librarians I recog-nized from class and in passing at the library. Pretty much every witch and fae at the university seemed to be here, and then some.

I started noticing family units who must've come back to campus to celebrate Mabon and enjoy the huge upcoming feast. Sometimes, families were just happy couples...but more than half the time, there were groups of three or four men with one woman, or vice versa.

Craziness. I started imagining the kind of heart attack I'd give Mom if I came home with more than one boyfriend. Stifling a laugh at the thought, I passed a fae lady at the table set up with drinks and little snacks, doing a double take when I saw the lustrous lilac mane flowing behind her. "Your hair is beautiful," I said. More varied in hues than mine, with icy undertones that veered more toward a silvery-blue.

She flashed a sweet smile. "Aw, thanks! So is yours." She had a giggle like a peal of bells, twinkling and pleasant. We went our separate ways from there.

I settled in the shade of a few trees, looking down at the feather. I'd passed within arm's distance of a lot of folks, but it was still cool to the touch. There on my own, it began to warm up again until it was like holding a sunbaked stone. I looked around in confusion, expecting to see Ben following me. Instead, I felt the sensation of a strong arm closing around my waist and yelped.

"A cupid's arrow. Where does it point your heart?" murmured a low voice in my ear. My heart just about stopped.

"Phaeron," I breathed. I'd expected our paths to cross again, but here and now? In the light of day with so many people around?

Cold sweat sheened my back instantly, and I trembled against the sensation of a warm, muscled chest pressed to my back. I was going to die and traumatize all these people on Mabon.

"Hello, Cress. Don't be afraid." I'd forgotten the smooth purr of his deep voice, like the enticing brush of silk. "I haven't had the chance to talk to you while you've been under your guardian's watchful eye."

"What's there to talk about? You killed my friend," I whispered fiercely. Something told me I shouldn't antagonize the man who'd sliced up Geo like he wasn't made of stone.

"I would not perpetrate such a heinous act," he replied. I glared over my shoulder, catching only a hint of his glowing topaz eyes in the shade. The rest of him was functionally invisible.

"And you wouldn't attack Geo either, I'm guessing?" I demanded.

His eyes narrowed to catlike slits. "That is different. I only wanted to speak to Morgana. She owes me some answers. If your guardian had cooperated, I could've done it without hurting him."

For a moment, I simply stared. Phaeron was a murderer and a monster, yet he didn't sound like one. Old fashioned, perhaps, but not evil to the point of consuming souls.

And the best serial killers are the most charismatic, I reminded myself.

"What do you want?" I asked. I spotted Geo cooling his heels at a table close by. He'd nicked my phone again and was distractedly scrolling, but he was still within shouting distance. Granted, I didn't think he was faster than Phaeron if I pissed the dimensional off.

"I understand your hostility, so I will be brief," he said. "I have been unable to properly thank you for releasing me from my prison. Allow me to award you a boon."

"A...what?"

His chuckle blew warm air over my ear. I shivered despite myself. "A gift, Cress. My possessions are meager, but I can still offer magic." I felt him lift my left arm by the wrist, turning it over. I nearly yelled out for Geo as the claw on Phaeron's thumb traced a little pattern over the delicate skin of my inner wrist, but it was done within a breath. A circular rune the size of a dime, as gray as Phaeron's skin, now stood out where he'd touched. It looked like an intricate knot.

"When you are in need, find a patch of darkness, touch the rune, and say my name. If I am able, I will come to you," he promised.

I stared at the little mark in surprise. Didn't he realize I could use this against him? "Why would I ever use this?" I breathed.

With my hair shifted to the side to look over my shoulder at him, my neck must've presented too clear a target. His grip around my waist tightened, and I clearly felt his mouth brush the rapid pulse hiding just under my skin.

I bit my lip to keep a noise from escaping, swallowing it as he sent pleasure straight to my core.

Then the sharp points of his fangs grazed my neck, and I moaned out loud, followed by a flush of mortification. "Perhaps after I convince you of my innocence, you will understand why I want to protect you." His deep voice was right in my ear, turning my knees to jelly.

"S-stop. I don't want this," I said. I didn't want him turning my body against me like that.

He straightened immediately, clearing his throat. "Then I must ask you to leave this place and take any dear to your heart with you," he said. I stiffened with immediate fear at how ominous that sounded. "A dark presence nears, and I am not at my best to combat it, thanks to your guardian."

He tapped my right side, and I glanced down, shocked to see his right arm bound by white bandages and a sling. He made it disappear back into his shadows, but several questions pushed at me. I touched what I thought was his arm around my waist before realizing it was the muscled cord of his tail. Clever.

"You were the one who attacked him," I said.

"Alas, the details don't matter. The healer I saw said it will be several days before even advanced healing will repair my shattered bones. I cannot face what's coming on your behalf, so you must leave."

I chewed on my bottom lip. "*What* is coming? And why would you fight anything for me?"

"To speak of it will bring its presence. Just trust me, Cress. Go." He released me so suddenly I stumbled.

I turned around and felt for him, but it was like he'd vanished. "I don't trust you," I said to empty air.

"Then I'm sure your soul will be a delicious treat." His voice drifted down to me. I craned my neck up, spotting him fully visible in a bough of the nearest tree. His tail dangled, twitching like an agitated cat's, while his face was drawn in a look of censure. My breath froze.

Even a disapproving Phaeron was a sight. The high cheekbones and unusual skin tone that marked him as a dimensional had a sort of alien draw. A lock of glossy black hair had escaped the tie keeping it back from his curled horns. Its length fell just past his collarbone, soft compared to the masculine cut of his features. His eyes gleamed like polished topaz in the light of afternoon.

He'd found a shirt somewhere, a short-sleeved tee. My imagination reminded me of the perfect abs that hid underneath it. As I stared, his expression shifted to something nearly coy. "I do not have your trust, but perhaps I have caught your eye all the same?" he said in a low purr. "Does cupid's arrow point my way?"

The feather was pulsing urgently with heat in my palm. The last thing I needed to know was whether this man and I were compatible on a deep level...even though I feared how likely it was with the patch on my neck still tingling.

I was destined to put a silver sword through his heart, right? No matter how his presence drew more of my attention than I cared to admit. There was no sense in flirting with the enemy.

"No," I said, forcing a scowl up at him.

His smile widened. "Is that so? I await the day you change your mind." With a wink, his presence disappeared into a curl of black smoke.

I knew he was gone this time, because the feather's heat dimmed instantly. Blowing out a tense breath, I wondered what the hell had just happened. I lifted a skeptical brow at the feather as it heated again, right before Geo rested a hand on my shoulder and asked, "Who were you talking to?"

He scanned the woods, expression fiercely protective. "No one. Just taking a breather," I lied, hoping I didn't look too flushed.

"I thought I heard the dimensional's voice," Geo said. His quicksilver gaze turned to me for explanation.

I pretended I didn't know what he was talking about, wide-eyed and shrugging. But I made a quick decision as I walked him back to the celebrations. "I think I've had enough Mabon."

Geo looked increasingly confused. "As you humans say, I believe you are acting...sus." He said the half-word stiffly. "The feast hasn't started."

"People don't say 'sus' out loud, Geo. Like, you would say 'suspicious.'" I bit down on a laugh. He was still learning, after all, listening patiently to my explanation. "I just want to go early."

Man, this was going to be a hard sell to everyone else if Geo was doubting me. Roe was the center of attention at one of the tables too, having drawn most of our coven and friends. I doubted I'd be able to convince them to leave early, but I still drew Roe aside for a private moment.

"Hey, I had a bad feeling," I whispered. "Kind of like... that awful day."

She understood instantly, a look of sympathy taking over her expression. "You're leaving?" she asked.

"I think we all need to leave. Like something bad's about to happen," I said, holding my breath as she considered. It was clear she loved Mabon and the sense of community it brought together.

"I might leave a little early too. But it's probably nothing." She rubbed a couple circles into my back. "Go take the time you need. We love you, girlie."

I realized what I looked like as the wide-eyed panic set in at the idea of losing her or any of my other friends. She thought I was overreacting on some whim, and it wasn't like I could tell her the dimensional himself had told me to leave. "I just want you guys to be safe," I said. "It's not worth the free food, you know?"

She started to frown. "Would you feel better if I promised to leave after the feast, then?"

"Yeah. Definitely." It would probably still be light out when it ended, transitioning to the evening bonfire.

"Then I'll go home early too," she said.

I promised to see her later and said a round of goodbyes to the familiar faces like Willow, Áine, and Heath sitting at her table. But Ben wasn't with them. I actually found him exactly where I'd left him, but now Dr. Aurina was on her knees, consoling her crying daughter and murmuring instructions to one of her mates, who flew off in haste.

"What happened?" I asked.

Ben glanced up from his phone and shrugged. "She got hurt playing, I guess. Did you find anyone worthy of the quill?" he gestured to the red feather I twirled idly between my thumb and forefinger. It was growing hot again as I stood next to him.

"Yeah, actually." Since I was leaving, I didn't see a point of hanging on to it any longer. So I offered it back to him, holding the bottom of it.

He sat up from his slouch with a gasp. "Oh! Let's see if it really works." He closed his hand around the soft filaments, and the feather quivered before disintegrating into a puff of crimson dust. My palm itched.

Turning it over, I saw I had a different rune on my palm,

this one resembling a long line with several smaller lines crossing it. Ben gasped as he revealed a matching one on his hand. "Anam cara," he said.

A gentle wind blew away a layer of red dust still clinging to the mark, and I rubbed at the red lines now crossing my skin. I wondered how permanent it was. "Do you know what this means?" I asked him.

"Yeah...you don't know the anam cara symbol?" he asked in disbelief.

"I'm still kind of a new witch," I muttered.

He breathed a little laugh, getting up to hug me tightly. He drew back with his hands on my shoulders. "It's one kind of soul mate," he said, a big grin crossing his face. His giddy happiness gave him a boyish charm, taking away that edge of worry he seemed to always carry.

"We're...soul mates?" Whoa there. I hadn't expected this at all.

"Of a sort. I'm surprised your gal friends didn't tell you all about this," he said. "Anam cara are technically soul *friends* but...it explains a lot. Everyone's supposed to have an anam cara, someone they can be so close with. They basically have the same aura. Someone they miss deeply if they're parted for too long. It's romantic and...quite intimate."

Emotion stirred in his green eyes like a play of light and shadow. There seemed to be a deep yearning there that had his fingers flexing on my shoulders, like he didn't want me to escape now that he'd found me and learned what we could be.

And I had no intentions of running. "It does explain a lot," I agreed. How after only a day of knowing him, I'd really felt connected to him. Why I'd felt his absence so much. "I was going to leave early. Maybe you want to come with?"

"Definitely. Where are we going?" he asked.

"My dorm room? I'm allowed guy visitors until, like, nine at night," I suggested, getting a little jump of butterflies.

He chuckled. "Works for me." He caught my hand as I led him away from the festivities, and we walked with our fingers entwined to my dorm room.

I snuck glances at him, so happy I'd saved the feather to offer to him. To think something like anam cara actually existed and I'd found mine within a month and change at university. I couldn't help a silly daydream. He was a freshman too, so we had four years of too-late dates over pizza and notes before major exams, dances and socials to attend, and so much more. And if I was fated to face Phaeron with the help of three men...chances were now so much higher that Ben was one of them.

I was also quite aware that Geo was following us at a polite distance, probably wearing a stony mask of disapproval. Well, I'd have to get my gargoyle guardian to come around somehow. They'd probably gotten off on the wrong foot. He had a seat in the garden as I took Ben up to my dorm room.

Ben glanced around and raised a brow at me. "Do you live alone right now?"

"Yeah. Just me and my cats," I said, closing the door after us. "I'm like a crazy cat lady. Sorry you had to learn this after the anam cara thing." I noticed neither Milo nor Bella popped up to inspect and greet the newcomer, which was unusual for them.

"It's cool you have familiars. I haven't found mine yet," he said.

It occurred to me that, for all my daydreaming, I hadn't thought through what we'd do now that we were here in my room. I turned to Ben, my offer for Myth-Flix drying up when I noticed how close he was. He reached up to toy with a bit of my purple hair; his knuckles grazed my cheek, and his smile turned tender.

"I want to kiss you. Is that all right?" he murmured.

He waited while playing with that lock of hair, running it between his fingers. Boys in the past had just taken any hint of interest as an opportunity to mash their lips against mine. But Ben wanted to cross that boundary with respect, and it magnified that quivery feeling in my belly a hundred-fold. "Yes," I breathed.

He cupped my nape and drew me into a careful, testing brush of our lips. I'd read in some of my books that a first kiss should feel like a firework, a dazzling explosion of sparks within. Good enough to make a gal's toes curl. But until Ben came back to deepen the touch of our mouths, I'd felt like all those descriptions were nonsense.

Now, I thought they didn't describe it intensely enough. I wrapped my arms around his shoulders, drawing him closer, breathing in the clean and minty taste of him. Our tongues brushed, sending shockwaves of sensation down to my core. We only surfaced for air when my phone began to ring.

I stumbled away from Ben, touching my fingertips to my sensitive lips. I felt how inexperienced I was, and with a kiss of that caliber, Ben had to have a lot more familiarity with the opposite sex. He had a knowing twist to his lips.

Blushing, I checked my phone to see it was Roe calling. I nearly let it go to voicemail, but I suddenly had a queasy sensation in my belly. "Hey," I said, answering.

"Cress! Are you okay?" she exclaimed.

I lifted my gaze to Ben's, flooded with concern at my friend's frantic tone. "Yeah, I'm fine. I'm in my dorm."

"Oh, thank the gods," she sighed. "The feast is canceled. They found a body out in the woods."

I covered my mouth, feeling sick. Suddenly I felt like I was thrown into the past, standing on a sidewalk again, watching the lifeblood leave Lanie as Phaeron loomed over her like a gray reaper. "No," I whispered, nearly pitching sideways. Ben's strong hands caught me, and he helped me sit on my bed before I slumped to the ground.

"They say the girl had purple hair. I thought of you immediately," Roe was saying. My face went numb. That was an unusual enough color that I thought to the fae I'd met, with her beautiful length of purple-blue hair. "Can you come to the clubhouse? Bring Ben and Geo if they're around."

I'm sure your soul will be a delicious treat. That fucker. He'd planned on taking another victim the whole time, with a side of messing with me again, distracting me from what was important. I glared at the shadowy knot on my wrist. Phaeron wanted to play games, but I wasn't up for that. I was going to take him down.

19
PHAERON

Yᴇᴛ ᴀɢᴀɪɴ, I found myself closing a dead girl's eyes. She was a fledgling high fae, with natural hair in icy shades of purple, straight from a polar aurora borealis. She had no pupils, her body left without a life or soul and her expression etched with horror.

I'd sensed *it* somewhere at this gathering. Waiting. Watching. But it'd struck and consumed with great haste, undoubtedly knowing I was also here to stop it.

I lifted some of the fae girl's hair, watching the multi-colored strands fall through my fingers. First the seer with a hood like Cress's, and now a fae with hair like hers. I was no longer convinced this was a coincidence.

Nor did I believe my blackouts were an unrelated occurrence. Another had taken my mind within moments of leaving Cress, and my wits returned just to see this latest victim of the Hungering Darkness. There was no sign of it, other than its prone victim.

With growing dread, I had to confront a terrible possibility. I'd spent significant time hunting the monster from my original world and found no trace of its corrupted white fire. It could have taken root in myself instead. Laughing within me as I turned over every rock searching for it.

It would explain why I was still constantly sensing the monster of clawed darkness and endless hunger. It could have the ability to flare its presence, toying with me and my sensibilities before using me as its jaws to fulfill its dark desire for souls.

I flexed my good hand, and the shadows wove themselves into pitch-black talons to overlay my fingers. I turned them over, inspecting for any speck of white burning at their edges, but they were pristine. My shadowborn blessing appeared to be completely intact.

Perhaps it was time to surrender myself to Moongrove Library. An experienced custodian of dimensional magic may be able to detect the evil hiding from my own senses.

However, it was more likely I'd be killed on sight. There was something I needed before I even considered that path: Morgana's soul and the answers only she could give me.

She was a gargoyle for a reason, carrying a heavy sense of duty as the first librarian witch. Perhaps her betrayal was as simple as that... She'd been doing her duty, making sure the Hungering Darkness was locked away. But duty was a cold companion when it meant I was left in containment with the monster for two hundred years.

I balled my hand into a fist and stepped away from the girl, leaving her to be discovered. It was only a matter of time.

I didn't doubt that Cress would blame me for today's murder. Without concrete proof of my innocence, I deserved her contempt. I couldn't shake thoughts of her, one gargoyle protector away from consumption. Her soul, shockingly bright compared to those around her. This creature of the night couldn't help but crawl back into the radiance rolling from her like a beacon, despite how she felt about me.

If I was harboring the Darkness, this obsession was the biggest danger to her. It was clear she was a target, but I was missing a crucial piece of this puzzle. Why Cress? Was it because she'd released me from the library? The Darkness could be seeking revenge for siccing its most fervent hunter back on its trail.

Or perhaps it sought to harm her in order to hurt me. I thought of the reluctance on Cress's face when I'd asked if we had a connection. It was clear something brewed there, made bittersweet by her hatred of me. My body responded to hers. I wanted to know her, to bask in her radiance, to serve in her shadow. It'd taken every ounce of my willpower not to bite her, to mark her as mine to others of my kind.

I'd felt the heat radiating from the feather in her hand, which had nearly melted in my presence. I knew I was growing attached, but there was just something about her. Perhaps fate wasn't so unkind to leave me mate-less and alone into the rest of eternity. But she had to see something in me as well for this to work. If only I could prove to her that I am a guardian, not a murderer, tasked as a sacred shadowborn to protect everyone I met from within the darkness that was my constant companion.

I'd failed to kill her gargoyle protector and take Morgana's soul for one last conversation. It could've been as easy as severing his head, but at a crucial moment, I'd hesitated, earning myself shattered bones and broken ribs. That moment also lingered at the forefront of my mind, because I'd considered the results of my actions a second too late.

If I killed her gargoyle and the Darkness found her, I would have personally doomed her. The danger had refreshed itself in my mind upon seeing that fae girl. How could I seek closure if my actions directly led to Cress's death and consumption, life and soul alike?

I would consider at another time what it meant, that the most important person in my life had become the young witch who despised me. If it weren't for the gargoyle and her unfortunate misunderstanding of my intentions, she would find it hard to be rid of me.

Despite how disliked I felt, at least I had one companion. He was drunk already, but that appeared to be David's general state of being. I could tell it muted the pain fracturing his soul, so I didn't comment.

"Hey, man. How's the arm?" the shifter asked as I settled on the opposite side of the alleyway.

The Moongrove librarians would never find me here in the middle of the most run-down section of New Salem. The dregs of supernatural society made their homes here, such as they were.

David didn't mind me coming and going at what must've seemed a fickle whim. I may have sweetened that pot by using my shadows to steal him more tolerable liquor. He passed me the bottle today, and it ran smooth on my tongue before searing a path down my throat. I could've finished the whole bottle to muffle the most recent memory of the fae girl's dead face and Cress's distrustful expression. My latest failures.

I gave the bottle back to him. "Fine. I have had worse."

"You're funny. Sorry you got all banged up," he said.

I hadn't expected anyone to care for my well-being, let

alone someone who'd lost everything. When I'd arrived to the alleyway in the dead of night, stained with blood, he'd jumped into action immediately with a roar of, "Holy shit!"

That's how I learned he was a bear shifter under all the unshaven hair. He'd practically slung me over his shoulder and taken me to a charity place run by a verdant witch man covered head to toe with tattoos. No questions, just healing, a meal, and a new set of clothes.

Gang violence was apparently prevalent in the area. Somehow, that'd turned me into a badass in David's eyes. Though he certainly thought the story of how I'd gotten to this place in my life was a work of total fiction.

I'd tried to tell him about my home dimension and the Age of Decay that'd driven me to lead my people to a safer land not ruled by an insane goddess and her monsters.

He'd laughed. *Laughed.* Then said, "I think I played that video game!"

I decided to forgive him when he sobered up that morning and told me how his true mate had ripped his metaphorical heart out by rejecting him. The cracks in his soul had pulsed, growing worse before my eyes.

"Then she doesn't understand that she is doomed to never find someone better than you, David," I'd said. "And one day, you will find a woman who calls to your heart and soul in an entirely different way."

"You really think so, man?" he'd asked, looking down at himself.

As I shared his latest bottle with him tonight, I remembered my vow to him. I'd try to find him someone else with a compatible soul, someone kinder than the woman who'd broken him. All he needed to do was let the alcohol go. One sip less each day. We'd clean him up and set him back on the right path.

Deep into his drink, he started telling me again of a place he was dying to visit. Aurora Heights, where forsaken and rejected shifters were given a second chance. I think he would forget that he's already shared tales of this frozen utopia in what sounded like a pocket dimension to the far north.

"If this place is your dream, then you should go," I said quietly. Maybe someday I would get a more sober shifter to tell me if Aurora Heights even existed, and where to find it.

"I couldn't leave you behind, man."

But he should. If there was even a small chance the Hungering Darkness had its claws in my soul, he should've already started running.

"Maybe we could go together someday," he suggested.

"Perhaps," I agreed. I thought of Cress again, wondering if she was safe in her dorm by now. If the too-close stars in Earth's sky were kind, I would see her again under less hostile circumstances. I was far too eager to see where we stood when that day came.

20

BEN

I SPENT most of the afternoon on a couch in our coven's room in the clubhouse, my arm around Cress as she hugged tightly to my side. It was like the fae girl's death had set her back to that grieving place after her seer friend died. I did my best to comfort her, but in reality, I was usually the one to break things, not help the mending process afterward.

Geo had demanded he come inside too and watched us with a crease between his brows. I couldn't help a smug smile. She'd wanted me, not him. One point for Ben. Her anam cara, I reminded myself, occasionally glancing at the mark on my palm with a softer expression. She and I were meant to be, soul friends with our spirits cut just right to fit together.

I stuck around as long as I could. The deadline started to burn deeper in my chest, sending radiating waves of pain through my whole body. I had only a couple hours left before it killed me if I didn't return to Garroway with my task completed.

My phone buzzed with several annoyed messages from

Bianca, demanding to know where I was. I put her off as long as possible, too. Despite the circumstances, there was a little bubble of peace around my heart as I held Cress and helped her through the news as it came to us in bits and pieces.

The fae who'd died was not a target I expected Lucas to strike, though. The university released a report in haste to explain that she'd come from the Winter Court, one of the many grandchildren of the Winter King.

I needed to talk to Seth, see if there was anything we could do for Lucas. Because this was another blood witch killing, confirmed by the university. A different spider had a hold of my brother's strings, and I would sever them if I could simply *find* Lucas. Mabon was celebrated in a huge area, but I still simmered in frustration, knowing I'd been in the same place as him.

"I'm sorry, I have to go," I whispered into Cress's ear as the sunlight started to wane through the window. She had her head on my shoulder, eyes closed but not asleep. She stirred with a low sound, her big brown eyes fixing on me. When she gave me a look like that, I was ready to do anything for her, except stay and run the risk of not meeting my deadline.

"Okay," she murmured.

"You should go home too. You don't want to miss curfew," I said. I'd read the email off her phone, pretending it applied to me too. All students were to be in their dorms by eight at night. It seemed the university wanted everyone inside by nightfall, and it'd canceled any activities and games outside of curriculum requirements for the time being.

Worse, they were implementing increased security for

those coming and going from the university grounds. Cress had sighed with relief, but I took the news with a sinking heart. They were partnering with the SPDI to allow only students and authorized personnel onto campus grounds.

I may be able to trick Cress and the others into thinking I was a guardian witch with a little blood trickery, but trained supernatural police would be much harder to fool and much less likely to have a sense of humor about it. So when I left the clubhouse and turned to say goodbye to Cress, I knew this could really be the last time I saw her.

"See you tomorrow?" she asked, hope lacing her voice.

"I hope so," I murmured, opening my arms to her. I lifted her off her feet and into my waiting kiss, swallowing her startled laugh. She held on with her arms around my shoulders and her legs clinging to my waist.

I kissed her with everything in me. She didn't hold back either, matching me tongue for tongue, clinging like I was her only anchor. My cock began to harden, pressed against the covered heat of her, and I felt the shiver that went through her when she noticed and tensed for a moment. I expected her to wiggle her way free of me, bashful as she could be, but she surprised me by relaxing and leaning further into my lips.

I only put her down when someone catcalled us from the other side of the road. I gave him a stink eye until he kept walking.

A flush took over Cress's cheeks again. "God, Ben. You know how to kiss," she said.

"What can I say? I was motivated to learn for a moment like this." I brushed the hair out of her face, smiling when I saw some of the light had returned to her eyes. She'd come back from the low place she'd visited today.

I took her hand in mine, pressed the lingering red

symbols in our palms together. "It might not be tomorrow, but I'll come back to you, anam cara."

"You'd better," she said. "Or I'll go find you."

Part of me trembled at the idea of her ever stepping foot in Garroway's lair. "Let's not let it get to that point," I said before stealing one last peck on her lips in farewell. I forced myself to leave before I was tempted to linger for too long.

The deadline on my chest pulsed with a few warning warbles of deeper pain, leaving soreness in my muscles. I donned my gloves and checked the pocket of my hoodie, looking over the four rose gold cupid feathers. They were still perfect and gleaming.

Out of nowhere, strong hands seized my arm and ripped the glove off my right hand. "Ben, what the fuck?" Bianca hissed.

I already had a dagger in my left hand, halfway poised to strike her. "What the fuck, yourself," I muttered, putting the weapon away and jerking my arm from her hold.

She'd snuck up on me out of nowhere. Now that we were away from the clubhouse and together, we started jogging back toward the manor.

"I thought you were smarter than this," she practically growled. "What are you going to do when the master sees you have an anam cara mark?"

"I was hoping to convince him to try calling Lucas back to the manor and cancel his mission to kill Cress," I said. I knew I could talk the master into it. By his twisted logic, Lucas was his property, and I knew he had to be furious at someone else stealing access to Lucas's blood rune.

Bianca looked over at me in stark disbelief. "He's not going to call your brother off because she's your anam cara."

"I wasn't going to tell him that part," I admitted, snapping the glove I'd placed back onto my hand. He wouldn't see it today as I revealed what I knew about Lucas and his activities.

"And you shouldn't bind your fate to someone who's got a hit out on her," she added, glancing over at my palm. "It might be too late for that, though."

She was probably right. Our less than traditional education didn't include much about anam cara or other forms of soul mates, but I understood the anam cara bond kicked in right away, no matter what Cress or I wanted. We'd always be drawn to each other as friends and even lovers; now we just understood why. I was thrilled and terrified for what it meant for Cress to be pulled toward someone like me, though.

"I have a plan," I said. "I'm going to tell him that we have no concrete proof that she is actually the lost Darkmore heiress and that Lucas hesitated too long because of that and got himself captured by an enemy. I'll put it in his language. He's losing money having Lucas out there, drawing attention to rogue blood witch activity. We're getting unwanted exposure that he will have to work around, especially on the NSU campus, which is locking down on the free flow of visitors."

"Okay, fair," she said, tipping her head for a moment.

"You think it's going to work?"

"Fuck no. Because the next thing he'll do is assign the mission to someone with better follow-through. Someone on hand, trying to manipulate him. And when he assigns *you* to kill her, what will you do then?" Behind her glare, I saw the emotion she lashed out with: fear.

It was something we were both intimately acquainted with. An unhealthily overwhelming fear of Master Garroway and the way he always seemed to twist situations into nightmares. Because that was what an order for me to kill Cress would transform into. A living, breathing nightmare come to life. I slowed to a walk, barely able to breathe past the clog of terror in my throat.

"Let me handle the master, all right?" she asked more quietly.

I frowned over at her. "What will you tell him?"

"I can't think past this damn deadline," she muttered, rubbing right next to one of her breasts. "But I'll think of something better than your fool plan."

True to form, Bianca thought of something better than my fool plan. The master called me back into his office after accepting the proof that we'd both finished our missions as directed and ending the pressing pain of our deadlines. She spoke to him first, and then I had my turn on the comfortably upholstered chair in front of his desk.

Garroway's nostrils flared. "You smell different, little Ben."

The blood nearly froze in my veins. Could he somehow sniff out that I'd found a bubble of happiness, or even the cupid magic forming the anam cara mark on my palm?

His lip curled, and he steepled his fingers. "Some sun did you good. Bianca tells me you believe Lucas's blood rune was hijacked by someone else."

"Yes, Master. There have been two amateur blood witch murders on the NSU campus," I stated. "Neither of which you've ordered. And Lucas has been off grid for more than a month."

"Has it not occurred to you, in your desperation to see

him again, that these facts could be unrelated?" he asked in his slow drawl.

I considered rather than blurt a hasty answer. "I think they're too related to be coincidences," I said carefully.

He sniffed, immediately dismissive. "Coincidences or not, the lockdown of the university poses an interesting problem. I have interests in New Salem that cannot be blocked." The wheels were turning behind his dark eyes, and they were fixed on me. I shifted uncomfortably until he came to some sort of decision. "Bianca made an excellent point earlier. You are currently of little use to me."

Gee, thanks Bianca.

"Perhaps you are the best candidate to station in the city until further notice. I will allow you into one of my properties, and you will continue a few simple ventures until the lockdowns cease."

I kept myself very still, barely daring to breathe. He was going to set me loose in New Salem? I could go see Cress more often, maybe every day.

"This is not a reward, little Benjamin," he said sternly. "You will work yourself around the clock if that's what's required. But in the meantime...I am agreeable to the idea of you hunting down your errant brother."

I began to nod. "Yes, Master. Whatever is required, I will do it."

"Anything to find him again, hmm? If he has indeed betrayed me, you know it will not end well for him," he said with quiet venom.

I felt myself pale at the implications but forced another nod. "I understand."

"Good. And if the jumped-up pink Barbie that leads the university acts against me again, you will be on hand for retaliation as well." He spoke mostly to himself, looking pleased.

I thought of his missions for Bianca and me today. A warning in the form of hurting Dr. Aurina's child and plucking a few feathers from the cupid demigoddess's wings. I hadn't realized they were the opening salvo of some personal vendetta.

21

CRESS

Monday evening was the earliest I could come see Dr. Voidbinder for extra training. With the curfew looming over my head, we had to move the time to seven at night rather than eight, which meant I'd barely gotten a meal scarfed down before running to the library.

He directed me to the small room where the practice weapons were kept and steered my shoulders toward a lineup of dusty silver swords. "It's time you learned some magic. Pick one," he said, acting like he hadn't just invited me to my own personal candy shop.

I picked up and inspected each one and found them all to be nearly identical. Straight-edged, plain, and more lightweight than I expected. Most were battered from practice, reminding me of old band instruments that'd been loaned out, dented, and returned a few times.

I ended up choosing one with a grip that felt right in my hand, and Dr. Voidbinder magically assigned it to me and let me store it in the tall, slim locker assigned to me on floor negative one. This was it. I was really going to learn magic!

My excitement soured to frustration quickly. If only

practice was as straightforward as picking a weapon. On the first day with a real sword, I made the same motion with it until my wrist ached. "Criss-cross. Just an *x*," Dr. Voidbinder had said like it was no big deal.

Just an *x*, my ass. My first rune was a study of precision and patience. Each line had to be the exact same length, formed by a figure-eight swish of my sword's tip. The length of metal grew heavy in my hand as I made the motion over and over while saying the name of the rune, Lux, with each attempt.

Our time together was too brief. I tried again on Tuesday to no avail, and then Wednesday, channeling the pitch of my frustration into increasingly choppy strokes through the air.

"Lux. Lux. Freaking...LUX!" I shouted before tossing the sword to the ground in frustration.

The professor looked on, disapproval and concern tugging at his lips. "Young lady, it is a snappy gesture." He showed off how to do it again with his sword, creating the rune with a couple stiff motions of his wrist. The *x* lingered in the air, two clean and translucent librarian-purple lines, until he said, "Lux." The rune disappeared, the magic sucking back into the tip of his sword. It began to glow from within.

"Now you try." He stooped and put the leather hilt back into my hand.

I heaved a sigh, thankful at least that Geo wasn't here to witness this particular practice session. He'd been more distant than usual since Mabon, transitioning back to a stony, businesslike persona. I wouldn't be surprised if I walked out of the library tonight to find him turned back into his form of obsidian and quartz, if he wasn't scrolling the Internet on my phone.

It was probably my fault. Upon learning that Phaeron had taken another victim, he'd muttered, "You lied to me. He was there, and you spoke to him." I didn't deny it. A look of shock had crossed his face before the distance he imposed.

Yet I needed Geo now more than ever, and his protection may be the only thing warding Phaeron away from eating my soul next. Needing to apologize to the gargoyle weighed on my stress even now. I'd taken a glance at the search history he'd left behind...it was focused on emotions and regulation. It stung to know he was seeking out this kind of thing without asking me to help.

Distracted by my thoughts, I moved my sword in another figure eight, saying tightly, "Lux." When light erupted from it, I nearly dropped the weapon in shock. I gaped at the shining length of metal. After three days, there it was, beautiful, *real* magic that I'd cast with my own hand.

"Mighty fine light you have there," Dr. Voidbinder said, grinning. He lifted his sword up to mine, showing how I'd lit mine brighter than his somehow. "I think that's enough for the evening. Let's get you to the powercore and home before curfew."

I nodded, blinking away the dazzled spots in my eyes. "Thank you, sir," I murmured, following him to the elevator. He scanned his badge to take us down to the level with the library's powercore.

I asked something that'd been lingering with me ever since my librarian's handbook had mentioned power levels. "What do you think my power level might be?"

Dr. Voidbinder lifted a skeptical brow. "It's a little too soon to tell. Your first few years as a witch are for learning and challenging the boundaries of what you can do with your magic," he said. "Usually, we test after that. Even modern machines run the risk of harming a new witch through the defensive and magical conduction power level tests."

All I really heard was the "usually" and turned a hopeful look his way. "No, Miss Cress. I think you need to be patient," he said.

I deflated as the elevator doors opened. At this time in the evening, we didn't see any other librarians as we went to stand before the powercore. The sight of the massive orb resting in its stone loop still lifted all the hair on my arms and neck. Its magic electrified the air, forming a soundless call to come forward and commune with it.

It'd only spoken to me one time, when it'd bonded me to the librarian witch affinity. Ever since, I'd seen it twice a week and siphoned more of its power in wordless communion. I'd gotten the sense that it wanted to give me as much magic as possible to fuel my spells. The more powerful I was, the better equipped I was to defend its library.

As I placed my hands within it, I expected more of the same, just for a force to slide me forward several inches. My arms plunged into the powercore to the elbow, covering my skin with a cold jelly-like sensation.

"Hello again, dearest and brightest soul."

Its ancient, electric presence filled my head, rendering me wordless and frozen.

"You bear my prince's mark of protection."

A little lasso of pressure surrounded the shadowy knot of magic Phaeron had left on my wrist. His boon, before going and killing again in cold blood. I tried to flinch back, shocked that the powercore acknowledged the murderous dimensional as its prince.

"I wish to commune with him. He has not visited since his release."

I shook my head stiffly. There was no telling what would happen if Phaeron got access to the raw energy of the powercore.

"Your distrust is high. I have a task for you before I allow you to commune with me again. Call to him. Ask him about the Age of Decay. See if he is truly the monster you think he is."

Electricity flowed into my body, courtesy of the powercore, far more than it'd ever given me. I trembled and pulled back, thinking its magic was going to burst out of my veins at this rate. Numbness coursed over my whole body, leaving me limp when it pushed me away. I ended up on my back, hair dangling over the first step down from its pedestal.

"Are you okay?" Dr. Voidbinder asked, helping me up slowly. My limbs felt heavy, too full of the library's coursing electricity. I felt like I could draw a thousand Lux runes, but that was my only outlet for all this magic other than losing it over time.

"Yeah, I think so," I mumbled. "Is it normal for the powercore to order you to do something?"

"Quite so," he said, giving me a curious look.

I decided to keep the task to myself. The powercore also likely knew I was too much of a coward to do as it ordered, so it kept further communion with it hanging over my head.

Sometime soon, I needed to talk to Phaeron again. The thought was a stone of dread in my stomach.

TRUE TO ITS WRITTEN WORD, *The Librarian Witch's Handbook*

told me Phaeron's last recorded power level the next morning since I'd successfully cast a Lux rune.

Well, I kind of lied. His fancy-pantsy dimensional magic defied the testing methods of the time. So he's somewhere north of where a demigod starts, which is PL9.

I nearly spat a mouthful of cereal and milk over its open pages. It flapped at me in distress.

1. Gross.

2. Regretting this little vendetta yet?

"Frick! Why couldn't you just tell me he was that powerful?" I muttered, ducking my head when I felt the attention of others also eating breakfast in the cafeteria.

It replied by quickly sketching out a photorealistic version of my face on its next page, with a dunce cap on top of my head. "Captain Oblivious" was written across the hat.

I smacked it closed with a scowl. "Rude-ass book," I muttered.

After a minute, its front cover flipped open.

C'mon, Cressie-poo. You know you love me.

I glared at it harder. "Don't call me that."

It flipped another page and started aggressively spamming me with ink hearts.

"Just let me eat my breakfast in peace, and I'll forgive you," I sighed. It dutifully closed itself for me.

My bad mood persisted as I let my cats out for the day and strolled out of the dorm. Bella and Milo sensed my mood and stuck close to me, while Jin went off to cat around on her own for the day. I sighed to myself. Another day, another chance to get frozen out by Geo and look around hopefully for...

Ben stepped out of the garden path, offering forward a small bouquet of multicolored flowers. "Good morning," he said, flashing his crooked smile. It was like the clouds parted, and the sun warmed that little sad spot in my chest. I gasped and flung my arms around him.

"Aww, you missed me already?" he teased, pressing his lips to my cheek.

"Says the guy who disappeared for, like, two weeks," I said.

He handed me the flowers, and I took a happy sniff of their sweet scent. "Well, I'm gonna be around a lot more now," he said. "Walk you to class? What's first?"

I heaved a sigh. "Latin. My least favorite class."

He laced my free hand with his and let me lead the way. I didn't even glance back to see if Geo followed us. "Why'd you sign up for that?" Ben asked, wrinkling his nose.

"It's kind of a requirement. Most librarian runes are Latin-related," I grumbled.

"Oh, that sucks."

"Wish I had guardian magic sometimes," I admitted. Their magic replied to will and strength after they spoke a rune's name aloud. No making shapes with a weapon like librarians had to do. At least I wasn't a celestial witch, who had to keep complex strips of runes pre-prepared for most of their spells.

He pulled a face. "Yeah, you know, every affinity has its pros and cons. When do you get out of class for the day?"

"About two. You?"

"Yeah, close to then. What do you think about going out, just you and me? No need to bring Geometry. I'll keep you safe." His evergreen eyes glimmered with mischief.

I glanced over my shoulder, spotting Geo trailing us. It would be kind of nice to go somewhere without him always in my shadow. But the last time I'd been even partially parted from him, Phaeron had latched on to me.

I *did* need to talk to the dimensional if I ever hoped to

commune with the library's powercore again. Eventually I'd run out of magic and be as useful as an ordinary woman with a sword. But I was skeptical that Ben's presence would keep me quite as safe as the gargoyle who'd already humbled Phaeron once.

"Sounds like a great time. I just don't think Geo will go for it," I said.

"Well, he's your assigned gargoyle, right? Just order him to go do something else," Ben suggested. When I hesitated on that idea, he threw up his hands. "Or give him the slip! What's the matter with a little fun? It's not like he has any emotions to be upset with you when you come back."

I raised a brow over at him. "No. I do need him. If we want more privacy later, I can ask, though."

Though frustrated, Ben didn't argue anymore, and we met up again after all my classes. He ignored the gargoyle doing some doomscrolling on my phone, standing at a polite distance away, when we met up at the library and settled at the first floor study area on a well-loved couch.

"Guess we need to use my phone," he teased, and that was the only acknowledgment he gave Geo before pulling out his device and pulling up some Myth-Flix for us to watch. I got the left earbud and he took the right one.

In the midst of us trying not to laugh too hard and interrupt people actually studying, I turned and said, "Hey, Ben. Are there theaters around that show these movies?"

"I'm sure. I'll look one up later," he promised. In the meantime, we finished the episode we were watching. So engrossed, I didn't realize he'd slowly inched his arm around my shoulders until we were cuddled closer together. I felt a little blush but settled into his side with a glance up at him.

We'd cuddled like this after the news of that fae's

murder at the Mabon celebration, but that'd been a little different. Or was it? I was so aware of Ben now, getting a little shivery feeling from his fingertips brushing the skin right under my shirt's cuff. His breath smelled of mint...

His kiss had tasted like mint, too. I wondered how the smell made me want to kiss him again so much.

Ben didn't leave my side until dinnertime, only going to get to his off-campus apartment before curfew. "Same time, same place tomorrow?" he asked.

I smiled eagerly. "Sounds good."

His goodbye kiss left me with butterflies and I smiled through my dorm food meal, a big bowl of spaghetti. I pulled out my handbook and propped it up a safe distance away from the potential splash zone of red sauce. "Hey, *The Librarian Witch's Handbook*," I recited.

Its front cover lifted up. The first page simply said: *Hey.*

"Can you tell me more about anam cara?"

Are you asking me about...

It flipped the page and surrounded two big, bold words in a circle of hearts.

TRUE LOVE?

I stifled a surprised giggle. "I suppose I am!"

Okay, toots, let's see here.

Someone drew out the chair opposite mine at the little cafeteria table. I glanced up in surprise to see Geo with his own bowl, giving my handbook a confused look. "Are you talking to the blank book again?" he rumbled.

"Yes," I said. Now I was the one giving simple yes or no answers and staring. Geo rarely ate and usually didn't sit when he needed to scarf down something small.

The handbook was blank to anyone but its owner, a fact I'd learned with some surprise when I'd tried to show Geo one of its more kooky explanations to my endless stream of magic-related questions. While he twirled his fork with far more attention than the simple task required, the handbook flipped a page to give me an answer to my question about anam cara.

It displayed a sketch of the same mark on my palm. *"Anam cara" has come to define a phenomenon experienced across the greater supernatural community. Some believe one whole soul is split into two before birth and that a person will never feel complete without the person who received the other half of their whole soul. Because no supernatural power exists that can verify this, it is simply a theory. However, it's pretty widespread and accepted by those who have found their anam cara.*

An anam cara pair can establish their bond as either platonic or romantic. Either way is defined by a deep bond of friendship. Would you like me to tell you how to fix the bond in place and strengthen it?

My heart skipped along happily. I definitely felt like Ben and I were heading down the path of a romantic bond.

"I wish to speak with you about Ben," Geo said, drawing my attention out of daydreaming about the next time I'd see the man in question.

"Oh yeah?" I drew myself up, the handbook's question forgotten.

"He is your anam cara." He pointed to my hand. I'd explained what the mark was after Mabon, since he'd been curious. "I have noticed...you prefer his company."

I heard the words hanging unsaid and bit my lip. This could easily be an emotional minefield for the gargoyle who'd never experienced the nuances of relationships. It almost sounded like...well, he couldn't be jealous. I sincerely doubted it, at least.

"I have feelings for him," I said, weighing this explanation carefully. "You have to understand, that's separate from you. Just because I'm dating Ben doesn't mean I think any less of you. You keep me safe, and I appreciate that. But...there's going to be times when I will want to be alone with him. You'll have to trust him to keep me safe."

He frowned immediately. "But you are my purpose. I cannot simply entrust him with my job."

"I'm just asking you to be a bit flexible with that," I said. "I'm not in trouble if I'm with Ben." His expression shaded to distrust of that statement.

"I am a gargoyle. Stone. Rigid."

I reached across the table and poked his arm. "Not right now. You're flesh and blood, and part of that is being flexible. Bend like a reed and all that," I said, hoping he'd understand.

He looked down at his skin, where the imprints of pressure from my fingertips were rapidly fading. "I'm not sure... I am capable of what you're saying," he said slowly.

"Maybe with time," I suggested.

His face took on a neutral, stony expression. "Perhaps."

22

CRESS

Ben and I took the shuttle into New Salem that weekend to visit a supernatural movie theater. A new experience for both of us, I'd learned, and I was excited to see how it was different from an ordinary trip to see the latest blockbuster.

Geo rode along in the seat behind ours, and I could tell Ben was getting frustrated with the other man's constant presence. Honestly, so was I, but I hadn't gotten through to Geo that I would be okay. Therefore, he sat behind us through a showing of a superhero movie composed of a star cast of varied supernaturals while Ben playfully fed me popcorn and chocolate-covered peanuts.

In those moments in the dark, it was almost like it was just Ben and me there. But the moment we took a walk through New Salem, I was aware again of Geo following us. Unhappily. It felt wrong, like I was teasing the gargoyle, forcing him to watch me have fun without him. But at the same time, he refused to leave even for a few hours.

"I've got a lot of...classwork to do tomorrow," Ben said apologetically at the end of our date. "I'll see you Monday night? Maybe Tuesday if it's a lot."

It would be Tuesday, I found out, spending Sunday and Monday catching up on my own work before my grades could slip from the time I spent hanging out with Ben and training with Dr. Voidbinder.

Monday evening, I picked up my silver sword and learned a slightly more advanced rune called Repello. It was...basically what it sounded like. Cast with a diagonal cut of the sword, in a motion that took it up and back toward my chest, it activated when I turned the hilt of the sword so the flat of the blade was facing outward.

"Now, young lady, be aware that this is the weak version of a rebounding spell you'll learn later," Dr. Voidbinder told me once I successfully cast it. A squared-off section of air glowed with translucent magic in front of me, prepared to cancel out the next spell aimed at it. "It will stop most magic in its tracks, but only one spell per shield. If you face an opponent that casts multiple spells at the same time." He made a popping sound and flared out his hands.

"Got it," I murmured.

"Luckily for you, you can layer up to three shields on top of each other..."

Casting Repello once was easily enough, but I didn't quite grasp how to put one shield on top of another by the time our session ended. Still, I knew two runes now. I was so proud of my progress.

I was riding that high when I put my sword away for the night and retrieved my phone. Geo hadn't wanted to use it tonight, and I was relieved when I saw what was on my screen. Ben had texted me a string of short messages, which I put together in my head. *Want to go somewhere, just you and me? No Geo?*

I shot a guilty glance over my shoulder, toward the

gargoyle waiting outside the locker room. *Yeah. Where do you want to meet up?*

Thoughts of my upcoming date with Ben lasted me through the drudgery of Latin and the dry facts in Introduction to Supernatural Society, and by the time I was in Introduction to Fashion, I was in full daydream mode. It was a sunny autumn day outside. I wondered what Ben wanted to do on a nice day like this.

I snuck a glance at Geo standing in the back of the class with his arms crossed. His expression wasn't quite blank, but he certainly looked bored. I'd decided that tricking him would be for the best, but that didn't mean I didn't feel guilty as hell about it. I just didn't want him stuck so stubbornly to his duty, to the detriment of his budding emotional state. Maybe he'd thank me later for giving him the slip.

When class was over, I went to Geo and whispered, "I'm going to go to the bathroom real quick. Meet you back here?"

He nodded stiffly. "I shall wait."

I walked out at a normal pace and then booked it down the stairs, taking them two at a time. By the time he realized I wasn't coming back, I was probably way down the street and spotting Ben standing on the sidewalk with two steaming cups in hand. He fell into a jog next to me.

"This way," he said, somehow managing those cups without a spill. We took several turns down side streets on campus until slowing. "Unless he flies after us, we should be fine. Here, I got this for you. Extra sugar."

I took a deep breath of the white chocolate mocha he handed me and beamed. "Thanks! Where to now?"

"Just follow me, babe. I know the perfect place. Hope you have some walking shoes on." He glanced down at my dusty sneakers and nodded in approval.

We crossed to the fae side of campus, passing varied species of fae. They had one thing in common despite their varied looks, which were black clothes of mourning. "I thought I could show you the best part of Mabon you missed," Ben said, drawing my attention away from the dark thoughts threatening my headspace.

"Oh yeah?" I asked. He motioned forward with his chin, toward the approaching tree line. Two trees had their branches so intricately entwined that they formed a natural archway. Stepping past it was like a gateway to another world strung with the autumn rainbow.

We followed a dirt path further into the forest and my gaze fixed above us with awe. The trees here didn't simply rust. Their leaves turned into shades of ruby and gold, carnelian and bright yellow and bronze. Little creatures flew around the branches—I recognized that they were much like the diminutive people that the university sometimes used to deliver letters.

"Wow," I breathed. "My friend Áine told me that New Salem used to be the Fall Court. I can totally see it here."

"This isn't even the best part," Ben laughed. We walked hand in hand deeper into the forest together. The colors grew richer, like someone had turned up the saturation filter even as the trees spaced out more and grew impossibly taller, towering over us and releasing carpets of jewel-toned leaves with each gust of wind.

Wisps of light danced around the biggest tree, set apart from the rest in a clearing heaped with leaves. I inspected it curiously, realizing I'd need about five of me to encircle its massive trunk with my arms.

"Here, hold these for a sec," Ben said, passing me his empty coffee cup and backpack. He dove headfirst in a mountain of leaves he'd vaguely shaped up, scattering them everywhere with a boyish laugh.

He stacked an even higher pile of leaves for me to jump into. They were fresh and dry, crackling perfectly under my weight. I popped my head out of the pile, watching Ben open up his backpack and start drawing out a towel and all the fixings for a little picnic.

"You came prepared," I giggled. Together, we made a mostly flat surface of leaves for the towel, and he lay out a lunch of sandwiches and other goodies.

"What can I say, I'm a good boy scout," he said with a hint of humor.

His food had gotten a little squished, but I didn't complain, instead tucking in and relaxing to the sounds of wind rustling through the massive branches of the huge tree. When we were done, I laid out with my head on the towel, more content than I'd been in a long time.

"Ben," I said, breaking the companionable silence between us. "I had a thought."

He settled next to me, close enough that I could count the sun-kissed gold flecks in his eyes. "Hmm?"

"I've told you all about my dreams. What are yours?" I asked. Not once had he mentioned his major or what he wanted to do with his life after college.

"Oh, I dream of being free—" He coughed suddenly, turning away from me and having a fit of painful-sounding coughs.

"Damn, are you all right?" I asked, catching him

rubbing the corner of his mouth with a leaf before tossing it away.

He turned back to me, nodding. "Sorry, yeah. I mean, I do have dreams, but they seem so far away." He lifted his shoulder. "Still feels like I could do anything and go anywhere with half a reason to. You know what I mean?"

I considered him before smiling wide. "I think…you don't know yet. That's okay too. I thought I wasn't going to get the hang of all this magic stuff, but I know how to cast two runes now."

"I think you'd make a good librarian. I mean, you've already got the look down." He ran his fingers into my hair, dislodging a couple leaves, and let the purple strands catch the light.

"Completely unintentional."

"Still. It works. You're beautiful, babe." He continued playing with my hair, and I lidded my eyes, enjoying the brush of his fingertips over my scalp and the nape of my neck. His featherlight touches turned a brush down the curve of my cheek and neck into a shivering sensation.

Ben paused when he hit my neckline, shifting closer, closing the space between us until I could feel his heat through my shirt. My breath quickened as he resumed his gentle perusal of my body with his knuckles skimming around my arm. I shifted into him when he traced the curve and dip of my waist, and by the time he stopped to give my hip a firmer squeeze, his lips were on mine again.

He was unhurried now, exploring my mouth with the same patience. This wasn't like his fevered goodbye on Mabon, when I swore he was trying to fit all the affection of two more weeks into a few passionate moments. Something had changed in him, like he knew he could take his time and fully intended to.

I asked myself, was this handsome, mysterious man the one I wanted to be my first? I wasn't so inexperienced that I didn't recognize where this was going. Perhaps he took it slow for my benefit, as my first touch on his chest was shy, nearly unsure. A voice much like Mom's in my head reminded me that I'd just met him, and he certainly seemed like the type who could get anyone he wanted.

That wasn't why I was drawn to him, though. The answer lay on my palm, the red cupid magic seeming as permanent as a tattoo. He was my anam cara, a friend to my soul. Being apart from him had been hard already, but being with him...it just felt right.

I found the contours of his muscles through his shirt, surprised at how defined he was without a bulky hoodie on. His strong arms looped around my waist, pulling me to straddle him in one smooth motion. His hair made a golden halo around him, kiss-swollen lips drawn in a confident smile. This was exactly where he wanted me.

Until we began to slide. Squealing in surprise, I tumbled off him as the pile of leaves under us shifted with the sudden change of our weight. We landed at the base of the pile, limbs awkwardly entwined, and laughed together. "Hey, Ben?" I licked my lips, chasing away the nervous feeling in my belly until I realized it was a squirm of antici-pation. "Why don't we go somewhere more private?"

23
CRESS

It was late afternoon as we crossed the campus back to my dorm. "We'll go into the front," I said, knowing Geo would probably return to the garden out back to wait for my return. I was not feeling up to a confrontation with him, not when I had Ben by my side, eager at the promise of alone time.

"Lead the way," he said. I walked a little faster than normal, not that Ben was complaining. We approached my dorm from the opposite direction I usually took, going through the front with a swipe of my student ID. Unfortunately, that meant we needed to pass by the service desk, and the woman working this afternoon gave us the stink eye as we passed through the foyer and to the stairs.

That particular woman was why I didn't like going in through the front, preferring the side entrance that led directly to the stairwell. Oh well. I got Ben up to my room and locked the door behind us. I dropped my backpack next to my desk, and he did the same, taking in the little box that was my dorm again.

"It's just enough space without a roommate." Though

the blank side was a constant reminder of the time when Lanie's stuff filled it, my things were slowly creeping into the void she'd left behind. The posters of my favorite classic rock bands covered the far wall now, along with an analog clock to keep me on track.

But I didn't care what time it was. Not when Ben looked at me with such singular intent, only a few feet of electrified air between us. We met somewhere in between, tumbling onto my bed until we began right where we'd left off, with my knees around his hips. I jolted when his warm fingers tunneled under the hem of my shirt, spreading along the bare skin at the small of my back.

"Cress, you're sure?" he murmured between kisses.

There he was, making sure he respected my boundaries. He pulled back from my lips, resting our foreheads together as his gaze searched my face.

"Yes," I said breathlessly.

He smiled, broad and pleased. "Just know, I think this will strengthen our anam cara bond and bring us closer to a romantic bond," he said.

I considered and began to nod to that. I wanted to follow the magic, which sang with happiness any time Ben was around. We already had a romantic bond forming, and the magic would just affirm that. "But what about protection?" I asked.

He lifted my hips with his as he pulled out his wallet, withdrawing something before flicking it to the side. He had a condom tweezed between two fingers. "Being prepared is sexy," he said with a smirk before moving his index finger to reveal he actually had two condoms in hand.

It was a little too late to be bashful, but I still felt a hint of embarrassment as I said, "Before we do anything else, you should know, um. This is my first time."

He set the condoms aside and hooked his thumb through the back loop of my jeans, sneaking a squeeze in as he lowered my core to press against him. "Don't worry, babe. It's natural," he murmured. He guided me through a bold grind against his groin, right against the bulge in his jeans.

I felt an answering jolt of wet heat between my thighs, rolling my hips into his erection as it grew underneath me. He trailed kisses over my jaw and neckline, and I moaned, a tender "oh." Questing hands drew my shirt up and over my head, his lips tracing back and forth on their way to my breasts. He paused to greet each one with a kiss and a teasing graze of his teeth that made my whole body hum.

I reached for the hem of his shirt, and he caught my hands. "Not yet," his lust-roughed voice whispered in my ear. With a sigh, I nodded. It was all I could do to keep my weight balanced on my palms while he played my body like a fine instrument.

He undid the button of my jeans, pushing the zipper aside and slipping his hand between my thighs. I practically trembled on a rush of excitement. This was really happening; I was going to lose my virginity to my anam cara, someone I saw myself staying with through college and even beyond.

His gentle touch spread my folds and his callused thumb found the button of nerves and desire at the apex. "Ah, fuck. You're already so wet for me, babe." My hands grabbed his shoulders as I felt him sink one, then two fingers into my eager channel.

I concentrated on doing what felt right, circling my hips and riding the wave of pleasure tinged with a fleeting twist of pain as he flexed his fingers and stretched those intimate muscles. Pressure built at the base of my spine, urging me to ride his digits. He felt deeper in my channel as his gaze fell to my lips. The pad of his finger brushed an intimate patch of skin that turned my legs to jelly.

"Ben," I moaned, on the edge of a cliff only his expert touch could push me over. He was watching my expressions like I was the hottest thing alive but pulled away before I found that release.

"Take the rest off," he ordered.

I sat up and pushed my panties and jeans off my hips with shaky hands. His smoldering gaze seared every inch of skin as I exposed it. He knew how to make me feel attractive rather than experiencing even a moment of doubt being this vulnerable with him.

Once I was naked, I reached for his shirt again, and this time, he obliged by holding his arms out. I gasped in surprise, taking in a broad, circular tattoo over his right side. The thing was at least six inches in diameter, covering a sizable portion of his ribs. "What does all this mean?" I asked, my gaze taking in the spiky, foreign-looking runes lining the inside of the circle, with one large rune standing out in red at its center. A few uneven lines stretched from the edge of the circle, crossing his broad chest.

"Tell you after. C'mere." He made a grabby motion and helped me into the bed and onto my back. He shucked his jeans and boxers in a quick motion, his erection bobbing free. As he reached for one of his condoms, I stroked the length of him.

He was velvet wrapped in steel, throbbing with desire. My fingers barely circled him. He laced his grip through mine, encouraging me to hold him firmer. "That's right, just like that." He let me take a few moments to admire the size and strength of him, milking out a bead of slick arousal as I slid my hold up and down his cock.

He checked my expression one more time. I smiled back, flushed with anticipation, and soon he was rolling the condom on and nudging me to lie back. He rested over me, and our lips met, tongues dueling as I felt his crown pressing to my entrance. He kissed me all the more intensely, swallowing my moan of pained pleasure as my pussy stretched to take his cock to the root. "Good?" he paused to ask, and I nodded eagerly, pulling him back to me.

My discomfort was quickly erased as he took my body to new heights. I rocked my hips into the pace of his thrusts. It *was* natural, like I was made for him, and I sank into the sensations of the moment. Already primed for him, I quickly found my first release as he shook the aging bedframe until it creaked in complaint.

"Damn, you're beautiful," he whispered, watching me ride that high. He continued a stream of praise between open-mouthed kisses and I hung on every word, holding them within like they were precious and fragile.

When we parted for air, my mouth drifted to his neck, kissing and nipping the taut skin. I wanted him to find the same completion, the same level of pleasure from me as he delivered each time our bodies rocked together. His moans were my reward as he panted and gripped my hips harder, holding me steady for the pounding of his thrusts. Our skin slapped together in time with the constant chorus of moans I breathed.

My fingernails sank into his shoulders as I felt pressure building again, swiftly detonating in a second, bigger peak on a rush of liquid heat. He followed me over that edge with a hoarse shout, finishing with a few slower thrusts before he came to a panting stop.

As we held each other afterward, I felt a tingling on my

palm. I'd noticed this morning that the cupid magic that'd formed my anam cara mark was starting to fade, making the mark watery around the edges like a juice stain. Now, to my astonished eyes, it firmed up around the edges and deepened to a rich maroon.

Ben scratched at his skin before lifting his hand too, tipping it to show me his mark was now librarian witch purple. "Huh. I didn't know it'd do that," he murmured.

"You didn't?" A bit of nerves tickled my insides, threatening to tear down my afterglow.

He sucked on the inside of his cheek as he considered his purple mark. "As far as I know, it's cosmetic magic. It came from a cupid, after all." It seemed like he was trying to laugh it off, but I was relieved nonetheless. "I bet it could be removed if you didn't want it."

I shook my head. "I wouldn't want to take it off." It was like a memento of our time together, something I could show off to show that I had a romantic bond with my anam cara. Intimate, but subtle. A mark only fellow supernaturals would fully understand.

"Me neither," he said, accompanied by another kiss, which led to roaming hands and...it was a good thing he came prepared with two condoms.

NIGHT HAD FALLEN by the time I saw Ben out of the dorm. I didn't really want him to go, but I also didn't want to be caught with a guy in my dorm room after curfew. He promised I'd see him tomorrow, and I was going to hold him to that.

"I know it is not my business." Phaeron's voice rose

from behind me. "But all the same, he is the one cupid's arrow led you to? Really?"

I whirled around with a startled gasp. Sitting casually on the bench right outside my dorm was the dimensional man. He had Bella cradled like a baby in the crook of his arm, and the sight of his claws resting on her tender belly was like a bucket of ice water over my good vibes.

"Phaeron," I said carefully, edging toward him.

"Yes?" He quirked a dark eyebrow. I realized Bella was making air biscuits, purring thunderously as he rubbed her. I released a tense breath.

He jerked his chin in the direction Ben disappeared down. "He is a blood witch on the wrong path. His soul is tainted with dark magic."

"Right," I said dubiously.

"Don't stop," Bella squeaked.

He turned a smile down to her. "Mrraw," he replied, jiggling his hand between her front legs as she slow blinked at him. Aw man, why'd he have to be a cat lover? He'd turned Bella into a content puddle.

I cleared my throat. "Could you put my familiar down?"

"Oh, this sweet girl is yours? All the better," he said offhandedly, but he didn't put her back on the ground. "Come sit with me a moment. There are matters we must discuss."

The powercore's demand came to the forefront of my mind, and I bit my lip. There wasn't a clearer chance than this. "I'm supposed to ask you a question," I said. "Something about decay?"

He slanted a look sideways, his topaz eyes seeming to blaze. "She is quite meddlesome, isn't she?" His tail twitched.

"She?" I echoed, confused.

"Many facts about the object you know as a powercore are secrets closely guarded by my people. When you last communed with her, she sent a bolt of pure power through you, to me, with a short message to come find you." He lifted his right arm, which appeared to be completely healed. I hadn't realized the powercore could send anything *through* me to him, let alone the kind of power to heal broken bones. "So...here I am."

I wet my suddenly dry lips. He seemed irritated to be here, summoned and forced to interact with me because of the powercore.

"Y-you could just go. You came, I asked, and—"

"No." His expression softened as he placed Bella on the ground and patted the bench next to him. "It appears I am required to give you a history lesson. She wanted me to tell you about the Age of Decay for whatever good it may do us both."

See if he is truly the monster you think he is, it had said. She? Could an orb of pure power have a gender?

"She wanted you to come commune with her in person," I murmured. I sat next to him, close enough to touch. His gaze flashed toward the bare inches between us, clear awareness in his expression.

Then he sighed, tilting his head back and folding his hands in his lap. "Do you know something I never grew accustomed to in your world? The stars are so much closer. You can count every spark in your constellations. My world, Soiluire, had few stars. None so close to us as the sun, especially. On any given day, the light of our closest star would send red-tinged light over only half of our cities and townships."

I startled again when a furry shape jumped into my lap. It was just Milo, apparently jealous of Bella getting attention. He bunted my chest as Phaeron chuckled at my expense. "Two familiars. Good potential, bright soul," he said.

My hand paused halfway down Milo's back as I slanted a glance at the dimensional. "The powercore called me something like that," I said.

"I know. It is literal." His topaz eyes slanted back in my direction, admiring for a moment. "As I was saying, I came from a place of darkness. The only major source of light was a flare of sudden light across the sky one night that fell from the heavens. It was...an egg of sorts, and even when the goddess hatched from it, her vessel remained and glowed like a pure white sun. We worshiped her immediately, this being that emerged fully formed. The goddess of light, Myuna. Any touched by her grace glowed with her radiance. She turned our shadow magic from black to white, a phenomenon that makes it look like fire. We emerged from the darkness to surround her anointed Torchbearers.

"Our civilization was rebuilt around her vessel. Great temples, high powers. The three tribes of my people came together and crowned a king and queen." He finally turned back to me, a bittersweet look on his face. "My parents. They ruled for an entire age before deciding to have children. My royal mother birthed twins. First my brother, Endaeron, and myself a few minutes after."

He extended a hand, two wisps of shadow taking form on his palm. One was extra broad with a pair of bat wings and horns that stuck outward. I recognized Phaeron in the second shadow, which was shorter and leaner next to his twin, without the wings. His brother had to have been huge to be even taller and broader that the already massive Phaeron.

"Myuna chose him from the cradle to carry her blessing.

I cannot summon white shadow to show you, but her magic's presence bleached his skin stark white, and when he summoned his shadows for the first time, they glowed from within with her radiance."

"What about you?" I asked, my brow knitting.

"I bear the blessing of the land itself. I am shadowborn, a guardian of the spaces untouched by the sun. Don't be alarmed," he cautioned before shadows wrapped around his hand and extended his fingertips into massive, sharp talons. I watched them with a surge of fear anyway, imagining what damage they could do to myself or my familiars.

When he stopped flexing his hand, the talons retracted, and the little shadows he'd summoned warped and were now facing each other. I recognized the silhouette of the same ram-horned wolf creature that my librarian's handbook had shown me, and his brother's true form was like a mirror to it but with forward-facing horns and more bulk. "Technically, Endaeron was also shadowborn, but Myuna turned him into...something else. They called him lightborn, and as crown prince, he was celebrated and loved."

I frowned, not sure I liked his tone or where this story was going. "We had a very deeply rooted problem," he murmured, closing his hand on the shadows. "I was many centuries into my existence when Myuna revealed her true face. She was no benevolent goddess at all, but a monstrous creature who'd bided her time and ingratiated herself in our culture, spreading her influence until the right moment."

"Oh shit," I muttered.

He inclined his head. "To say the least. The Age of Decay tore down our society within a day. Myuna's Torchbearers died instantly, their souls enslaved and forced to bring a steady stream of my people to Myuna for her to feed upon.

She glutted herself on the souls of millions." Phaeron's gaze was years in the past, dulled by the grief of what he described.

"The white shadows of Myuna turned instantly from a blessing to the worst of curses. My brother's corruption was the direst of all, as he was afflicted by the same hunger for souls as the goddess who chose him as a babe. He transformed into a monster and became known as...well."

When he hesitated, I blurted out what I thought he was going to say. "The Hungering Darkness?" I asked in a small voice.

"Don't say its name! You don't want its attention," he hissed, going bolt upright.

I sucked in a fearful gasp as a chill wind blew over us. Phaeron got to his feet, shadowy claws overlaying both his hands as he crouched protectively in front of me. "Cress. Go inside," he ordered. When I simply stared at him, fear having me by the throat, he roared over his shoulder. "Now!"

"*Cress?*" a soft voice, merely a thread of sound, hissed from the darkness. "*At last...*"

That certainly motivated me. I stumbled over my own two feet in my haste to book it to my dorm. My shaking hands made swiping my student ID a challenge, but when I got the door open, in bolted three furry shapes ahead of me as Phaeron bellowed, "Coward! Show yourself!"

With a flimsy glass door between me and trouble, I turned back. There was...nothing outside. Just a wave of shadow magic that eclipsed the light of the closest streetlamp. A little sting swiped over my shin. It was Jin, who hissed when I looked down at her.

"Sorry, sorry," I said, remembering myself. Phaeron

could handle himself, but I rushed up to my dorm to take shelter behind a solid wall of cinderblock.

All three cats pressed to my legs as I lay out on my bed. I could feel Bella and Milo's terror like my own, but Jin's presence was a shock. Her scratches may just have saved our lives. As we waited there, I heard nothing, no way of knowing whether a battle occurred right outside the dorm. I should've gone to bed, but I just lay there, sweating, waiting for any sign that the Hungering Darkness wasn't outside, lying in wait to consume my soul.

Eventually, I met Jin's eyes. She was curled up by my hip, but she raised her head when she realized she had my attention. "It wasn't him, was it?" I whispered.

The cat simply stared for a moment. Lanie had trusted her familiar immediately to explore the campus and chose when she wanted to come and go from our dorm room. A little-known fact about that night: Jin had been there. But I'd never asked, assuming this whole time that Phaeron was the murderer.

Finally, Jin meowed, and Milo stirred. "She says no," he translated.

"This whole time," I murmured in a broken whisper. "It...it wasn't him. But then...who was it?"

"She wants to remind you that Lanie left you answers," Milo squeaked.

24

CRESS

Dearest Cress, began the hardest read of my life.

Lanie's pages and pages of frantically typed notes filled my computer screen at last. I'd let her email get buried under the mundane traffic of a college student's life, but no longer.

I'm sorry I left your life so abruptly. I knew you would try to stop me if I'd tried to warn you. We may not have known each other long, but you were a good friend to me, and I appreciated getting to know you.

"Ah, fuck. I can't do this," I said tearfully, closing my laptop and holding my face in between my hands. A small cat jumped into my lap, and at first, I thought it was Bella, come to comfort me. I stroked her back and glanced down in surprise, because Jin's fur was longer and softer than I expected.

She couldn't talk to me like my two familiars, but when she pawed at my laptop, her message was still clear. I couldn't keep pushing off reading the message…and disrespecting her deceased witch because of my own pain.

"You're right," I sighed, and she settled into a tight, not-purring ball in my lap as I opened the computer and started reading again.

I know you're not going to read this right away. But the pathways of fate have shown me you do eventually, sometime in early October. Jin is there to offer what comfort she can, and you've just had a scare.

I nodded along, my lips twisting wryly at just how correct she was.

It is very difficult to scry events that happen after one's death, but for the first time, I must brag on my Graygazer heritage. I've opened up small windows into the future to give you tidbits of what is to be. Be careful what you do with it all, because scrying this way is usually pretty inaccurate.

First, I don't know who it was that killed me. For years, I had nightmares of a man painted with blood witch runes but with claws of white fire for hands. I knew he was my destiny.

Pausing, I read that line again. White fire for hands... It sounded a lot like the white shadow Phaeron was just talking about. If I was right about his brother, she *was* killed by the Hungering Darkness.

But the Hungering Darkness *wasn't* Phaeron. He wasn't wearing any sort of runes that night, nor did he need to.

I wondered what else he'd told me that I hadn't believed, my gaze falling to the maroon-tinted anam cara mark in my palm. I minimized Lanie's note for a minute, pulling up the document where I kept my class notes instead and searching for auras. We'd covered them in both my introductory classes, and I'd pasted images from the slideshows to have a reference for aura colors I could return to.

I zoomed in on the image that had all seven witch affinities side by side. Librarian purple, verdant green, celestial yellow...

Guardian witches were oddballs, with auras that were either a soil brown or a neon green accompanied by the shapes of spiked geodes. I'd seen spikes and that same shade in Ben's aura countless times. Yet the mark in my palm was in the range of crimson to maroon that was associated with blood witches.

A sour feeling stirred in my belly as I compared my mark to the chart, double and triple checking to be sure. *Shit. Things are not as they seem at all.*

I didn't fully understand how this could've happened… but one thing was for sure. Ben had lied to me somewhere along the line. I could still feel the ghost of his touch on my skin and hear his praising whispers, but the pleasure had turned to ice. He'd concealed what he was, but his soul couldn't lie. Not to the anam cara mark and not to Phaeron, who'd mentioned that his soul was tainted with dark magic.

I took a shaky breath, muttering some of my handbook's more colorful euphemisms for "shit" as I returned to Lanie's letter.

As far as I can scry, the monster that killed me is a parasite of sorts, jumping from host to host and bringing out the worst in them. It is fed entirely by souls and absorbs their power. Considering it has no body of its own, it can hide for ages, slowly breaking down the willpower of its host.

I think you know by now that dimensional monsters are really scary and alien. I may be biased, but this is the scariest one. That's why you have to kill it, Cress. For good. But you can't do it alone. Only you can bring together a team capable of defeating this creature.

I read the paragraph again, frustration needling under my skin. It was asking too much to think she'd give me a convenient list of everyone needed for this team, but who could kill the monster that even Morgana Voidbinder, a demigoddess, had failed to destroy?

By the way, you have to know that Geo woke up only to help you. He has no emotions to understand it is the pull of a true mate bond between you two that constitutes his "duty."

"What!" I yelped.

I know it's hard to believe, but he needs you to show him the way. Then he'll understand and maybe even embrace who he is.

I sat back, clutching my head. The cupid's feather *had* heated in his presence, though. Perhaps if I'd offered it to Geo rather than Ben, I wouldn't be simmering with a knife of betrayal buried so deeply in my back. If Geo was anything, he was brutally *honest*. And he'd been right about Ben all along. I needed to do better for my gargoyle guardian, then perhaps we could say the words "true mate bond" out loud.

That was the end of Lanie's most world-shaking revelations for me. She shared other, smaller facts about the people, friends and otherwise, that I spent the most time with. Things to say to Wren to get her to think rather than react. A research path for Roe so she could find out what "fae trickery" Grant was involved in, which made me feel all kinds of uncomfortable for just assuming he was usually high off his mind.

She encouraged me to tell the truth of what I'd seen and experienced since before her death to Roe and anyone else I trusted. At the end, she signed off with love and a blessing to adopt Jin. And a PS: *You will have to hurt Ben to help him.*

I closed my laptop with the finality of another goodbye and rested my forehead on its cool lid. It was still the middle of the night, and instead of giving me the kind of concrete answers to go forth and conquer, it felt like Lanie had dumped an unmanageable end goal on me.

Bring together a team capable of helping me destroy an unkillable creature.

Take down said creature, the Hungering Darkness, a dimensional parasite currently latched in secret to someone else.

Pass my classes. That was kind of important too.

If Ben was in class tomorrow, somehow, I needed to not tip off that I knew he was lying about...maybe a lot of things. Because as I sat there thinking, I connected a few circumstances too neat to be mere coincidences.

I strongly suspected that the man who'd appeared right after Lanie's death with a strong curiosity for me...

A guy who I hadn't kept tabs on for hours at the Mabon celebration...

Someone who'd still be within a couple blocks of my dorm when I'd said "the Hungering Darkness" aloud...

A blood witch in disguise, hiding who knew what else.

Ben had to be the true host of the dimensional monster who'd killed my friend. He was someone I had to hurt to help, because I wasn't letting the Hungering Darkness nibble away at my anam cara, even if he was a liar with a lot to answer for.

SINCE I HADN'T SLEPT, I felt like absolute trash when my phone's alarm went off. Jin stirred in my lap with a low chirp before putting one of her front legs over her ears. That was about my mood, too.

I shuffled through the morning motions before exiting the dorm out of my usual door. I quickly spotted Geo in the garden, since the bulk of his gargoyle form's wings was unmistakable. He'd frozen the clothes he'd been wearing yesterday into solid stone over his figure. My heart sank somewhere in the vicinity of my knees when he turned stiffly to look at me, his expression coldly blank.

Pausing mid-step, I gulped a swallow. Lanie's words about a true mate bond flowed through my mind. I'd truly made him miserable, making him watch Ben and I together, none of us knowing he had a different kind of supernatural draw to me. It was easy to see in retrospect, and now my fuckup was staring me in the face.

"Hi, Geo," I said tentatively.

"Greetings," he ground out.

I figured it was best to address the elephant in this garden. "You're in your stone form again." I braced myself for his reply as his stone lips dipped toward a frown.

"You left me in the cold. This was more comfortable." Between the gritting of his stone voice, I recognized a steely thread of anger. He lifted his heavy arm and pointed at my chest. "I searched for hours for you. Just to learn you were off with Ben."

My shoulders drew in. "Look, Geo, I'm sorry."

"Then I find the dimensional murderer here this evening. Yelling into the night," he continued as if I hadn't spoken.

"Was he okay?" I asked, wondering how long after I took shelter that this happened.

"I chased him away. Neither of us felt like another fight." Stone scraped as he tilted his head at me. "You ask after his wellbeing while ignoring mine."

I put my palms up. "That's not it at all."

He stood straight again, withdrawing his accusing finger. "It is fine. You are still my duty. Killing Phaeron is still my purpose. And then I can go back to the library, where I belong."

"Geo, no, I—"

"To Latin?" He turned away, starting to head that way.

I watched him turn his back on me with a sinking sensation in my chest. Damn, this was bad, maybe irreparable. That would be what I deserved, stuck with the liar I'd chosen rather than the loyal man I'd upset.

"Geo, please listen. I didn't want to hurt your feelings. I just wanted to go out for an afternoon without an escort," I said to his back as we started down the sidewalk.

"What feelings?" he said woodenly. "I have none. They are nothing but trouble."

I winced, feeling his words like a physical blow. "And I've discovered some things that you should know. I think we've been mistaken about who killed my friend this whole time."

He stopped abruptly, and I nearly ran straight into his wings. Whirling faster than I thought was possible for his stone form, he glared hard enough that I took a step back. "Is he so charming that he can disarm you so easily?" he demanded. "Have you been playing with not one, but two distrustful men behind my back?"

"No, I just...I actually listened to him last night. We were wrong. Phaeron and the Hungering You-Know-What are two different people." I spoke rapidly in the face of his rage.

He stared, considering. "The Hungering—"

"No, don't say its name!" I burst out.

"—Darkness."

I tensed with a rush of terror, remembering all too well that little voice from the shadows that'd appeared nearly instantly when I said its name.

Geo's expression softened a fraction. "He will not attack you in my presence. You are safe. That is what you said before, yes? That I help you feel safe."

I touched my chest, where my heart raced with a burst of adrenaline. "Y-yeah. And that hasn't changed. I just made a dumb mistake."

He released a dry huff and resumed the trek to my first class. Well, forgiveness wouldn't be easily earned, but he still stopped and waited as I took a pit stop at the campus coffee shop. The line was long today, but I absolutely needed a caffeine fix.

The person at the back of the line turned when the door slammed closed behind me, and I sucked in a gasp. It was like looking at a ghost come back to life. I'd seen that face dozens of times, with its slightly crooked smile and a hint of chub stubbornly clinging to the apples of his cheeks. Lucas. A younger, slightly shorter version of Ben here doing something as mundane as ordering a coffee.

"Excuse me," I said, tapping him on the shoulder. "You look so much like someone I know. Are you related to Ben?"

"Oh!" He lit up immediately. "Yeah, that's my big bro! Have you seen him lately?"

I tilted my head, wondering if he knew Ben had been looking for him for ages with a reaction like that. "He's in one of my classes," I said, extending a hand. "I'm Cress."

He shook my hand quite firmly. Ouch. "Lucas," he said. "I've been looking for...for him for a while."

I chuckled, rubbing at my palm. "No kidding?"

"Yeah, family stuff, you know? Things aren't so great back at home. His affinity turned out to be blood, and he didn't take it well. Our family expects us to be guardians." He shrugged, putting his hands casually in his pockets. "He just ran off one day."

"Well, I can get you in contact with him, no problem," I said, taking out my phone. I snapped a quick picture of him, to his half-formed protest, and texted it to Ben.

"Missing something?" I sent with the picture.

He responded immediately. "O shit brt."

"Y-yeah," Lucas was saying, scratching behind his head. "He been doing okay? How do you know him?" My phone buzzed several times as he spoke.

"We have a class together and...I think maybe we're going steady." My smile was sad, though, considering the gulf of secrets I'd just discovered. I didn't trouble Lucas with any of that, though, especially as I started to really consider his presence and obvious lies. He wasn't nearly as slick as Ben.

He was, like, sixteen at most. What family sent a kid who should still be in high school onto a college campus? Especially one now on lockdown after two gruesome murders. I peered at my phone, frowning at the series of short messages.

I pieced it together in my mind, reading it in a panicky tone with how much Ben repeated my name. "Cress, don't go anywhere with him. Stay there. Okay? Cress? Make sure you have Geo! Cress, read your messages."

My brows rose steadily as I turned my attention back to Lucas. He was beaming and saying, "Aw, he got a girlfriend! Look at how much I missed."

He was next at the counter and ordered his coffee quickly, as did I. We stood at the bar together, waiting for our drinks. "It's only been about a week or so. You haven't missed much," I said.

"Cool, cool. Maybe I could walk you to class or something?" he suggested. "I gotta know the girl that's caught my bro's eye."

"Yeah, sure," I said, only feeling a twinge of unease because of Ben's messages. Something weird was afoot, and I needed one of the brothers to explain.

We stepped outside with drinks in hand, and Geo turned to acknowledge me with the barest of nods before glaring at Lucas. "Oh shit," the young man murmured.

"Lucas, this is Geo, my guardian from Moongrove Library," I said, watching the uncertainty play over his face.

It wasn't a surprise when he laughed nervously and hitched a thumb over his shoulder. "Actually, I think I should be going. It was nice to meet you, Cress!"

"But your brother—" I said before cutting myself off. He'd already turned and was power walking his way to the corner where two streets intersected. I watched him take on a burst of speed as he hooked a left with the sidewalk.

"Good riddance," Geo muttered.

I was about to ask why the sudden hostility when a pair of hands seized my shoulders. It was Ben, who looked me over with a frantic air. "Where'd he go?" he demanded. I pointed and started to answer, but he was already taking off in hot pursuit.

I turned back to Geo instead. "What the fuck," I said under my breath.

"So, Latin?" Geo asked.

"...Fuck Latin. I want answers," I decided. I pointed at his stone wings. "How well do those actually fly?"

"They are adequate."

"Let's follow them from the air," I suggested, waiting impatiently for him to consider before offering a single, grinding nod. He scooped me into his arms, bridal style, only jostling a dribble of coffee onto the sidewalk.

I held on to the cup despite the obvious dangers of dropping or spilling it. Geo lumbered into a running start, flaring out his gigantic stone wings before lurching into the sky. He was unsteady at first, listing to one side, and I cried out, certain we were about to crash. With a few mighty pumps of his wings, we accelerated and lifted higher into the sky.

Cold wind streamed by, but pressed to Geo's solid presence, I gained more confidence that we weren't about to suddenly fall out of the sky due to his weight. Obviously, he could still fly despite being made of solid stone. I wasn't questioning it, not when we gained rapidly on the brothers. I spotted Ben's golden head first, dodging around people and obstacles with all the agility of a parkour expert.

Two blocks up was Lucas at a full sprint. He glanced over his shoulder before hooking a sharp left. I was tempted to shout directions to Ben, but he wasn't so easily shaken. Geo slowed to follow Ben, staying over buildings so we didn't throw off a noticeable shadow.

"What do you think this is about?" His voice grinded next to my ear.

"Lucas said he was looking for Ben, and Ben's been looking for Lucas for ages," I answered.

"Then this makes no sense."

"Exactly."

"I have never trusted Ben."

"Yeah, I get that. He's been hiding his blood witch aura." I glanced over my shoulder at Geo's serious expression, backlit by the blinding halo of the sun. "That's what you really meant by him having a chameleon aura."

"Indeed."

"Couldn't you have just *said* that?"

"You were not ready to listen," he rumbled.

I breathed a sigh. "You were right all along, and I'm listening now."

For a moment, Geo smiled. Just a faint tilt to his obsidian lips, but a small victory nonetheless.

I ducked my head as he banked hard, slowing further when Ben finally lost sight of Lucas and came to a stop, bending over and grabbing his knees. Distracted as I'd been talking to Geo, I hadn't noticed the younger brother disappear, but there was no sight of him even from the air.

"Shh. Let's see where he goes," Geo said in his quietest voice as we landed a few buildings back, on the side not facing Ben. A good thing, too, as the gargoyle's weight made a noticeable thud when he came to a stop. I could just imagine Ben startling and looking up, but if we couldn't see him, he couldn't see us.

Geo held up a finger for me to wait, and a couple excruciating minutes passed before he motioned for me to go to the other side of the roof. I crouched and stepped over a clutter of old junk being stored up here, taking to my hands and knees before the lip of the roof and peeking over the edge.

Ben's golden-brown head of hair was just passing underneath, heading back the way he'd come at a slow, defeated pace. I watched to see if he would turn right with the sidewalk, but he glanced left to right and crossed the street instead.

I returned to Geo and nodded. His takeoff was a lot smoother this time, with several stories of air between us and the sidewalk below. We circled around and went higher into the sky, to the point our shadow shrank. I hoped Ben would simply return to the coffee shop, but he didn't, instead taking a turn off campus grounds and down the main road leading into the city section of New Salem.

Leaving the campus was a lot easier than entering, and I knew that Ben had mentioned having an apartment in the city. "He's probably going home after all that," I said. My phone buzzed with a few messages, likely from him, but I didn't trust myself to take out my device with the possibility for the wind to snatch it and dash out its innards several stories below.

"You wanted answers. We will demand them," Geo replied.

That sounded damn good to me.

25

BEN

I'd just unlocked the door to Garroway's private property when a *whoosh-thud* sounded behind me. I whirled around in one smooth motion with a dagger in hand, just to see Geo unfolding from a landing crouch and letting Cress down from his arms. *Shit.* I jabbed the weapon back into my sleeve before she could notice it.

"Cress? You followed me...from the *sky*?" I asked, uneasy by the tight look she spared me.

"Hey. We need to talk."

"Ah. The four words a guy dreads most," I said, sparing a nervous laugh when Geo squared up behind her, his bulky arms crossed. He flexed one of his wrists, and I heard the hiss of air.

She licked her lips, tucking a bit of her bright hair behind her ear. "I need you to come with me to Moongrove Library," she said.

I cocked a brow. "Why?"

"Well, um. I think I understand why you were gone for two weeks now. You've been feeling kind of sick, huh?" Sympathy mixed into her tone, and she held out a hand.

"The librarians should be able to sort you out. Let's go now."

I glanced from her proffered hand back to her face. "Babe, you're scaring me," I said, trying to laugh it off again. "I feel fine. Why don't we catch a movie or something since you're here? You can even bring Geocentric in if he promises not to break anything."

"Look, Ben. Try not to freak out, okay? But I think you have a dimensional monster tagging along in your soul right now, and we need to get it out," she said. Even Geo turned a confused look her way.

I put my hands up. "I have no idea what the fuck you're talking about."

"There is no harm in getting tested," Geo rumbled.

"I'm not sick," I protested. "You two are coming at me right now with some shit. I'm not going to the library."

Geo cracked his stony knuckles and smiled. Fucking smiled. He was going to force me to go along with this mess and would enjoy every moment of it.

"This is...this isn't how I thought this conversation would go." Cress heaved a sigh, rubbing her forehead. "Something really weird is happening with you—and your brother, too. He didn't say much to me that actually made sense with how he was acting."

That's because he was only in the coffee shop to kill her, I thought, still quivering with nerves at the thought of how close a call she had. "I don't really know what he's doing, either," I admitted. If he had a new master, then his first mission assigned by Garroway shouldn't matter to him anymore. "I'm on your side, all right?" As much as I could be, at least.

"I know," she said faintly before coming to some sort of decision internally. She lifted her shoulders and took a deep, steadying breath. "But I also know you're a blood witch. You've been lying about that and probably a lot of other things, too." She tipped her hand, flashing the blood-witch-maroon mark on her palm.

A queasy feeling settled in my belly, and my veins chilled with ice water. I should've known I would get caught, but this was so much sooner than expected. "You're right," I said, and each word emerged from my throat like razor blades. I winced at the sudden taste of blood in my mouth. I was dangerously close to admitting too much about myself. "But...that doesn't change the fact that I'm on your side."

At last, with the truth revealed, I started trying to word the impossible. My warning that she needed to leave, forgotten in my own greed for more time with her. I'd acted like Lucas would never find her, like she would be mine forever...like I could escape Garroway's iron-clad grip on my blood.

As if I'd summoned him, my blood rune began to heat. "Oh no. No," I murmured in horror. Crimson light erupted from under my shirt, and Cress gaped as I bent double from the sudden searing agony of Garroway's singular attention.

"*Benjamin!*" he snarled in my head. Somewhere in his manor, he had his black dagger raised and his eyes closed. My own eyes blazed with red light as he hijacked my senses. "*I have watched you lead these two to my property. Do you think I didn't install security? 'I am on your side,' hmm? She is your brother's mark to kill.*"

"*Master, please.*"

"*No, little Benjamin. You haven't been doing your job.*" A jab of pain lanced my head, like he pressed his finger a little too firmly into my temple.

"Ben?" Cress asked fearfully, but I was blinded and reeling from the sudden assault on my nerve endings.

"I believe you have been...incredibly distracted." I felt my hand uncurl from the heated rune on my chest, held stiffly in front of my watering gaze. Garroway laughed, the sound echoing in my head. *"As I suspected. Return to the manor."*

He manipulated my body like the puppet master he was until I was standing stiffly upright with two of my hidden daggers now unsheathed and deadly in my fists. My vision swam back into focus as Garroway started relinquishing his hold on me. Geo had pushed Cress behind him, and she looked over his shoulder in horror, her slim hands wrapped around his muscled arm to try holding him back.

"Return to the manor," Garroway repeated, his voice now holding the echo of an order I could not defy. *"Do not let anything stop you. Between fight or flight, you will fight first."*

"Yes, Master," I had to answer, though every cell in my body screamed defiance.

His presence left, as did the sudden knife of pain he'd jammed into my ribcage. But even with the lightshow dimmed, the danger was far from over. Geo had his arm lifted, and light winked off the needle-sharp tip of a quartz spike aimed straight at my heart.

I threw myself to the ground as he fired it. With a *thump*, it sank to the root in the solid wood door behind me. "That was rude, Geology," I snarked before cursing when I realized he had a second one primed and ready to go in his other arm.

"Put down your weapons at once," he demanded.

"No can do," I replied. My fingers would literally not uncurl, except my thumb and pointer to seize the little vial of Garroway's blood I flicked out of the ring on my right hand. I shattered it, coating my fingers in vampire blood, and deftly painted the runes for speed, strength, and regeneration up my arm as the gargoyle took aim at me.

"Geo, don't!" Cress screamed. "He's not himself. We can still save him!"

He shot the second spike at me without hesitation. Honestly, I didn't blame him. But with a vampire's preternatural speed, I flipped out of the way and landed in a crouch. Aggression pulsed under my skin, Garroway's command urging me to leap out and try to damage the gargoyle's obsidian skin. I'd probably just break good steel in the attempt.

Cress jumped out from behind Geo's aggressive stance, and I had a new target. I judged whether I had enough control to pull off what I was thinking of and leapt out at her. She gasped in surprise as I held the edge of a blade to her throat, my hand shaking with the effort to hold back from following up with any number of other attacks.

She looked at me like I was the worst kind of monster, her wide brown eyes filled to the brim with fear and betrayal.

"Forget about me," I shouted. "Go! Far from here. Not just to campus!"

Geo lunged at me, and I peeled away from her just in time to avoid the grasp of his stone hands. I pulled back with effort, taking off at a run before my compelled body could launch another attack at either of them. My primary directive was to return to the manor, so I did, running at an impossibly fast pace until the speed rune on my arm dried and flecked off into blood-red dust. Those never lasted long enough.

I tried to stop and catch my breath, but Garroway had tied his web too tightly around me for any hint of rest. I climbed one of the high walls that'd been lifted on this side of campus with sheer strength, bypassing a need to go through campus security with obvious blood witch runes on my skin. At least for the climb, I'd managed to sneak my daggers back into their sheaths.

As I took back streets to avoid most students on campus, it really sank in. I was compelled to run straight toward my funeral. Garroway had glimpsed the anam cara mark through my eyes. *As I suspected.* His smug words played on repeat in my head. How long had he been on to me?

All I knew was that it was over. Ruined. Even if I survived Garroway's punishment, there was no way Cress would ever trust me again. Cress knew I was a blood witch and, now that I'd held a dagger to her throat, probably figured out I was an assassin too. She would regret the anam cara mark on her palm, just like how I kicked myself for wearing such an obvious sign of affection for her for Garroway to find.

Hopefully she took my words to heart and got the fuck out of town.

I finished my marathon of a run to the manor's pocket dimension and nearly collapsed right outside the front steps. Two men caught me, Seth and one of the other senior blood witches. "I'm sorry, son," Seth murmured.

Panting hard, I turned to see my mentor's face twisted in hard sympathy. Yet he followed orders with the other witch. They marched me inside on my jelly-weak limbs and took an immediate turn for the room Garroway kept connected to his private rooms.

His torture chamber, a box of tiny red tiles that were painfully textured on bare knees. No matter how much we scrubbed and bleached it, it always smelled faintly of dried blood.

I was thrown to the ground, forced to kneel in front of Garroway seated in the only chair in the room. He wore a black satin night robe and a disgusted expression as he looked down his nose at me. After dismissing the other two witches with a nod, he lifted the night-black dagger and activated my blood rune, leaving me on the ground before him like a limp marionette.

Seth closed the door behind him and plunged us into near darkness, except for the dim red light Garroway preferred to work under in this room.

"How eagerly I have waited for this day," he drawled. His voice was deeper in here, every edge of his slow cadence magnified with sharp edges as I quivered in helpless fear. Under the red lighting, he was a demon with blood-red skin and half the planes of his face in shadow.

What he said sank in as he drank in the moment. My brow twitched the barest bit from confusion. Eagerness was not something I associated with Garroway. He'd lived long enough that I doubted he even felt the joy of being eager for anything.

"Going on sixteen years, in fact." He set the black dagger down, a minor relief. There wouldn't be any more pain through my blood rune for a while if he was settling in for a lecture. "Are you familiar with the butterfly effect?"

With my mouth sealed and my body frozen at his feet, I merely stared at him.

"A small action having a greater aftereffect, of course." Garroway answered his own question without missing a beat. "I have made millions just by being there to take advantage of whatever aftereffect was started by my clients' requests. Let me tell you a story, little Benjamin."

Dread pooled in my stomach. I hated Garroway's lectures and stories, because ultimately, there was some analogy that looped back to our current situation and a punishment to come along with it.

When I was fifteen, I was caught stealing medical supplies. The infirmary was available to everyone except during a particular part of our training, when Garroway carved the blood rune into our skin. It was the most painful thing in existence, and when he'd given me mine, I'd sworn for days that he'd killed me as I came in and out of sober consciousness as the blood rune's magic seared its way into every pore of my body.

For Lucas, that'd been when he was eleven. When Garroway was done with him, I'd snuck into his room with painkillers, antiseptic, and ointment to save him some of that agony.

After I was caught, Garroway sat me down in this room, just like this. He'd described in detail how a blood rune could take root incorrectly if it healed too early. A similar case came about in the early 1900s, when a blood witch managed to drag herself out of bed and treat her wound with a healing potion. The rune bonded incorrectly to her body, resulting in constant pain no matter what she did until she committed suicide to make it stop.

He'd described her death in vivid detail before taking a mallet to my hand for stealing and had me stand outside the door as he "reapplied" the rune to Lucas. I wasn't allowed to heal myself for three days, and Lucas took a whole week from there to recover; the initial application of the rune should've taken him four days.

"I once was acquainted with a celestial witch by the name of Marie Evenstar," Garroway began, sitting back like we were sitting before a fire, sharing stories. "She was rather powerful, but of course, most witches of her affinity are. She had a business reading star charts for supernatural children. With unerring accuracy, she could tell a parent what was in store for their child. I imagine there were a few embellishments. Not everyone is destined for greatness under the stars.

"Marie came to me with a tale of woe. You see, misfortune had struck her in a series of three acts. The stars had not warned her that her business partner, Eris Darkmore, would meet an untimely end along with the rest of her family as part of an electrical failure in their house."

Seth must've burnt the house to the ground to hide any evidence of the truth. A sour feeling began to squirm in my belly. Why would he bring up the Darkmore job again?

"She was not, in fact, all that skilled at celestial magic, as it turns out. But her best friend Eris was and could channel great amounts of celestial energy into and through Marie, who had a power level of five, but only in that skill. Without Eris, she was useless with star charts. Her business tanked, and she started taking on debts she couldn't pay.

"Then her husband passed away in a car wreck. Marie was inconsolable as she sat on my couch, explaining how desperately she needed money. She'd lost everything at that point. Her husband, her best friend, and soon her business as well. She begged me to loan her a sum every bank balked at and promised to sell the business, her home, and most of her possessions to afford paying me back. Bankruptcy was out of the question for a woman who'd married into such a storied family as the Evenstars. She still had appearances to maintain, she explained."

He tilted his head, a smile playing at his lips. His fangs flashed red in the low lighting, and I realized he actually was looking eager to tell this story. I didn't like the way he looked at me at all, like I was about to deliver him the most delicious feast.

"You see, Marie was desperate to move forward on a good foot as a single mother," Garroway continued. "For she had two young boys at home, Benjamin and Lucas."

My lungs spasmed with a gasp I wasn't able to utter. He was talking about my fucking *mother* right now, more details than he'd ever spared. I didn't know her name, her affinity, or anything past the incredible sum of five million Garroway had paid her to take my brother and me off her hands.

"She'd said you both had such promise in your futures. Tearfully, she even admitted that one of you had a star chart linked with the sweet girl who'd perished in that fire, little Luna Darkmore."

Cress. He was talking about Cress. Holy shit! Hot needles seized my shoulders as I tried to move, to scream, to react at all.

"She just wanted enough money to get by. And do you know what I gave her?" He took up the dagger at last and gestured, loosening my jaw so I could answer him.

"Five million dollars," I said through a mouthful of dry sandpaper.

"No. I gave her nothing at all, in fact. But in the dark of night, I sent a team to her door, and *they* gave her a bullet to the brain and made it look like a suicide." His eyes flashed with satisfaction as I moaned quietly, just a small echo of the emotions rending my heart in two.

He'd made me hate her, the nameless, faceless woman who'd abandoned me. What kind of monster sold her sons to a sadist like Garroway? Not my actual mother, it turned out. She'd made the incredibly unwise mistake of trusting him, though. And he'd murdered her for it.

I could barely breathe as he gave me time to really feel her loss and the crushing guilt that threatened to choke me.

I didn't cry, though. I couldn't. Garroway had already had his fill of them from my childhood and training. Every bit of pain, physical and emotional, had taken their toll until I couldn't release another tear. My sobs were completely dry as I mourned the mother I didn't remember.

But something else crystalized in me as Garroway breathed in, savoring the medley of emotional pain I was feeling. I hope it soured the taste. There wasn't a witch under Garroway's command that didn't hate him, but the level of animosity I felt reached blood-boiling levels as he enjoyed the fruits of ruin he'd sown in my family.

Eventually, my vampire master continued his little story. "The butterfly effect in motion. Eris Darkmore dies, and I end up taking Marie Evenstar's precious sons as my own. And so far, you have paid me back with about what I've invested in you...next to nothing." He scowled at me as he toyed with his black dagger, flipping it through his fingers. "But your pain has been extra delicious, little Benjamin. You've taken more than your share for your brother. Would you like to know how he repaid you?"

"No," I said flatly. I just wanted it to stop, even as I knew he would twist the knife as hard as possible.

He raised the dagger, making a come hither gesture with his other hand. The door leading to the rest of manor opened, and backlit by the sudden glare of light was a familiar face, not a hair out of place. "Lucas," I croaked.

"Hey, big bro." He flashed me an apologetic look like he was begging me to understand what a sucker punch it was to see him, whole and hale, after he'd given me the run around for over a month.

"Lucas here has done an outstanding job at his first mission." Garroway gave him a brief golf clap. I stared at my brother, wondering what the hell this mission was since

Cress was still alive and untouched. "When he felt no draw to the Darkmore girl, all I had to do was wait. You snuck out of the manor and went to her all by yourself, little Benjamin. And what do you know...Marie's star charts were right." He pointed the tip of his blade at my right hand. "You even took the bait to steal an extra cupid feather to test your connection to her."

Of course that had been bait. Garroway was about five steps ahead of me on whatever demented chessboard we were playing on.

"And now we come to a special time in your life," he said, gesturing Lucas into the room. The darkness closed over us once more. "I do not permit my witches to have anything so pedestrian as a soul mate or anam cara."

He gestured for me to stand, and my body did, pulled up like a puppet with its strings tugged. His last statement was beyond ominous, and cold sweat beaded my back as I realized exactly what my punishment would be. "Master, please. I promise I won't see her again. We can put this behind us," I begged.

The vampire bared his fangs and patted me on the cheek. "When will you learn, little Benjamin? You are mine, body and soul alike. Therefore, this is not a punishment, only destiny. *I* am your destiny. Lift your shirt."

Sensation returned to my fingertips. He wanted me to bare my blood rune with my own hand, ready for the forthcoming mission.

"She's innocent, Master. She doesn't deserve this," I said instead.

"Lift your shirt," he repeated tonelessly while lifting a brow. Even that minute expression told me he wasn't all that amused.

"Just do as the master says," Lucas whispered.

My nostrils flared as I resisted the impulse to turn and glare at him. I knew he didn't want to see me punished worse, but he could at least have the dignity not to pile on with Garroway.

The vampire got tired of my resistance, though, and compelled me to bare my blood rune to him. The moment the tip of the black dagger dimpled the skin over the edge of the rune, I went unnaturally still from the touch of its dark magic. The rune prickled with a feeling like a thousand tiny beestings and glowed from within with crimson light.

"Your next mission is to carry out the assassination of Luna Darkmore, also known as Cressida Rollins, by any means," Garroway intoned. The point of his dagger dug into my flesh, and I cried out. My pain was much more than physical as he damned me with one flick of the weapon. "I give you until Samhain to make a ghost of her."

The weapon left an inch-long red line under my skin, extending out from the wound. My new deadline, active until I did as he ordered. "And as an added incentive to carry out your task, I invoke Agonia." He traced the jagged red marking in the center of my rune, making it burn all the brighter.

I staggered away from him, covering the rune with both hands as it heated and circulated a sudden pinch of pain across my whole body. It wasn't the full agony spell, not like the one that'd knocked me unconscious recently, but I knew this punishment well. It wasn't going to go away until my mission was complete. I would carry constant pain with me, no matter what. The further my thoughts and actions strayed from the mission at hand, the worse it would be.

"I hate you," I hissed, nearly blinded by the sudden hot, needling feeling as it settled in my spine and radiated outward. I could barely keep myself upright, staggering into the wall where I stayed propped up with a fist. "Every waking hour of the day, every breath I take as I rest, I despise you."

"Ben, stop. Please," Lucas said in a begging tone.

It was too late for that. I clamped my teeth through a wave of vertigo as I stared down the vampire who assessed me with a cold stare. "If given even a fraction of a chance, I will cleave the head from your shoulders," I gritted out. "I will shove your body outside and dance in your fucking ashes, Garroway."

"Is that so?" the vampire asked.

"Yes—"

I was on the ground in a split second, gasping for air. The rush of agony from his kick to the center of my blood rune nearly threw me straight into the arms of unconsciousness, but I couldn't be that lucky.

He seized the front of my shirt, pulling me upright until we were nearly nose to nose. There was nothing human in his eyes as his stale breath washed over my face. "You and every other blood witch I own," he practically purred. "But there are no chances like that here, little Benjamin. Now run off and plan how you will kill your anam cara before you provoke me to tear your throat out instead."

He released me, and I fell limply to the ground. Everything hurt, pounding to the wild pulse in my chest. Light rushed over me as the door opened, but I remained down, making a low sound in my throat like a wounded animal.

Someone tentatively touched my shoulder. "Let's get you back to your room," Lucas said.

"Don't touch me," I muttered, shrugging off his hand.

I scraped myself off the ground without his help, staggering from the red-tilted room. "You know he made me do it, right?" Lucas asked in a small voice, trailing after me.

"Did he make you kill those two other people, too?" I asked after coming to a stop braced against the back of a sofa. It would be a long walk to the stairs when I couldn't walk straight.

"What two people?" He sounded bewildered.

"Never mind," I said curtly. "It doesn't matter."

I slogged all the way up the stairs and to my room, refusing to even look at him. Logically, he was just fulfilling a mission by leaving me in the dark for a whole month...but he could've at least hinted that he was okay. There were ways around almost every directive from Garroway's mouth to lessen the pain they caused.

Except times like now, when he'd turned my blood rune against me. I was exhausted already from exertion and now the bone-deep agony that clawed me with every step. When Lucas opened the door to my room, I had nothing left in me to argue. I thumped onto my bed fully clothed and tried to lie as still as possible.

My foot lifted, and I felt Lucas start picking at my shoelaces. "Go away," I muttered into my comforter.

"Please let me help you," he said in a small voice. "I'm really sorry, Ben. I hate that you're in pain right now."

I didn't respond. I couldn't find the words right now. Lucas tugged off my shoes and set aside the wallet and phone that were in my pockets.

As the silence stretched between us, I caught the sound of thumbs on a screen and the familiar buzz of my phone. "What are you doing?" I asked no louder than a mumble.

"Setting up an opportunity for you. A chick named Roe is asking if you want to go to a party. She says that Cress will be there."

The icy feeling of dread was soon replaced by even more needling viciousness as I resisted my mission. "I'll help you, big bro. We'll put this past us," Lucas said, a thread of hope in his voice. "We'll kill Cress together."

His words caused my rune to let up on the pain, and for a moment, the absence of it felt like the headiest relief.

I hope she's running away right now.

And then the Agonia spell returned with all the force of an avalanche, and I finally sank into oblivion.

26

CRESS

By late afternoon, I stood in the middle of my dorm room. Roe straddled my desk chair, while Willow sat cross-legged on the floor and Áine was on the spare bed, keeping Milo spellbound by pulling out single cat treats from her pocket dimension and had him looking around in awe.

Geo, in his human form, leaned against the door with his arms crossed. He was reluctant to leave me and deeply unhappy to transform back into the form that gave him unwanted feeling. It still gave me hope that he'd come to this little meeting of the minds as I came clean to my friends.

About everything.

How I'd freed Phaeron from Moongrove Library and how it'd been him who I'd seen over Lanie's body that awful night. I shared how I'd been studying for weeks to learn magic two years ahead of schedule, with the express purpose of killing the dimensional I was sure had murdered my friend.

They listened with sympathetic expressions, knowing I wanted to share everything before the questions came. So then came Ben…and the mystery he turned out to be. I set out the pieces of his puzzle for them and how I suspected he was the one possessed by the Hungering You-Know-What this whole time.

Roe's fingers turned white around my chair. "So you're telling me Ben lied to us and held a dagger to your throat?" she demanded.

"Yes, but—"

"That bastard!" she exclaimed.

"He's not really himself, though. I've seen the real Ben and…he's sweet and thoughtful." I showed them the anam cara mark on my palm again. "He just needs to meet an experienced librarian who can yank the Hungering You-Know-What out of him."

"Let's just call it the Hunger," Áine suggested.

"Are we just going to ignore the thing with his brother?" Willow asked in her wisp of a voice. "Because that's too weird."

"He had a blood witch aura too, but it was much weaker," Geo supplied.

Roe's tanned skin reddened further. "Nothing to it, then. They're both liars."

I nodded and cleared my throat awkwardly. "I'm sorry for keeping all of this from you. I didn't want to get expelled from NSU…this place is just incredible. But the situation has gotten so far beyond me."

"Aww, girl. C'mere." Roe got up and bundled me into a bear hug, which Willow and Áine joined after a moment. "You're not going to handle any of this alone anymore. We gotta stick up for each other."

I practically cried then and there; her words were so welcome. It felt like a weight off my shoulders at last that my friends finally knew everything and could help me figure out what to do from here.

"And it just so happens that I have an idea," Roe said. She sat down and started fiddling with her phone. "You want to catch Ben and haul him off to Moongrove Library, right? Well, there's a party this weekend at the marina for a merfolk holiday. There's an attendance limit, of course, but curfew is going to be loosened to let the mer celebrate. It's the perfect opportunity. We can set a trap for him there."

"What kind of trap?" Geo asked warily.

"Well, if we're not getting the SPDI involved, it'll have to be a relatively simple one," she said thoughtfully. "I'll text him about the party and say that Cress will be there and see what he says. He could see right through it and say no, or he can pretend that nothing happened today and go so he can party with his girlfriend. Then we nab him."

"And how do you suggest we...'nab' him?" Geo asked with air quotes.

Roe smiled and rubbed her hands. "Well, my mama taught me a ton of runes before I came here. I can make shackles for him from rock and soil. Blood witches rely a lot on their hands, so that will neutralize him."

"I can summon vines to help immobilize the rest of him. And if anyone gets hurt, I know some healing magic," Áine volunteered.

Willow bit her lip. "My magic isn't really strong, but I can always help be a lookout or something," she murmured.

"And..." I sighed as I looked down at Phaeron's mark on my left wrist. "I will call Phaeron this evening so we can get his help too. It sounded like he's been dealing with the Hunger for a long time and wants it dead even more than we do."

Geo's mouth thinned with displeasure. "I would prefer that we did not involve the dimensional."

"I know. But you'll be there too." I smiled his way. "And you will keep us safe just in case something goes wrong."

He considered for a few long moments. "I will agree if you learn two specific runes first and that you will not talk to the dimensional anymore without me present."

I needed to convince Dr. Voidbinder to be on call to take the Hungering Darkness from Ben in the first place, so I started to nod in agreement. "So, we're doing this?" Roe asked.

"We're doing this," I confirmed.

She started sending off a couple texts. The air was tense in the room as we waited for Ben to reply. To my surprise, it was nearly instant. "He says he'll be there," Roe said.

GEO

I made sure my demands were difficult to meet. The two runes I had Cress practice in the mere days we had were Luminare and Inemos, both power-level-three spells she had little chance of mastering. Dr. Voidbinder had been hesitant to even start her on them, but then again, he was already wary of her request for him to be at the library this coming Saturday.

He was a good man, though. He agreed both to teach her and to be here, just in case.

And Cress succeeded at the Luminare spell within a night. My brows rose, impressed when she raised her sword to the sky and shouted the rune name before erupting into light. It poured clear and bright from her sword but with a purple glare where the magic flashed from her skin in its less pure form. She blinded me with a three-second blaze of brightness.

By Friday night, Inemos was still far from her control. The symbol was complicated to make with the tip of a sword; plus, it required precise timing as it charged within the sword before being shot from the tip. This one, I absolutely hoped she could get. Inemos was a stasis spell that could lock down a dimensional.

Should Phaeron turn on her—and I strongly suspected he would—Inemos would be the difference between her quick death and his when I finally had the excuse to bludgeon him to death. For all her talk about how she thought she was wrong about him...I still thought he was too dangerous to live.

She didn't get the Inemos rune correct and seemed in low spirits as we walked back to her dorm. It was evening, technically past her curfew, but my presence kept anyone from questioning her. Even in my flesh form, it seemed the authorities wandering the street recognized me as one of the library's gargoyles.

"Does this mean you won't come help us tomorrow?" Cress asked me finally. She had her hands in her hoodie's pocket. The silver sword she'd "borrowed" from the library swayed under the material with every step. I'd distracted Dr. Voidbinder while she slipped it from the locker room and let my guilt rest by telling myself she was going to return it very soon.

"Hmm?"

"I didn't figure out the rune," she said.

It was after a long, thoughtful pause that I said, "No."

She glanced up at me, a little crease between her brows. "Huh?"

"I will not try to stop you," I clarified. I disliked how my chest felt lighter when her expression became a beaming smile. I cared about her happiness too deeply in this form. The logical side of me thought I was taking liberties with her safety by allowing this plan to go through.

However, there was one thing that tipped my judgment further. As we stopped in the shadows of the garden outside her dorm, she placed her fingers on Phaeron's mark and tried calling his name. She tried three times. He didn't show up from the darkness.

She'd tried again and again, but it seemed he, too, had lied to her. Or he would not show his face with me by her side. Either way, the effect was the same. He would not be at the party, friend or foe. I could handle Ben all on my own if it came down to it.

Her shoulders lowered and she sighed. "We still have a solid plan," she said.

"He would be an unpredictable wildcard anyway," I said, putting a hand on her shoulder in an attempt to comfort her. "We shall capture Ben and put an end to this whole affair tomorrow."

Unexpectedly, she put her arms around my middle. "I'm not ready for you to go," she said into my shirt. My arms hovered awkwardly until I finally settled them around her. My first hug. It was...nice.

"Who says I am going anywhere?" I asked, puzzled.

She looked up at me, our faces inches away since I had learned to lean down to speak with her. Her wide eyes flicked to my lips for a moment before she nibbled on hers. "You did," she replied quietly. "You said once you fulfilled your purpose here, you'd return to the library."

I nearly had the kneejerk reaction to remind her that killing Phaeron was my purpose, but that wasn't the truth. *She* was still my duty, and nothing about our current situation felt finished. "I also said I would not take this form again. Yet here we are. It pleases you, so I have returned to it."

"I appreciate it," she said. "Does this mean...you've forgiven me?"

I tilted my head as I thought back to the conversation she was referencing. I'd been furious, angrier than I'd ever felt, and said many things that I now realized she'd kept a memory of. She thought I was going to abandon her while Phaeron still walked free and that I carried a grudge for her rash actions that I'd already forgiven after seeing her obvious remorse.

"I..." I hesitated. Saying I bore no grudge seemed so cold. "I am not angry. I just want you to be safe. That is all I have ever wanted."

"Yeah?" she asked quietly. "That's all you want from me?" Her gaze searched my face for something, though I could not fathom what.

"Is there something more you desire?" I murmured.

She started to smile, and I recognized that look, the same one she always had when she was about to give me a new experience. "I'll show you, okay?"

"All right."

She lifted to the tips of her feet and laced her hand behind the back of my neck, pressing our mouths together. Like with the hug, I didn't respond for a moment, too stunned that this was happening. I knew I was not charming like Ben or Phaeron, but here she was, kissing *me*. I trembled from a foreign rush of emotions as I finally returned her affection before she pulled away a moment later.

"Good night, Geo," she said, backing away slowly.

"Sweet dreams," I murmured, watching until she returned to her dorm. Usually, this was the point where I returned to my gargoyle form to go dormant for the night, but my stone heart was pulsing at double its usual speed, so I sat on a bench instead to catch my breath.

With my lips still tingling from the touch of hers, I'd never felt so alive.

"The party's at the marina," Lucas reminded me as my numb fingers fumbled to fasten one of my daggers under my left sleeve. He rushed to help me. Evening had fallen already, and I was sluggish on purpose.

I hadn't surrendered to the sweet abyss of painlessness that plotting to kill Cress brought me. Garroway's trick was wearing away at my self-control, though, because every day that passed made it more tempting to stab something to make the awful screaming of my nerves stop. I knew it was by design.

The vampire undoubtedly waited with his version of eagerness for me to fulfill his sick mission. He'd harvest my pain like the finest vintage of wine and continue to do so. The loss of an anam cara came with a permanent yearning for someone who was no longer there, after all.

"Look at me," my brother commanded. His hands on my shoulders set off a stinging sensation, and I blew out a hiss of pain. I forced myself to meet his gaze. "You have to do this."

I glanced away, muttering, "No, I don't."

"Ben, you *have* to do this," he repeated. "You're going to die if you don't!"

"You don't understand. I'm already dead," I sighed. I was only agreeing to go to this party to deliver one last, dire demand that Cress leave. Once she was gone, there was no way I could end her life, and the deadline would end mine instead by Samhain.

"Do you love this chick? Really love her?" he asked, raising a dubious brow. "Nothing's more important than staying alive. There will be other women."

Mutely, I went back to strapping on my weapons and checking my ring. A new vial of Garroway's blood was primed and ready to go, just in case. "Do you remember talking to Seth about principles?" I asked finally, determining I was as ready to go as I could get.

Lucas shrugged. "Yeah."

"There are some things you just don't do," I prompted.

His lips pursed, and for a moment, he sneered. He'd never scoffed at wisdom from Seth before, our mentor more like his idol. "That's stuffy and out of touch when your life's on the line," he said. "Let's go."

He led the way as I limped after him. The touch of fresh air and the night-kissed wind on my skin outside was a fresh torture as it ghosted over my raw nerve endings. Still, I went, and Lucas sighed impatiently as he had to slow walk so he didn't outpace me too much.

"Are you allowed to help me?" I asked. Ordinarily, I wouldn't ask, but I really wanted him to turn around and go back into the manor tonight.

"Yes. The master gave his permission." He flashed a thumbs-up over his shoulder.

We traveled the back streets of Salem before I caught my breath enough to ask, "What was your real first mission? Last I remember, it was to kill Cress and make a stop at Moongrove Library for something."

"It was just to hide from you," Lucas said with a shrug.

"So, what was up with the library thing?" I asked. "Did you go there too, or was that another misdirection?"

He turned to glare. "I told you my mission, all right?"

I put my palms up. "Sorry." I didn't know what'd gotten into him. He seemed so impatient to get to this party. That wasn't like Lucas. My brother still hadn't drawn the blood of a real victim, compelled by the blood rune on his body to put his deadly skills to use for Garroway.

We disguised ourselves by mingling with a big inbound group of partygoers. I saw picnic baskets and blankets for those who couldn't stand being in freezing cold water, while the merfolk just wore big, excited smiles along with jeweled nets and shiny shells in their hair. We followed them to the marina. Lucas hummed a happy tune under his breath while I gathered the tatters of my self-control for what needed to be done.

The party stretched from the marina on back to the grassy shoreline, which teemed with bodies bouncing and swaying to the bass rumbling from several speakers bigger than I was. Lucas bounced his head to the beat while I glanced around, wondering how the hell I'd find Cress in this crush of people.

He grabbed my elbow and pointed. There was a better lit area past the main party, where a series of picnic tables held a small group not interested in dancing. Cress sat right below a streetlamp, the distinctive purple of her hair standing out like a beacon.

My mouth ran as dry as a desert breeze. *Kill her. End it.* My thoughts grabbed on to the relief of imagining fulfilling my mission here and now rather than suffering the prolonged agony of the death that awaited me if I didn't.

I headed her way. My palms itched to grab my daggers. I could surprise her with a strike to the heart. Quick, painless, done.

No. No, I'm not doing that. I won't hurt her, I vowed. I staggered like I was drunk. Fuck, I didn't know how I would endure more than a minute in her presence.

Cress stood and turned to me, a smile already shaping her lips. She was lovely in a dark lipstick, with dramatic makeup giving her eyes the kind of seductive flare that made my heart pump. Soon I was only feet away from her, and my mind filled with dozens of ways to take her out nearly instantly.

"Hi, Ben," she said, holding both of her hands out. She caught both of mine, as I couldn't help myself even now. It felt like I closed my hands around glass shards as Garroway's Agonia spell made sure I would never enjoy her presence again. My sight swam alongside the vicious jabs of pain.

Something closed around my wrists. When I blinked, I realized Roe had rushed over and clamped onto me.

"What the—" I started to struggle, trying to jerk away from her strong hold.

She uttered a rune, Figura, and the earth under my feet rippled and sank a few inches, rapidly feeding her a stream of soil and rocks that became unbreakable shackles that pinned my wrists together. It was done, and I was bound within a few seconds.

"That's for threatening Cress," Roe said tightly. "And this is for lying to us." She cocked back a fist and smashed it into my jaw.

As I stumbled back, the night erupted with a flare of eerie white fire.

PHAERON

I emerged from another blackout somewhere on the NSU campus, hearing the infernal thumping of what modern supernaturals considered "music."

I approached with an uncomfortable sensation dribbling down my spine. The last time a big gathering had occurred here, the Hungering Darkness had struck with all the deadly agility of a venomous snake.

Gnawing pain sank its teeth into my gut. How long had I been wandering, out of my mind? I would need to find a meal soon.

"Come, brother. I will let you get a taste."

I froze to the spot, taking a wary look around for any hint of white shadow. "Show yourself," I said.

"We don't have to fight. You feel it, don't you? The same hunger that I do."

"We are not alike," I said stiffly. My shadows uncurled around my hands, forming knife-like talons.

Its laughter was thready. *"Not yet, but soon. Come join me. The witch with the bright soul is here."*

I rushed into motion, my senses screaming. There was a flare of dimensional magic ahead, past the heart of this party. "You will not consume her soul," I demanded, cold with fear that it was anywhere near her.

"Such beautiful purple hair. So soft. I could reach out and touch it right now if I wanted."

"Leave her alone, damn you." The music playing was so deep it was disorienting to my sensitive hearing. It was suddenly like I was slogging through air ten times as dense as I fought to keep my wits about me and find Cress.

The monster who'd once been my brother was close enough to threaten her, and instead of the clear-headed adrenaline that should've flooded me at the thought of him taking another victim, I was growing confused. Lost.

The people here partying started to scream and run away from my destination. It felt like it was growing farther away the more I labored.

"So, you will not eat her with me tonight?" That blasted voice was still in my ears. *"What a pity. Come back when Myuna has a stronger hold on you."*

I sank to my knees, clutching my face as its willpower clashed with my own, recognizing now the clawing blankness that threatened to send me into another blackout. It'd been its voice in my head all this time, triggering the episodes so I wouldn't be able to interfere with it.

Dread left me breathless. How had it gained such a power over me?

One of the last things I saw before I turned into a curl of shadow was Cress only a few yards away. Blood streaked down one of her cheeks, and her soul blazed a bright halo around her, brilliant and beautiful in its intensity. Our gazes met, and I just barely registered her scream, "Phaeron! Help!"

28

CRESS

Ben staggered back from Roe's punch, falling like she'd hit him much harder. I glared at her. Striking him was definitely not part of the plan.

"How dare you hit my brother," Lucas said. Well, the words came from his mouth, but they were soft and hissed. The young man's head jerked to the side, screwing up with pain and twitching like it'd gotten stuck that way. My eyes rounded to the size of saucers as white fire leapt out of his palms, quickly overlaying his arms and forming long, pointed weapons in place of his fingers.

Not white fire. White *shadow*.

"Oh shit," I yelped, reaching behind me frantically for the sheathed sword I'd rested on the picnic table. I snatched it up and drew the silver weapon out, casting Lux before holding the brightly lit metal up to Lucas's face.

He stumbled away with a sound like boiling water in a kettle, shielding his head. His body jerked the next moment, blood spraying as the pointed tip of a quartz spike emerged from his chest. "Hmm," he uttered.

He inspected it for a moment while Ben screamed hoarsely, "Stop! That's my brother!"

Lucas wrapped a white clawed hand around the foot of bloodied mineral sticking out of him and pushed it back out. With the leisure of someone who knew he was in little danger, he drew a rune in his blood over the wound.

The first person started to scream and point, which scattered most of the group sitting at the picnic tables. They ran off into the night while Roe stood there, her mouth a shocked "o." She slammed her foot down into the grass and muttered a rune's name, causing the ground to shake in a circle around her. It buckled and cracked, which was her signal to Áine. The fae lifted her head from behind a table to circle her hands, and a gnarled pack of whip-like vines burst from the churned earth, aimed straight for Lucas's ankles.

He leapt to the side, so I saw Geo charging forward in his gargoyle form, a club of pure quartz held above his head. He brought it down, and Lucas evaded with the lightning-quick movements I'd seen Ben using after painting himself with runes.

Ben himself stumbled forward as the gargoyle and his brother squared up. "I said stop! Don't hurt him," he said on a gasp.

Geo, who'd been about to swing again, paused as Ben threw himself in between them.

Lucas didn't pull the strike of his talons. They raked over his brother's back instead, and Ben jerked, his expression going slack with shock. He tumbled to the ground.

When Lucas brought his bloodied claws to his lips and licked one clean, I realized he wasn't in control at all. The Hungering Darkness sighed as he tasted Ben's blood. "Such a tease," he breathed before launching at Geo.

I exchanged a glance with Roe, who was trembling. We both were, actually. "Is that the thing you thought was in Ben? The Hungering Darkness?" she whispered.

His head whipped our way. He already had one of his clawed hands deep in Geo's chest, dealing him a grievous wound. "You're in luck, Morgana. It seems they want to be eaten first," he purred, withdrawing his talons and leaping at us.

"Uh. Uh. Figura!" Roe shouted in a rush, making a lifting motion and drawing up a compacted ball of soil out of the ground about twice the size of my head. She grabbed it and threw it to explode in Lucas's face. Dirt flew every-where, and he stumbled, snarling.

I cast Repello as he came for us again, only momentarily distracted by Roe's magic. For once, I was glad for the endless drills Dr. Voidbinder had put me through. On pure muscle memory, I took a ready stance as Lucas rushed at me. His white talons descended on my shield.

For a moment, the magic held him back, and I took a chance to jab my sword into his shoulder. The shield shat-tered a moment later, his swipe slowed but still grazing my face. Pain exploded across my cheek, and I flinched back.

Roe grabbed his forearm when he tried to follow through by impaling me on his other hand's talons. She hissed in pain, smoke sizzling from her skin, but she still pulled him into a punch she reinforced with stray rocks over her hand like an improvised knuckle weapon. The Hungering Darkness staggered backward from the force, his head whipped to the side.

I cast another Repello shield and held my breath as I quickly repeated the gesture, successfully layering a second one over the first. That might last me a second longer, because it seemed we'd barely harmed the creature. He leapt for Roe, and I pushed her out of the way, letting my shields absorb the impact that could've killed my friend.

"Baby witch magic," he hissed, smashing his way through my magic. "Have any more tricks?"

"I do, actually!" Roe exclaimed. She'd cast another guardian rune and had two sharply pointed rocks floating above her. With a gesture, she sent them smacking into his wounded shoulder and face.

Motion caught my eye to the left, toward the roadside. A mass of partygoers were fleeing the scene, but closer to us was Phaeron, skidding to a stop and clawing at his face. His eyes were replaced by two pits of white fire, but still, I think our gazes met. "Phaeron!" I screamed. "Help!"

His shoulders heaved, and the mass of his body disappeared into the shadows. Out of habit, my right hand flew to my left wrist, the sword hanging to the side as I touched his mark of protection. "Phaeron, come back!" I called desperately.

He took shape again from the shadows, on his hands and knees. After shaking his head viciously, he leapt into motion.

"Uh, Cress," Roe shouted, pulling me back as the Hungering Darkness approached again with his talons raised.

I dragged myself out of Roe's hold and whipped my sword over my head, using the only other rune I knew. "Luminare," I whispered, and light exploded from my sword and skin like a ground-level firework.

The dimensional monster took shelter behind a picnic table. I blinked the spots from my eyes and saw Phaeron just standing there, his otherworldly features slack with admiration and a kind of awe. *Of me.* He looked at me like I was the sexiest woman alive. His eyes, blessedly, were back to their shined topaz state, reflecting sparkles of my light, and dark shadows swarmed up his arms as soon as the spell faded.

Phaeron turned, and the moment was broken with his sneer. He pointed a claw where the Hungering Darkness hid. "Cowardly wretch, hiding in the body of a boy. Face me!"

"Gladly," the thing within Lucas hissed, leaping out at him. Phaeron caught him by the elbows and threw him further away from the dregs of the stampeding party, into the darkness of the space between the marina and the next building.

Phaeron was soon running straight at me. He plucked the hilt of the sword right from my hand with an incline of his head. "Thank you, bright soul," he said.

"Wait...I needed that!" I shouted after him. It was still glowing with my Lux spell, but he didn't seem to mind.

Another shadow passed overhead. Geo landed hard, silvery liquid leaking from his chest wound. He and Phaeron exchanged a glance and a nod before rushing the Hungering Darkness at the same time.

With no weapon, I ran away from the fight, picking my way back to where Ben had fallen. He lay face down in the grass with Áine bent over his back. Green magic flowed between the hands she hovered inches from his gashes. "I ain't touching your blood, so stop asking," she was snapping as I skidded to a stop on his other side.

"Cress," he moaned. He tilted his chin to fix me with one bleary eye. "Please. Healing runes."

"What do I have to do?" I asked. Unlike Áine, I was willing to do anything to get him to survive this.

With a shaking fingertip, he drew a rune in his own blood on his forearm. Two lines with a third bisecting them. "Like that," he croaked.

"Eugh, why?" Áine asked as I began to make the mark around his open wounds with his blood. It was nasty work, but it made a noticeable difference when combined with her efforts.

"It's working. It's part of his magic," I said. The gashes crossing down his back started to knit closed before our eyes. It was a bloody affair to watch the bits of muscle and veins combine themselves again, and had I had any sort of meal before this, I would've thrown it back up on the spot.

Ben worked his jaw. "My brother attacked me," he whispered.

"That wasn't your brother. He's possessed by...what I thought was in you," I admitted. "Look, I'll explain later. Can you walk?" I offered a hand up before realizing he was still shackled by Roe's first spell.

He glanced down at where I was looking. "Don't take them off," he murmured. "Just...leave me."

"What? No," I said immediately.

"No way are you getting left behind after I spent so much magic healing you," Áine protested. She and I helped heft him to his feet as a cloud of darkness rolled over where we stood. Phaeron's gray figure jumped in front of us. Gashes dripping purple blood covered his arms, and four jagged lines nearly cleaved his tail in two where it was most slender.

He brandished my sword in front of him. It was still glowing, and everywhere its light touched him, his shadows receded. Its edge was coated in blood.

"Know why this way is superior, brother?" asked the monster puppetting Lucas's body as his white shadows cut through the gloom of whatever spell Phaeron had cast. His clothing was cut to ribbons, but the skin underneath was flawless. "This body heals nearly instantly. Yours does not."

A whistling sound pierced the night, courtesy of a rock the size of my fist hurtling through the air and smacking the Hungering Darkness in the shoulder, staggering him. "Hah! Take that!" Roe called.

Phaeron surged into motion, holding the sword up to Lucas's face in a mirror to what I'd done earlier. His shadowy claws sank into the space behind the young man as he cringed away. Phaeron tugged like a fisherman with a prize catch on the line.

For a moment, I could see the true creature of white fire as its head emerged. Phaeron had him by one forward-facing horn. I watched with my mouth popped open. Just like the drawings of him and Phaeron's other form, he was much like a horned wolf, and when he opened his mouth to howl and thrash, white teeth bristled from his jaw.

He went berserk, squirming in Phaeron's hold and making Lucas's arms swing. Fuchsia blood spilled in twin arcs as he gouged two swipes into Phaeron's chest before he was forced to let it go. "This isn't over," he hissed before compressing into a curl of white shadow and disappearing.

The dimensional man took a knee, planting his fist in the dirt. I cautiously went to his side, gasping when I saw how much blood he was losing. A stream of it stained the grass. "Áine!" I called.

She bounded over and reeled with both hands over her mouth. "Mother Tree!" she practically squeaked before going to work with her green healing magic.

"Phaeron...what happened to Geo?" I asked. I had my head on a swivel and counted my two friends, Ben, and him. The marina was deserted otherwise, blankets, food, and other knickknacks discarded in the group's haste to leave. Willow had left with them as we'd agreed on before-hand, only acting as a lookout since she wasn't sure of her magic yet.

He met my gaze, his pupils shrunk to tiny slits while his expression was tight with pain. "The gargoyle lost too much of his enchanted oil. He's frozen until he can turn human," he answered.

"He's alive?" I breathed.

Phaeron nodded tightly. "You still need him. I made sure his injuries weren't fatal."

A relieved smile crossed my face. "Thank you. I...I don't know what I'd do without him."

He stared at me in his probing, intense way for several long moments. "Do you see now that I am not a monster, bright soul?" he asked.

My throat clicked in a dry swallow. It was hard to think when he looked at me like that. "Y-yes," I murmured.

Those topaz eyes flicked down to where Áine was finishing up with staunching his bleeding wounds. "I shall live, faeling. Thank you for your help," he said with a bow of his head. "I owe you a debt of gratitude."

"I accept your admission of debt," Áine answered gravely. It sounded like a fae formality. She helped him to his feet, and he immediately turned and towered over Ben, who'd collapsed back into the grass.

Gently, Phaeron lifted him under his back and knees and walked to a picnic table that'd survived the battle. He laid Ben down on top of it, then peeled back the hem of his shirt to reveal Ben's tattoo. Phaeron made a little *tsk* noise. "This is some of the cruelest magic I've seen," he murmured.

I joined them on Phaeron's other side, noticing that the

skin around the tattoo was puckered and pink, with reddish veins spreading from it. The last time I'd seen it, only the big rune in the center was red, but now every line pulsed crimson and glowed faintly. "Do you see this?" He pointed toward the center rune. "That is Agonia. Something...or some*one* has triggered it. He is in a lot of pain right now."

"Who did this to you?" I looked up at Ben, who lay motionlessly with his shackled hands resting to the side. He was breathing, but his skin was pale with blood loss and the effects of the Agonia rune.

His only response was a weak couple of coughs. More blood dribbled from the corner of his mouth.

"Is there anything we can do for him?" Roe asked. She was behind me, looking over my shoulder.

Phaeron tapped his chin. As he deliberated, I noticed Áine had bounded off into the gloom. I recognized her distinctively bouncy stride as she returned alongside Geo in his human form. He was looking remarkably shiny with new silver gouges in his chest and limbs. He shambled toward us, powered on sheer willpower alone.

The dimensional man glanced that way as well, a thoughtful frown on his face, before he said, "There is something that can be done, yes. It will be extraordinarily painful."

"Do it," Ben mumbled.

Phaeron crooked his fingers, and shadows descended over them. He pulled them back until only his index was coated in a hooked talon. That wicked point was pressed to the edge of the circular rune. "Three...two..." There was no one. He raked his claw across the diameter of the rune in one fast swipe.

Ben nearly flopped off the table before Roe and I caught him. "Son of a *bitch*!" he shouted hoarsely.

"Don't heal it. Let it scar," Phaeron said. He pressed what was left of Ben's shirt to the wound he'd made.

Ben released a relieved sigh after a few moments, going completely limp. "No more Agonia. That feels...so damn good," he murmured. "Did you...am I free?"

"You may speak freely. But without the tool used to carve this rune into you, nothing can stop this." He pointed to a single red line among the ones fading back to black. It was like the others that streaked across Ben's chest, aiming for his heart, but it was only a couple inches long.

Ben lifted his head and then let it thump back down with a groan. "Ah, shit, the deadline's still active. What about hurting..." He stopped and spoke the next word on a whisper, like he was testing if he could speak it. "...Garroway?"

"Who's that?" Roe demanded.

"Just the vampire who had my mother murdered and magically enslaved my brother and me," he muttered. "I really can talk about this with you all. That's incredible." He sounded like he was going to pass out at any moment, though.

I recoiled in shock. "Did you just say...enslaved?" I asked.

"Yeah." He struggled to open his eyes and flashed a hint of his crooked smile. "I have so much to tell you, babe. But I promise you're going to know everything. No more lies."

After this bloody night, I wasn't sure if I could handle the truth. *Enslaved.* What the actual fuck.

"To answer your question, I believe you will be able to resist direct orders from this Garroway individual," Phaeron said. "But attempting to attack him may cause the damaged Agonia rune to try and finish you."

"I'll take it...for now," Ben sighed. He mumbled something about stopping a deadline next as his eyelids flagged downward.

Phaeron sighed as well. "The authorities are here."

I looked behind us. The first arrival was a winged woman who landed next to a toppled picnic table. Dr. Aurina was bundled up for a cold evening, her expression pinched with fury as she took in the damage and the remnants of the abandoned party. The force of her emotions was so strong I could feel the ominous press of them against my skin. Her two mates who could also fly landed close by and flanked her protectively.

Now that I was paying attention, I picked up the sound of approaching sirens. Better late than never, it would seem.

The cupid demigoddess's angry gaze swept over the lot of us. Phaeron and Geo, hurt but still standing. Ben, prone on the table with his wrists bound. Roe, Áine, and I...mostly unharmed but definitely what seemed like a random gaggle of NSU freshmen.

"Well," Dr. Aurina said, hands curling to fists at her sides. "Which one of you is going to explain what happened?"

Cress and her men return in Shadow Slayer!

Consider joining my Facebook group: Ella Hendricks Library Nest! Stay up to date with planned releases, chat about favorite books, and enjoy the occasional giveaway!

. . .

PLEASE REMEMBER TO REVIEW! Reviews help other readers find stories they may love. Consider leaving a review for Librarian Witch on Amazon and other websites.

ABOUT THE AUTHOR

Ella Hendricks is an author of romances with dark roots and steamy twists. She loves getting lost in fantasy worlds, especially if the monsters are naughty and the lady saves the day in the end. When Ella is not writing about swoon-worthy men, she's off collecting video game achievements. She holds a master's degree in journalism and lives in Texas with her family.

Find out more about her books at: www.ellahendricks.com